Peterson, Tracie
A love transformed

O9-BUB-614

A Love Transformed

Books by Tracie Peterson

www.traciepeterson.com

SAPPHIRE BRIDES
A Treasure Concealed
A Beauty Refined • *A Love Transformed*

BRIDES OF SEATTLE
Steadfast Heart
Refining Fire • *Love Everlasting*

LONE STAR BRIDES
A Sensible Arrangement
A Moment in Time • *A Matter of Heart*
Lone Star Brides (3 in 1)

LAND OF SHINING WATER
The Icecutter's Daughter
The Quarryman's Bride • *The Miner's Lady*

LAND OF THE LONE STAR
Chasing the Sun
Touching the Sky • *Taming the Wind*

BRIDAL VEIL ISLAND*
To Have and To Hold
To Love and Cherish • *To Honor and Trust*

STRIKING A MATCH
Embers of Love
Hearts Aglow • *Hope Rekindled*

SONG OF ALASKA
Dawn's Prelude
Morning's Refrain • *Twilight's Serenade*

ALASKAN QUEST
Summer of the Midnight Sun
Under the Northern Lights
Whispers of Winter
Alaskan Quest (3 in 1)

BRIDES OF GALLATIN COUNTY
A Promise to Believe In
A Love to Last Forever
A Dream to Call My Own

THE BROADMOOR LEGACY*
A Daughter's Inheritance
An Unexpected Love • *A Surrendered Heart*

BELLS OF LOWELL*
Daughter of the Loom
A Fragile Design • *These Tangled Threads*

LIGHTS OF LOWELL*
A Tapestry of Hope
A Love Woven True
The Pattern of Her Heart

DESERT ROSES
Shadows of the Canyon
Across the Years • *Beneath a Harvest Sky*

HEIRS OF MONTANA
Land of My Heart • *The Coming Storm*
To Dream Anew • *The Hope Within*

LADIES OF LIBERTY
A Lady of High Regard
A Lady of Hidden Intent
A Lady of Secret Devotion

RIBBONS OF STEEL**
Distant Dreams • *A Hope Beyond*
A Promise for Tomorrow

RIBBONS WEST**
Westward the Dream
Separate Roads • *Ties That Bind*

WESTWARD CHRONICLES
A Shelter of Hope
Hidden in a Whisper • *A Veiled Reflection*

YUKON QUEST
Treasures of the North
Ashes and Ice • *Rivers of Gold*

❦

*All Things Hidden****
*Beyond the Silence****
House of Secrets
A Slender Thread
What She Left for Me
Where My Heart Belongs

*with Judith Miller **with Judith Pella ***with Kimberley Woodhouse

SAPPHIRE  3 BRIDES

A Love Transformed

TRACIE
PETERSON

BETHANYHOUSE
a division of Baker Publishing Group
Minneapolis, Minnesota

© 2016 by Peterson Ink, Inc.

Published by Bethany House Publishers
11400 Hampshire Avenue South
Bloomington, Minnesota 55438
www.bethanyhouse.com

Bethany House Publishers is a division of
Baker Publishing Group, Grand Rapids, Michigan

Printed in the United States of America

Library of Congress Cataloging-in-Publication Data
Names: Peterson, Tracie, author.
Title: A love transformed / Tracie Peterson.
Description: Minneapolis, Minnesota : Bethany House, a division of Baker
    Publishing Group, [2016] | Series: Sapphire brides ; book 3
Identifiers: LCCN 2016017969| ISBN 9780764213380 (hardcover : acid-free paper) |
    ISBN 9780764213267 (softcover) | ISBN 9780764213397 (large print: softcover)
Subjects: | GSAFD: Christian fiction. | Love stories.
Classification: LCC PS3566.E7717 L686 2016 | DDC 813/.54—dc23
LC record available at https://lccn.loc.gov/2016017969

Scripture quotations are from the King James Version of the Bible.

This is a work of historical reconstruction; the appearances of certain historical figures are therefore inevitable. All other characters, however, are products of the author's imagination, and any resemblance to actual persons, living or dead, is coincidental.

Cover design by LOOK Design Studio
Cover photography by Aimee Christenson

16 17 18 19 20 21 22   7 6 5 4 3 2 1

To my own dear Auntie Madeline and Unca Paul.
You have blessed my life with your love.
We don't get to pick our relatives,
but if we did—I'd pick the two of you!
I love you dearly.

*I*t was snowing the day Jack Brindleson showed up at Clara Vesper's door with the news that her husband was dead. He delivered the report with the same indifference he held for the snow outside. It was simply a matter of fact, and nothing could be done about it.

"Dead?" She shook her head. Her throat tightened. Her knees weakened. She had been married to Adolph Vesper for twelve years, and while their marriage had been arranged and no great passion engulfed them, Clara couldn't imagine how life would go on without him.

She sank into the nearest chair and looked at her husband's secretary. "What happened?"

"He was shot in an alleyway." Again Jack's casual telling of the matter bothered Clara almost more than the news itself.

"Shot." She murmured the word over and over as if repeating it could make more sense of the situation.

"Otto said the police believe it to be a robbery gone wrong. Nothing was taken, however, so they also believe the assailant was interrupted by the approach of others." Jack flicked off snow from his coat, mindless that it fell onto the medallion design of the expensive Wilton carpet.

Clara found herself just watching the snow melt into the velvet-like fibers of the rug while Jack went on about her brother-in-law Otto coming later to see her. At that moment, Clara found that nothing seemed quite real. She drew a deep breath and looked up.

Jack offered her a tolerant nod. "I know this is hard news to hear. I wish there were an easier way to break it to you, but I find just getting to the point to be the best. Now if you'll excuse me, I have to make several other stops at your brother-in-law's behest."

"Of course." She rose to accompany him to the door but found her feet wouldn't move.

Her husband's secretary seemed to think nothing of it. He gave a slight bow and headed out of the room like a man marching off to war. Clara watched after him for several moments before the butler showed up.

"Madam, are you all right?"

Clara turned to the man she'd come to trust almost more than her husband. "Perkins, I'm afraid there's been bad news. Mr. Vesper met with an accident—a shooting." She shook her head, still trying to let the truth sink in. "He's dead."

His eyes widened. "Are you quite certain, madam?"

She nodded. "Mr. Brindleson just delivered the news. He tells me my brother-in-law is soon to stop by."

"I am sorry. Is there anything I might do for you?" Perkins looked at her with an expression of complete sympathy. "The staff is at your disposal."

"I'm not quite sure what I'm to do. I suppose I will wait until Otto arrives. He will most likely take charge of the arrangements."

"Of course. Will you receive him here?"

Clara glanced around the formal sitting room. She received most of her company in this room, but it seemed inappropriate for planning her husband's funeral. "No. Put him in the library. Have Cook prepare some refreshments. Hot tea and scones might be nice." She didn't know if such things were proper for discussing funeral arrangements, but at the moment Clara felt she needed the bolstering of normalcy.

"Very good, madam. Should I also send for the children's nanny?"

The children. She hadn't yet considered telling them about their father, a father they barely knew.

"Yes. Have Mim come see me in the library."

Perkins nodded, then departed the room, leaving Clara to make her way to the library. The house, a large four-story in a most fashionable part of New York, twisted and turned with halls, rooms, and stairs. The library was situated on the south side near the middle of the house. This was one of Clara's favorite rooms. She had always loved reading, and the shelves were stocked with volumes of her favorite books. Even Adolph had recognized the effect on her spirit and had put in a very ornate lady's desk for her. It was here where she was able to sketch and enjoy designing jewelry.

She sighed. Entering the room was akin to entering a sanctuary where one might find refuge from the trials of the world. Clara breathed deeply and let the silence wash over her. The door at the far end of the room drew her attention. That door led to her husband's private office. It seemed hard to imagine he'd never again sit behind the massive mahogany desk. She tried to shake off such thoughts. A numbing took hold of her. Her marriage had never been built on love, but over the years they had found a mutual respect and kindness for each other.

Clara hadn't been sure such an amiable situation could ever happen after the marriage had been forced on her by her mother.

Mother. That brought an entirely different threat. Once her mother found out she was widowed, Clara would no doubt have to deal with her mother's insistence on finding her another husband—one even more prominent and wealthy than Adolph Vesper.

The very thought of her mother invading her peaceful life sent Clara to the sofa. She had no desire to see her mother. The overbearing, opinionated Harriet Oberlin was well known in society for imposing her wishes on everyone and getting whatever she wanted. No one who knew her relished her arrival.

A light knock on the library door caused Clara to put aside her thoughts. After all, dreading her mother wasn't going to do anything to stave off her appearance. "Come in."

Miriam Wolff opened the door. "Perkins said you needed to see me."

Clara nodded. "Come sit with me, Mim."

The stocky, slightly older woman nodded and closed the door behind her. "Perkins said there's been bad news."

"Yes. I'm afraid there has been. It has to do with my husband."

Mim took a seat on the sofa beside Clara. "What has happened?"

"I'm sorry to tell you so bluntly, but Mr. Vesper has been killed."

The nanny, who'd become one of Clara's dearest friends, reached out to take hold of her hand. "Oh no. Whatever happened?"

"Apparently it was a robbery. They shot him, and he is dead. My husband's secretary was just here to give me the news. He said my brother-in-law will be by shortly."

"Have the police any idea of who did this?" Mim asked, stroking Clara's hand in a reassuring manner.

"I don't know. I suppose Otto is taking care of all of that. I must say, Mim, I am completely untrained for such events."

"Would you like me to tell the children?"

Clara shook her head. "No. I'll tell them later. It's not like they knew their father all that well anyway. He wasn't given to playing with them and was so seldom home when they were awake. I doubt very much it will matter to them one way or the other."

"I suppose not. However, you've always been good to speak kindly of their father to them. They might sense the loss and feel some sadness."

"Perhaps." Clara shook her head. "Given they're only four—well, almost five—I don't know that they will really comprehend death anyway."

"I believe they will understand well enough. We came across a dead bird in the garden once as you might recall. I explained to them about death at that point. It has been a long while since that event, but they may well remember."

"I will tell them tonight before dinner."

"Will you order new gowns or have some of your old ones dyed?"

The question didn't make sense for a moment, and then it dawned on Clara that she would be expected to wear black. "I hadn't given it any thought. Do you suppose I could have the dressmaker bring something over?"

"I'm certain she could arrange it. Why don't I have Perkins send a boy with a note? Given the large staff your dressmaker employs, I would imagine they could bring something later this afternoon. If not, I'm certain any number of stores might carry suitable mourning attire."

"Yes, do have Perkins send someone. Ask to have whatever is currently appropriate created as soon as possible. Perhaps I should order two or three such gowns."

Mim got to her feet. "I will go right now and see that it's done. Is there anything I can bring you?"

"I had Perkins order refreshments for my meeting with Otto, but I would like a cup of tea now. And perhaps someone could build up the fire. It's quite cold."

"The weather has been most unpredictable," Mim said, nodding. "Here it is April and it's snowing, with no end in sight. The skies are quite heavy and gray."

Clara nodded. "It seems appropriate."

"I'll speak with Perkins and the housekeeper. I'm sure between the three of us we can meet all of your needs." Mim padded across the room, pausing momentarily at the door. "I am here if you need to talk."

An hour later, with a fire blazing in the hearth and strong tea to bolster her, Clara rose to meet her brother-in-law as Perkins announced him from the library doorway.

"Sister," Otto Vesper said, crossing the room in four long strides. "I am so sorry to have been delayed. I had wanted to come give you the news of Adolph myself, but the police had me answering questions and . . . well . . . identifying my brother."

Clara nodded and allowed Otto to kiss her cheek. "It's quite all right. Please sit, and I will ring for refreshments." She pulled the cord that would ring in the kitchen. Otto drew a chair closer to the sofa where she'd been sitting.

Joining her brother-in-law, Clara reclaimed her seat. "I want to know everything. Do not treat me like some frail, simpering girl. I am stronger than I look."

"And might I say you look remarkably lovely for one who

12

has had to bear such bad news." Seeing she was settled, Otto took his seat.

"Thank you, but I am quite serious. I want to know what happened."

"Well, apparently sometime early this morning, Adolph was waylaid in an alley not far from our office. The police believe it was a robbery and that things must have gotten out of hand. Adolph was shot . . . in the head. He died instantly."

Clara steadied herself. "I'm glad he didn't suffer."

"No. He did not suffer." Otto fingered his mustache as Clara had seen him do anytime he was anxious. He looked so much like Adolph that for a moment this gesture alone reminded her this man was her brother-in-law, not her husband. As identical twins they had their similarities, but also their differences. This little habit was one that Adolph had never adopted.

"Where were you when he was . . . when it happened?"

Otto shook his head, his eyes downcast. "I had not yet arrived at the offices. Perhaps if I had, I might have been able to intercede." His expression grew quite dejected. "I wish I could have stopped it."

Clara nodded. "I do too." And truly she did wish that Adolph could have been spared.

"I came to let you know that I have made arrangements for Adolph . . . for the funeral."

"Thank you. I wasn't at all sure what I was to do."

He nodded and gave her a sympathetic smile. "That is what I am here for. I want to ease your suffering in any way I can. The funeral will be next Friday. It will be a large affair, given the fame of our business."

For ten years the Vesper brothers had enjoyed a growing popularity for their individually crafted jewelry using beautiful Yogo sapphires from Montana. Clara had been the one to bring the gems to their attention. Such sapphires were unavailable anywhere else in the world and were highly praised for their coloring. They were, in fact, so beautiful that they were now often requested instead of the once popular Ceylon or Burmese sapphires.

Adolph had won acclaim for the unique designs, and everyone who was anyone vied for a piece of Vesper Yogo jewelry. Now that would come to an end. Unless, of course, Clara wanted to continue designing the jewelry as she had these last ten years. Only Adolph and Otto knew that she was the source of the beautiful pieces. Early on Adolph had taken credit for the designs, telling Clara that the jewelry wouldn't garner as much attention and approval if it were known that the pieces were created by a woman. So he had taken the credit and Clara hadn't minded. She enjoyed sketching out the various ideas that came to mind as well as helping to create the wax molds. It didn't matter that her husband and his brother were the ones lauded and praised.

"It's certain to be a large funeral, but our own Grace Church is big enough to accommodate the mourners."

"Thank you, Otto. I appreciate that you would handle this for me."

He looked at her and nodded. "But of course. There is very little I wouldn't do for you, Clara. You know that."

"I suppose I do. What I don't know is what I am supposed to do now. What is to become of us? Has Adolph set aside money for us to live on?" She had never had to worry about such things, having gone straight from her mother's house to her husband's. "Is there . . . insurance that will see to us?"

"I don't want to worry you with such matters," Otto said, then hesitated. "There are . . . some issues, but . . . well, I will do what I can to resolve them."

"What do you mean? Otto, I want to know the truth."

He nodded. "Well, the truth is that Adolph was never any good at managing money. He had a love for luxury and gaming . . . among other things. I'm afraid over the years he turned to me more and more to bail him out of trouble."

This news shocked Clara almost more than hearing that her husband was dead. Adolph always had seemed the very epitome of control and fiduciary responsibility. "I don't understand."

Otto leaned back and crossed his legs. "I don't doubt it. I was quite firm with Adolph that I would continue to help him so long as you and the children were unaware of the problems. I didn't want you to have to worry with the details."

"But I want to know those details now."

He gave an exaggerated sigh. "I suppose I owe you that much. The fact is that Adolph left you very little. Even the house and its furnishings belong to me. Of course, I would never put you from it or take this lifestyle from you. I want you to know that I will take care of you, and the children."

Clara tried to make sense of it all. Why had she never discussed such things with Adolph? Early on he had set up a bank account for her that would accommodate all of her spending needs. Throughout the city she had accounts that were handled by someone else. Her only responsibility had been to spend the money at her leisure. She frowned. Why hadn't he told her that he had given over everything to his brother?

"Clara, I want to tell you something, although I know it's much too soon. However, it might give you peace of mind. As you know, I'm well aware of the fact that you are responsible for the Vesper Yogo designs. I think it's about time the rest of the world knew the true source. I want to move forward with creating the same quality of unique pieces, and I want to reveal to the world that you are the artist behind them."

"But I thought you and Adolph felt the pieces wouldn't be well received if it were known that they'd been created by a woman."

"The line is well established and the pieces speak for themselves. With Adolph gone, people will assume the line will stop, but of course we can keep it going. I presume you have some designs I might take to begin work on."

She nodded. There were five designs sitting on Adolph's desk even now. "Do you really suppose people will continue to buy them once they know about me?"

"I do. In fact, I would like to have a grand affair and reveal the new pieces. With America now involved in this ridiculous European war, it would do us all good to have a more festive event to take our minds off the rest. If you could create, say, a dozen or more designs right away, we could plan for this to take place as soon as the pieces can be fashioned. Say in a month or two, after your initial period of mourning has passed."

"I have five completed designs. I gave them to Adolph just a few days ago. I believe they are still on his desk." She nodded toward the closed door that led to her husband's private office. "I have an additional three in my desk that are nearly complete. I suppose I could come up with another four."

"That would be perfect. I know this is a hard time for you, Clara, but you and I also know that this wasn't a marriage of love. Even though Adolph was quite fond of you, I know that the marriage was forced upon you."

"Be that as it may, I have two children who are now father-less. I must think of them and their needs. And, frankly, I am glad to have these things resolved before my mother has the opportunity to come and insert herself into my affairs."

Otto frowned. "Is your mother expected?"

"No, but no doubt she will hear the news. They have newspapers even in Florida, and Mother moves in the circles where such information will certainly be the focus of discussion."

"I'm sure you are correct on that account. So Florida is where she spends her time these days?"

"Well, it is in the winter. I believe she has a palatial estate there given to her by my stepfather. I thought she might have sold it after his death, but she seems to enjoy avoiding the cold winters of New York and has kept it. I can't say that I'm disappointed."

"The woman is a terror." Otto put his closed fist to his lips, then slowly lowered it again. "I am sorry. That was most un-called for."

"Perhaps, but it's true. I cannot pretend I have any desire to see her arrive here and immediately set to work finding me another husband. And, of course, she will."

Otto shook his head. "The woman has no scruples or sense of concern for others. If she does come and proves to be difficult, get word to me. I will not tolerate her bullying you."

The serving girl arrived just then with the tea cart. A sense of fatigue washed over Clara, and even though it wasn't yet after-noon, she found herself longing for a nap. Perhaps Otto would take tea and then leave. After all, he had plenty to do, given the jewelry business and the funeral. Maybe once she provided him with the new designs, he would leave her to contemplate how she would handle her new responsibilities as a widow.

2

As Perkins saw Otto out half an hour later, Clara made her way upstairs to the nursery. She had tried to formulate the words she would use to tell her children of Adolph's death. She didn't want to frighten them or cause them undue pain.

"Mama!" Hunter yelled, careening across the carpeted nursery like an onion cart out of control. Clara had only a moment to brace herself before the child plowed into her and wrapped his arms around her. His enthusiasm made her smile.

Maddy, his twin sister, followed behind in a more sedate manner. Clara's daughter was quite reserved but very observant. In her dainty pink dress and white pinafore she looked rather like a little doll. When she reached her mother, Maddy raised her arms to be lifted.

"I will hold you in just a moment," Clara promised her daughter. "But first I need for you both to come and sit with me while I tell you some news." She glanced at Mim, who crossed the room to take up her knitting by the fire.

"Is the circus in town?" Hunter asked hopefully. "You said we would go to the circus when it came to town."

Clara led them to the window seat. She sat and pulled Maddy onto her lap while Hunter climbed onto the seat by himself.

"It's still snowing," Maddy said, pointing to the frosted glass.

"Yes, it is." Clara kissed her daughter's cheek and brushed back her long hair. She looked to Hunter. "I have no idea if the circus is in town, but the news I have to tell you concerns your father."

Hunter frowned and crossed his arms. Being out of dresses only a few months, he looked most uncomfortable in the starched white shirt, short blue pants, and black wool stockings. Somewhere there was a jacket that matched the pants, but Clara didn't reprimand him for its absence.

"But I want to go to the circus." His lower lip jutted out as if to prove his point.

Clara shook her head. "Do not pout, Hunter. It doesn't become a young gentleman." Hunter immediately relaxed his expression, and Clara nodded in approval.

"Now, I know you may not fully understand what I am going to tell you, but I will try to answer all of your questions." She drew a deep breath and continued. "There has been an accident and your father . . . he was hurt. He died."

The children were both quiet, their expressions serious.

"Like the bird?" Hunter finally asked, seeming to understand the gravity of the moment.

"Yes," Clara said, "like the bird, only . . ." She hesitated to say more.

"Only what?" Maddy pressed. "How did he get hurt?"

"It is hard to understand or explain, but some bad man shot him with a gun this morning."

"Will you put him in the ground like we did the bird?" Hunter wanted to know.

"Yes. There will be a funeral for your father. It will be quite large with a lot of people, so you will stay here with Mim."

"Will Father go to heaven?" Maddy asked.

Clara had raised her children to revere God and know something of the Bible, but Adolph had only seen church as a means to further his clientele. She had no idea of his holding any spiritual beliefs.

"I don't know, Maddy. Father kept such things to himself."

"Nanny Mim says you only go to heaven if you love Jesus." Maddy's face grew quite solemn. "If Father didn't love Jesus, then he won't go to heaven." Her words were blunt and to the point, and all Clara could do was nod.

"If he doesn't go to heaven, will he go to hell?" Hunter asked. "Will he go to the devil?"

She didn't want to give her children nightmares about hellfire and brimstone, but neither did she want to lie to them. "I suppose he might if he didn't love Jesus. However, I don't know if he loved Jesus or not. I would imagine only God knows for sure."

"I heard Cook tell Mr. Lawrence to go to the devil," Hunter announced as if it held great importance.

Clara might have laughed out loud at such a declaration had the moment not been so grave. "You shouldn't eavesdrop, Hunter," she reprimanded, but she didn't dwell long on the matter. "I don't want either of you to worry about this. I simply wanted you to know what has happened."

Maddy snuggled against Clara. "Are you sad, Mama?"

The question momentarily left Clara at a loss for words. She wasn't really sad. She wasn't even sure that she would mourn. Not exactly. She had her concerns about the future and the desire to shelter her children from the harsh realities of being fatherless and . . . penniless. She gave a sigh.

"I am feeling many things just now, Maddy. Are you sad?"

She nodded. "I'm sad that Father got shot."

"And that he might go to the devil," Hunter added with a seriousness that Clara couldn't ignore. Maddy nodded.

"It makes me very mindful that we must always be ready to meet our Maker. We don't have any way of knowing when we might die, but we needn't fear it."

Maddy straightened. "Not if we love Jesus."

"Exactly." Clara gave her children a smile. "Now, I must go and tend to other things, but if you need to talk to me about this, you can ask Mim to send for me. Or you can talk to Mim. She is very wise and knows all about such matters."

Clara kissed her children, then left the nursery hoping that she had handled the matter appropriately. She made her way past the grand staircase to the east wing of the house, where her bedroom adjoined that of her husband's. Entering the room, she was struck by the absolute silence. The snow insulated things to a point of leaving the world completely still.

She made her way to her writing desk and pulled out the chair. She often wrote to her aunt and uncle in Montana and felt it would help her to sort her thoughts by writing to tell them of Adolph's death.

Long ago Clara had spent a great deal of time living on her aunt and uncle's sheep ranch. Her mother had much too much going on during the summer to dally with a child home from boarding school and seemed grateful that her dead husband's sister would take Clara off her hands.

Clara had enjoyed staying with her aunt and uncle and learning about God. Aunt Madeline had often told her Bible stories, and Uncle Paul led them each day in morning devotions. She also learned the importance of work. Her aunt taught her all about a godly woman's role. Clara learned to cook, clean, sew, and lend aid to those who were sick or injured. Her aunt taught her how to cultivate flowers and grow a vegetable garden that would sustain the family through the winter. There were lessons about caring for the sheep and other farm animals, and there were wonderful camping trips up into the mountains, where Clara prayed summer would never end. It was during one of those wonderful summers that Clara had given her heart to Jesus. And it was upon returning to New York City and her mother that Clara had been forced to hide such beliefs deep within.

"I will not abide such nonsense," her mother had said when Clara had asked if she knew Jesus as her Lord and Savior. "Your aunt and uncle are steeped in their strange religious beliefs, but that isn't for us. This will be the last I hear of such foolishness from you."

After that, Clara kept her thoughts to herself. She managed to hide the Bible Aunt Madeline had given her just weeks earlier when she'd prayed to have Jesus come into her heart and direct her life. And she took the Bible with her when she returned to boarding school, where they were perfectly accepting of such an article. When summer came and she was hurried off to Montana, the Bible went with her. Clara smiled. She still had that same Bible.

Some of her happiest memories were of her time on the ranch. She had known true tenderness and love there in her aunt and uncle's care. She had also found her heart awakened to romantic love when she lost her young heart to a boy who worked at the ranch.

Clara opened the desk drawer and set the Bible atop her desk. It had been fourteen years since she'd lived with her aunt and uncle. The summer she was sixteen her mother decided it would be Clara's last time to go to the ranch. In fact, her mother had cut the summer short by showing up in July to take her home. It was time to introduce Clara to society so that a husband might be secured. Clara made the mistake of telling her mother in no uncertain terms that she had already fallen in love and planned to marry Curtis Billingham. Mother had been outraged, accusing Aunt Madeline of allowing Clara to run wild. Mother didn't even wait out the night but dragged Clara back to New York before she hardly had time to say goodbye to Curtis. Clara had been devastated, and her only comfort had been her Bible.

She lovingly touched the leather cover. The pages of the book were dog-eared and worn, but as her aunt had once teasingly told her, *"A person can never wear off the words, no matter how many times they read them."* In her sorrow, Clara had read little else, and over her twelve years of marriage she had consoled herself with God's words on many occasions.

"Lord, I need your divine direction. I never expected such a thing as this could happen, but now that it has, I am completely dependent upon you for guidance."

⌗⌗⌗

Grace Church proved the perfect location for the grand funeral of Adolph Vesper. Despite his German ancestry and the war, the elite of society overlooked this in order to be among the mourners. After all, it was certain to be noted in the newspaper who was in attendance and who was notably absent. The long drive to the cemetery, which overlooked the river, was made even more disagreeable due to the cold weather. Thankfully, most of New York's elite instead chose to return home to their warm fires and opulent furnishings.

Clara and a handful of others attended the graveside service, which was abbreviated due to the weather. At the conclusion, the mourners offered their final condolences to Clara, then slipped away. Clara remained at her husband's casket to say goodbye, while Otto stood speaking to the pastor some distance away.

"I know you aren't really here, Adolph, but it seems appropriate to pretend that you are." She gave a quick glance through her heavy veil to make certain no one lingered nearby.

"Ours was not a marriage of love, nor did we know the passion that so often surrounds those who wed. We were thrown together for the convenience and benefit of many, never giving thought to personal feelings or desires. You always knew I loved another, and I always knew you loved making money. Still, I am grateful for the amicable years and the two precious children you gave me. I pray that somehow before your death that morning, you found the truth about God. I'm ashamed to admit that it never much mattered to me. I should have done more to encourage your understanding of God."

She touched her gloved hand to the coffin. "I do pray that you made your peace with God before it was too late."

The snow was nearly gone from the ground, but the cold wind that blew off the river chilled Clara to the bone. That and the thought of her husband spending eternity in utter damnation and separation from God when she might have prevented it by sharing what she knew to be true. Of course, even if she'd been more vocal regarding salvation, Adolph might still have rejected such thinking.

Leaving the casket, Clara made her way to where Otto was saying goodbye to the last of the mourners. He turned as she approached and held out his arm.

"Are you ready to go?"

"Yes." Clara gave one final glance at her husband's resting place, then took hold of Otto's arm. "I'm quite ready."

3

urtis Billingham was lucky to be alive. He knew that better than most folks. He'd been blessed to be sure, despite his own attempt to ruin his life. Securing the last few buttons of his flannel shirt, he tried not to remember all the terrible things of his past. However, the demons that drove him then lingered to pester him now.

You're nothing but a drunkard—gambler—womanizer who has done time in prison, the voices echoed in his brain.

His friend and mentor Paul Sersland said that Curtis was a new creation in Christ, but the devil wanted to convince Curtis otherwise, and the devil had a much louder voice.

A quick check of the time caused Curtis to hurry his steps. Madeline and Paul would be waiting for him to start devotions and breakfast. He tied a kerchief around his neck as he made his way to the large kitchen.

"Sorry," he said, taking his seat at the kitchen table.

Madeline patted his shoulder as she passed by his chair to take her own. Paul sat with his Bible and offered Curtis a look of amusement. "We got you a watch for Christmas, thinking it would help you keep track of time."

Curtis laughed. "It does, but it takes a little of that time away each second I pause to look at it."

They all chuckled at this as Paul opened the Bible. "This morning I'm gonna read Psalm 4. 'Hear me when I call, O God of my righteousness: thou hast enlarged me when I was in distress; have mercy upon me, and hear my prayer. O ye sons of men, how long will ye turn my glory into shame? How long will ye love vanity, and seek after leasing? Selah. But know that the LORD hath set apart him that is godly for himself: the LORD will hear when I call unto him. Stand in awe, and sin not: commune with your own heart upon your bed, and be still. Selah. Offer the sacrifices of righteousness, and put your trust in the LORD. There be many that say, Who will shew us any good? LORD, lift thou up the light of thy countenance upon us. Thou hast put gladness in my heart, more than in the time that their corn and their wine increased. I will both lay me down in peace, and sleep: for thou, LORD, only makest me dwell in safety.'"

Paul looked up and smiled. "David is praying in earnest here, isn't he? He's begging God to hear him and have mercy on him."

Curtis nodded. "I know how that feels."

"I think we all do," Madeline agreed.

"David knows he won't find strength in himself. But he's seen God work. He's seen God give him increase and protection. Not only that, but David knows he's been set apart for God's work. And I think he's reminding anyone who sees these words that they need to revere the Almighty. A lot of folks take God for granted, but David knows he can trust in God—that God will give him peace of mind and safety. Of course, that doesn't mean bad things won't happen. Jesus himself told us we'd have trouble in this world. David is saying here that no matter what, when his trust is placed in God, even the bad things won't be a problem."

"I agree." Curtis sampled the coffee and smiled at the strong, earthy flavor. He put the cup down before continuing. "I remember how for many years I sought peace of mind and gladness of heart. But I learned it can't be found outside of God. I know, because I tried to find it in other things."

Paul closed the Bible and gave a nod. "The world tries to convince us that it can be had in things . . . in places . . . in people. But that kind of happiness doesn't last. It's gone when those things go by the wayside." He looked to Madeline.

She gave him a smile, then stretched out her hand to take hold of Curtis's. Paul closed the circle, clasping each of their hands in a firm grasp. "Let's pray."

"Father in heaven, for this food we thank you. For the hands that prepared it and for those who partake of its goodness, we ask your blessing. Amen."

"Amen," Curtis said before opening his eyes and raising his head.

"Well, let's get to it," Paul said, reaching for a platter of sausages. "We had forty lambs born in the night, and I would imagine there will be just as many today if not more. They're starting to drop at regular intervals, and the boys are plenty busy, so I can't sit around here all day." He winked at Madeline and gave her a smile. "Although I'd like to do just that. Spending the entire day with my best girl sounds like a mighty fine thing."

"I'll be out there lending a hand too," Madeline countered. "So you *will* be spending your day with me." She handed him a stack of pancakes as he passed the sausages to Curtis.

Curtis knew both Madeline and Paul were hard workers, but they were in their seventies and he worried about them. "I'll get stuff secured at the mine today and be back to help you when it's time to shear."

Paul nodded. "It's always good to have you working alongside."

"Sapphire mining has lessened quite a bit since the war started, and I heard last week that they'll soon shut down altogether and the miners will be put to work mining ores and metals needed for the war efforts."

"I heard the same when I was in town," Paul said. "War's gonna change everything."

"Well, for now the sheep are going to need our full attention," Madeline interjected.

Paul handed Curtis the platter of pancakes. "Weather's been good, but I don't think it's going to hold. Looks like snow out there."

"Once I get everything shut down and secured at the dike, I'll be able to devote my time to helping you." Curtis took several pancakes, then handed the plate back to Madeline.

"Do you plan to be out there all day?" Madeline asked, putting the plate aside.

"I shouldn't have to be. I need to make sure the bracings are holding and then get all my equipment packed up."

"If you like, Curtis, I'll come out with the wagon this afternoon and we can load up your things."

"That would be great." Curtis poured syrup over the cakes, then immediately cut into them.

"Well, don't go off until I pack you a lunch," Madeline told Curtis, getting to her feet. "You might get delayed and need to be out there for a longer period. I wouldn't want you going hungry."

Curtis hated to see her leave her food. "You don't need to do it right now. Come eat your breakfast while it's hot."

"Bah, it'll be just as good five minutes from now. I know you. You'll down your breakfast and fly out the door before I can put anything together. You'll tell me you need to get to work and don't have time to wait." She threw him a look that dared him to deny it.

Paul just laughed. "You can't win this one, son."

Curtis smiled and turned his attention back to the food. He liked it when Madeline and Paul referred to him as son. His own parents had been gone for nearly fourteen years. Their deaths had left a huge hole in his life. A hole that was made only bigger by the loss of Clara.

When he closed his eyes he could still see her smiling face and soulful brown eyes. He'd never known anyone like her. It had been easy to fall in love with her. They were only children with untried hearts, but the feelings they held for each other were strong and true.

"Are you already at the mine?" Madeline asked, touching his shoulder.

Curtis looked up and met her gaze. "Sorry, I was just thinking."

She gave him a knowing nod. "I asked if you wanted two sandwiches or three."

"Two's enough."

"I packed you a Thermos of coffee and a big piece of yesterday's pie. I know how you liked it."

"What's not to like about huckleberry pie?" He grinned and turned his attention back to the food at hand.

"As much as you like huckleberries, I'll have to try to can twice as many this year. Of course, it will all depend on whether or not I can get a good supply of them."

Paul reached over and took up a newspaper. "It doesn't look like the war is going so well for the Allies."

31

"How sad," Madeline said, coming back to the table.

"I was going to mention this earlier," Curtis said, putting his fork down. "I plan to enlist in the army." He hadn't told either of them that he had been contemplating what he'd do concerning the American war effort.

Madeline sank into her chair. "Are you sure? I thought since you'll be closing your mine, you might be content to help out here. The army is going to need wool and meat."

Curtis nodded. "I'm sure they will, but they'll also need men. And it's not like I have a family depending on me." He smiled. "Well, you depend on me occasionally, but I know I'm more of a burden than someone you need around."

"That's hardly true," Madeline declared. She looked to Paul. "We've come to enjoy having you here with us. Like we told you some time ago, you are free to stay on."

Paul nodded and put the paper aside. "She's right. After our boys moved off and you lost your folks, we kind of figured God gave us each other. We've tried to look after you in your youth and thought you could look after us in our old age."

"Of course I will. However, I also know you believe in a sense of duty." Paul nodded again and Curtis hurried to explain. "I feel it would be my duty to serve my country, just as you fought to keep the Union together back in the War Between the States. I know they don't expect the war will last long with America coming to their aid, and I pray that is the case. However, I figure no matter how much time it takes, I should do my part."

Paul picked up the paper again. "Well, we're proud of you, son, and we'll stand behind you no matter what you do."

Curtis knew he meant it. He knew both of them would support his decision even if Madeline worried about the outcome. They were like that. They didn't try to live his life for him but were there to offer advice when he sought it. Never reproachful.

Never taking an attitude of superiority. Even when Paul had pulled him from the gutter sick and nearly dead, Curtis had never felt condemnation from either of them.

"Of course, like I said," Madeline added while buttering a piece of toast, "you can serve the country by helping here at home. Wool is important for uniforms and then there's the meat we can provide." She gave Curtis a side glance. "I think you'd be doing just as great a duty in helping out here as to go overseas."

Paul looked over the top of the newspaper. "Now, darling, we aren't going to interfere in his decision. Besides, if he wanted to stay here, there are quite a few wild horses we could round up and break for the army."

Curtis grinned at them. "I'll give it some thought."

They were just finishing breakfast when ranch hands Joe and Phil came by to fill their Thermoses. "Kind of cold today," Phil said, reaching for the large coffeepot.

Joe nodded toward Curtis. "If you're heading over to the mine, you'll wanna wear a couple of layers. I'm bettin' it's gonna be cold all day long. Clouds are moving in, and it might even snow."

"That's all we need," Madeline said, going to the stove to help the men. "Poor little lambs. What a hard time to be born."

Paul put the paper aside again and chuckled. "Mother would have them all be born in a warm bed in the house if she had her way. The lambing sheds are quite adequate, however."

Curtis wiped his mouth and got to his feet. "Guess I'll go grab my heavy coat."

"It's hanging by the front door, Curtis."

He went to kiss Madeline on the cheek. "Thanks. Don't know what I'd do without you."

"Probably have to make your own coffee," Joe hollered after

him. "I know that's how it'd be for me." They all chuckled at this.

Heading to the front door, Curtis made his way down the long main hall. About halfway to the door and just outside of the living room, he couldn't help but pause by the large picture of Clara. He reached up and outlined her profile with his finger. The photo had been taken on her eighteenth birthday, two years after her mother had forced her to return to New York.

He hadn't been there when the picture arrived. Instead he'd been drinking away his sorrows and contemplating whether or not he wanted to go on living. Fact was, he'd happened across the photograph quite by accident. It was about a month after Paul had brought him back to the ranch to recuperate. Barely able to stand, he had hobbled down the hall heading out to the porch to sit and enjoy the warmth of the day. Curtis remembered the moment as if it were yesterday. The pain at seeing her looking so beautiful, so happy—without him. It cut like a knife. It wasn't that he didn't want her to have a good life. He did. But he wanted her to have that life with him, not some wealthy society man. And just as he knew he would never be happy without her, Curtis had imagined she would never be happy without him. The picture suggested otherwise.

He studied the photo a moment longer. She truly was the most beautiful woman he'd ever known. Her auburn hair had been curled and pinned in a beautiful arrangement with a wide, scarf-like ribbon tied across the crown of her head. She wore earrings and a corsage of flowers pinned over her heart. The photograph was void of color, but he could almost imagine the vibrant colors of her dress. Clara had always loved bright colors.

Curtis felt the age-old longing for what might have been. They had been meant for each other—of that they were certain. She had been as sure of it as he had been, and at sixteen they had made a pledge to marry. Then everything seemed to fall apart. Curtis's folks left for New Orleans, where his father, a doctor, was much needed to help with a yellow fever epidemic. They would never have made the trip, but his father's best friend from medical school had begged them to come. It seemed the city was overwhelmed with the sick and dying. Since one of Curtis's two older brothers also lived in the city, his parents were happy to use the situation as an excuse to see their son and his family.

Curtis was old enough to remain at home on his own, but having been helping out at the Sersland ranch for the past two summers, his mother and Madeline arranged for him to stay with them while they were away. Curtis hadn't minded that at all because it meant he could be with Clara. But then the un-thinkable happened. His parents contracted the fever and died. His brother sent word after the fact. The news left Curtis in a stupor, but that was only the start of his woes. Clara's mother arrived at the ranch not long after to declare it was time for her daughter to return to New York and make her debut into society. After all, if she were to get a rich husband, she would have to prove herself to be one of the elite.

Clara hadn't wanted to go, insisting that she and Curtis had made a pledge to marry each other. Her mother had laughed at that, telling them both that this was something that would never happen. Curtis was nothing more than a ranch hand, and her daughter was destined for a life far more grand. Then she had forced Clara to return to New York City. Two years later he heard from Madeline that Clara had married. After that, nothing mattered.

He let out a long, heavy sigh and gave the photograph one last look. He hoped Clara had found happiness and that her husband treated her well. As for Curtis, he knew he would never love another.

The ride out to the mining area cleared his head. The crisp April air did taste of snow, and the skies suggested it would come sooner rather than later. The mountains were still capped in white, but in the valley the snows had come and gone several times, and with each melting everyone thought—hoped, really—that it would be the last and that spring would finally arrive. Of course, a Montana spring meant anything from a foot of snow to chilly showers or bright sun-filled days. It just seemed the latter came far less often.

The Sersland property stretched for miles in every direction. They had part of the land farmed in hay and grain, while other sections were devoted to grazing land for the sheep. Added to this were leases and forest permits that extended their acreage considerably. Five thousand sheep required a lot of grass.

The mine, or dike, as it was often called, was situated to the west of the house, nearly six miles away on the edge of the Little Belt Mountains. Not far from this were the operating mines of the New Mine Sapphire Syndicate. The Syndicate had tried unsuccessfully to get Paul to sell the land to them, but he had refused. Year after year they'd attempted to purchase the piece, and year after year Paul had told them no. Then two years ago on Curtis's twenty-eighth birthday, Paul had deeded the mine and twenty surrounding acres over to him as a gift, and the Syndicate had settled for making an arrangement with Curtis to sell them whatever stones he found. It had worked out well for both parties, although neither would ever get rich off Curtis's small mine. And the Syndicate liked keeping all Yogo sapphires under their control.

Curtis dismounted and unsaddled his horse. He staked the gelding out to graze, then went to work. Getting sapphires out of the ground required a great deal of patience. First he had to dig up the ground, then let it weather. There were several piles of dirt around the mine that varied in age. Once the dirt was weathered, it was far easier to harvest the sapphires using a rocker box by the river to wash the dirt and knock the stones loose. But even with all of that work, Curtis had only managed to find a few stones of any consequence. Most were quite small—less than a carat. On occasion he had found larger pieces, including a sapphire that looked to yield five or more carats. He'd decided to keep that one for himself. Still, if he was diligent, he could make at least one hundred dollars a month on average. Most of that he saved after giving a portion to Madeline for his keep.

He gave a long look around the area. He didn't have any idea when he might see it again. If he joined the army and went to fight in Europe, he might never see it again. Snow began to fall. At first it wasn't much, but as time went on, it began to snow in earnest. This caused Curtis to pick up the pace. There was no sense wasting time, and if the snow continued, he'd have to take what he could and cover the rest with a tarp until Paul could retrieve it with the wagon.

Curtis went down the long trench, checking the supports and picking up any tools he'd left behind. The mine had been Paul's idea. After he'd gotten Curtis back to health, he'd brought him out here. He figured it allowed Curtis the ability to work on his own without having to deal with the questions and possible condemnation of others. And Paul reasoned that the mine would give Curtis time to contemplate his future and decide what he truly wanted to do. Curtis figured he'd eventually either take on sheep, as Paul had encouraged him to consider, or maybe he'd wrangle wild horses. Now, however, there was a war, and America was a part of it.

Curtis found a couple of the supports needed shoring up and went to work. Once he finished today, he would spend the next month helping with the sheep. By the end of that, Curtis would enlist. The thought of war was quite daunting, and yet Curtis almost welcomed the thought of being a soldier. Just one unknown man in a sea of thousands. Maybe then he could forget the mistakes he'd made. Maybe then he could let go of the regret he wore like a yoke.

He went deeper into the trench and back to where he'd actually dug a short tunnel underground. Here he found several of the supports less than sufficient. When he'd last been out here, he'd been in too much of a hurry. Wisdom dictated that he now take the time to shore up the tunnel properly.

Retrieving a couple of rough planks outside, Curtis couldn't help but notice the wind had picked up a bit. The snow was already several inches deep. He murmured a prayer for better weather, then returned to the tunnel and went to work nailing the planks in place.

One of the overhead boards came loose as he fought to secure the side boards in place. "One step forward and two steps back," he mused aloud. He stopped what he was doing on the side, but he'd no sooner begun to work the overhead piece back in place when dirt rained down on him. He gave it little thought, but when the onslaught continued and grew heavier, Curtis knew he was in trouble.

He had no time to move before a good portion of the tunnel around him caved in, along with the supports Curtis had hoped to secure. The first beam hit him hard across the shoulders and knocked him to the ground. The next hit him square in the middle of his back. Pain radiated throughout his body, but Curtis had no time to react before another heavy load of debris collapsed atop him. He saw stars when one of the smaller boards struck the back of his head. The situation was growing worse by the minute. Curtis knew he would have to make a final effort to escape and crawl his way out, but his leg was trapped, and every movement sent electrifying pain throughout his body.

What a ridiculous way to die, he mused as he felt his vision darken. His last thoughts were of the Bible reading that morning. *"I will both lay me down in peace, and sleep: for thou, Lord, only makest me dwell in safety."*

4

A month had passed since the murder of her husband, but still the police could offer Clara little understanding as to why it had happened. Otto had come to check on her and the children every few days, but he always brought up the matter of the jewelry designs. Now, as Clara stood warming herself by the library fireplace, she couldn't help but glance at the unfinished designs on the nearby desk. She didn't feel overly creative, and the quality of the pieces was suffering. Mim said it was because of the murder and the uncertainty of her life without Adolph. Perhaps she was right.

Clara left the comfort of the fire and went to study the drawings. On one page she had outlined a pair of earrings. The pinnacle stone at the earlobe would be a Yogo sapphire. From there the design fanned out to end in a curve of small sapphires at the base. She hadn't yet figured out how to arrange the center. Another drawing was for a brooch. This piece was a variation on one she'd done years earlier. It would be unique, but the foundation of it would start with a box shape of white gold and diamonds. Atop this would be a bow with tails that would flow down and over the side of the diamond box. The bow would be set in Yogo sapphires. The finished piece would give the appearance of a gift box, but Clara hadn't yet been able to make the bow just right. The other two designs were even less complete. She knew one would be an opulent necklace to match the earrings. The fourth would also be a necklace, but the design hadn't yet worked itself out in her mind. If not for Otto's insistence that he needed a full twelve pieces for the gala presentation to introduce Clara's artistry, she might have given up.

Despite his pressure on her to finish the designs, Otto had been very good to her and the children. She didn't want to disappoint him. Movement at the library door drew her attention. Perkins entered with Otto on his heels.

"Mr. Vesper, madam."

Clara nodded and crossed the room to greet her brother-in-law. "You look chilled to the bone. Why don't we stand by the fire so you can warm up?"

"It's been the coldest spring I've ever known in New York City. Who ever heard of it being chilly in May?" He went to the fire and stretched out his hands. "I hope you aren't suffering from it."

Clara came to stand beside him. "No. I haven't gone out at all. Not since . . . the funeral."

He nodded. "A widow can hardly be expected to go out in public after her husband's death." He noted her attire. "Black makes you look so pale. I don't think Adolph would want you to dress that way."

She smiled and gave a little shrug. "Visitors expect it, and it's of little interest to me one way or the other."

"Have you had many visitors?"

"Quite a few. Everyone wants to offer their condolences and see how I'm doing."

"And what of your mother?"

"I had a short note from her. She told me she would be here soon. She had numerous things to attend to in Florida in order to close the house. Otherwise I have no idea of when she will arrive." Clara didn't bother to add that she had already decided to be unavailable to her mother's tirades and insisting ways. However, she knew that if she told Otto what she had in mind instead, he would never approve of it.

"Well, we shall, as they say, cross that bridge when we get to it." Otto straightened. He looked at her strangely for a moment. His eyes narrowed slightly, and his expression became rather intense.

"Is something wrong, Otto?"

"I just don't like the idea of you being at your mother's mercy."

Clara shook her head. "I've always been at her mercy. However, I am dreading her return as well. Once she realizes that I'm destitute, she will no doubt make it her duty to see me properly placed in another arranged marriage. But I'm not a child, and she no longer has a right to manage my life."

"I agree. Furthermore . . ." He paused and ran his finger along his mustache. "Clara, I know it's only been a month since we lost Adolph, but I have been thinking on something. I wonder if you would hear me out."

Clara saw something in his face that made her uncomfortable. "I suppose you want to discuss the designs." She moved quickly to the table. "I have been working on the last four as you can see. However, they are nowhere near complete."

He came to her side and touched her arm. "Clara, that isn't what I want to talk about."

She looked up. "No?"

"Come sit with me." He led her to a settee that faced the fireplace.

43

Clara took a seat, her discomfort growing by the minute. It suddenly dawned on her what Otto might have in mind. When he pulled up the ottoman directly in front of her, she was certain.

"I hope this won't sound callous, but you and I both know that your marriage to my brother was not one of love. You were an excellent wife to him, however. I have nothing but the highest regard for how you have comported yourself over the years."

"Thank you." She barely breathed the words. It felt as though an iron band had tightened around her chest.

"However, what started out merely as high regard has developed into something more. I have grown to love you, Clara. Of course, I've kept it to myself because of Adolph, but now that he's gone and has left you in such a precarious situation, I feel it only right to offer you my hand in marriage."

Clara felt the blood drain from her face. For a moment a wave of dizziness made her wonder if she would be able to reply. But Otto squeezed her arm and hurried to continue his appeal.

"As I said, I know it's only been a month, and I wouldn't expect you to marry me right away. We could wait as long as six months if you like."

"That long, hmmm."

"Clara, I know you must be completely taken off guard, but I assure you that my intentions are only the very best. I love you, and I care deeply for your children. I want them to be my own."

"You are right, Otto." His expression took on a look of hope, which she quickly crushed. "It's much too soon."

He frowned. "I am sorry. I acted only out of concern for your well-being. I didn't want you caught up in your mother's games only to find yourself forced to marry someone you don't even know."

"And I appreciate your concern, Otto. Truly, I do. You are more considerate than most brothers-in-law would be, and I am grateful. I've given thought to what you said when you first told me about Adolph's lack of financial sense. I would like to continue designing jewelry for you. I presume from the high sums we can garner that my share would be enough to live on."

"Of course," Otto replied, nodding. "Of course. But how will you hold your mother at bay?"

Clara smiled. "I'm not the little girl I was fourteen years ago when she forced me from the only place I've ever been happy. She doesn't frighten me, nor should she worry you."

Otto let go his hold on her arm. He got to his feet so quickly that Clara thought maybe he was angry. "Perhaps if you just told her that I have proposed and you intend to accept, then she'll be appeased and once again leave you alone."

"I wouldn't feel comfortable lying to her. You see, Otto, I don't intend to ever marry again. I have only ever loved one man, and I have no desire to pretend to love another."

He looked at her with an odd expression. "So you actually loved my brother?"

Clara realized that if she denied it, she would have to explain about Curtis and the ranch, and she had no intention of telling Otto about either.

"Please, let us say no more on the subject. I'm afraid it's making me quite sad." That much was true. Anytime Curtis came to mind, it only served to remind her of what she had lost. Of what she could never have.

❧

That night Clara arranged for Mim and the children to join her for dinner. It was far too painful to sit at the table and pretend to be enthralled with the meal when she was so obviously alone.

"I don't like this green stuff," Hunter declared, holding up an asparagus spear. Hollandaise sauce dripped from it onto the tablecloth. "Do I have to eat it?"

Clara shook her head. "No. I know neither of you is used to such things. Just put it back on your plate."

"I think it tastes good," Maddy offered as if someone had asked for her opinion. "Hunter is a ninny."

"Maddy, that's not very nice. Don't call your brother names," Mim interjected.

The child fixed her nanny with a most serious look. "Well, he is. Ruth told me that, and when she explained that a ninny was someone who was silly . . . I agreed."

Clara looked down at her lap, lest the children see she was forcing back a laugh. Ruth, a young woman who acted as her personal maid, was quite right. Hunter could be very much the ninny.

"Be that as it may, Miss Maddy, it's not proper dinner conversation," Mim replied.

Raising her head, Clara smiled at her children. "Perhaps a better topic of conversation would be this: How would you like to go on a trip?"

"Where?" asked Maddy, ever the practical one.

"I thought I might like to take you to meet my aunt and uncle. They are very nice people who live on a ranch in Montana. They have horses and sheep, chickens and all sorts of other animals."

"Could we learn to ride a horse?" Hunter asked.

"I would imagine so." Clara looked at Mim, whose expression suggested interest. "I've been giving this a lot of thought. I wrote to my aunt shortly after Adolph's death. I told her I might like to bring the children and come for a visit this summer."

"That would no doubt do all of you good," Mim replied.

"Would we get to ride on a train?" Hunter asked.

"You are quite concerned with riding," Mim said, laughing.

Clara couldn't help but laugh as well. "We would most assuredly ride on the train. It's a long, long way to Montana."

"When can we go?" Maddy asked.

"I'm not sure." Clara hadn't completely thought through her idea. First she had to go to the bank and see if there was enough money left in her personal account to fund such a trip. She didn't want to ask Otto for fear he would disapprove and make her plans difficult. "I should know more in a couple of days. But in the meantime, say nothing to anyone—especially not to Uncle Otto or Grandmother Oberlin."

Maddy frowned. "Is she here?"

Clara shook her head. "Not yet, but she will be soon enough."

"I don't like her." Maddy's matter-of-fact statement was one Clara could completely embrace, but she didn't want the child to disrespect her elders. Even if those elders were difficult.

"You shouldn't say such things. It's not respectful."

Maddy shrugged. "You told me to always tell the truth."

Clara was momentarily stumped. The child had a point. Mim came to the rescue.

"Maddy, some people are unhappy with life and with themselves. I've a feeling your grandmother is one of those people, so you shouldn't be quick to judge. Instead, pray for her to find joy that her heart might be made lighter."

"Nanny Mim is right," Clara said, noting the time. "Now, if you both finish with your dinner, I happen to know that Cook has made some very special cake for dessert."

"Is it chocolate with cherries?" Hunter asked, most hopeful.

Clara nodded and laughed. "It is indeed."

He quickly pushed aside the asparagus and focused on finishing his roast beef, while Maddy daintily wiped her mouth and pointed to her plate.

"I have finished."

It was only a matter of minutes before Hunter made the same declaration and Clara signaled for the footman to clear the table. She suppressed a yawn and looked again at the clock. Although it was only seven, she found herself longing for a hot bath and bed. It seemed all she wanted to do these days was sleep.

"Maybe it would be better if the children enjoyed their dessert in the nursery." Mim got to her feet and looked to Clara.

"Perhaps so. I know it's hard for them to balance on these pillows."

Hunter wiggled from side to side on the pillows they'd put under him. "It's kind of fun." Mim helped Maddy down, while Hunter dove over the side of the chair. "I can get down by my ownself."

"Very good, Master Hunter. Now both of you kiss your mother and then go straight up to the nursery, and I'll ask Cook to have the dessert brought upstairs."

They did as instructed, then headed out of the room. Hunter took off like lightning while Maddy followed behind at a more sedate pace. Mim waited until the children were out of sight before speaking.

"I wonder if you would mind my accompanying you west. I have family in Bismarck and would very much enjoy seeing them." She looked hesitant. "In fact, I haven't quite known how to bring this up, but I am . . . that is . . . I would like to . . . put in my notice."

Clara couldn't have been more stunned. "Your notice? But why, Mim? Is something wrong?"

Mim smiled. "Not at all. It's just that I've had a proposal of marriage from a man I've long loved."

"Oh, Mim!" Clara jumped to her feet. "That's wonderful. I'm so happy for you."

"I hoped you might be. I had planned to tell you the day we got word about Mr. Vesper's death, but I didn't feel I could desert you, given all that had happened."

"Oh, my dear Mim. You should have said something. I would have understood." Clara looked beyond the dining room and into the hall to make certain the children were gone. "I wasn't quite forthright with what I said to the children. The fact is, I do not plan to return to New York."

"I had a feeling," Mim replied.

"You did?" Clara couldn't hide her surprise. "I hope I'm not so obvious to everyone."

"Not at all. I know how much you love your aunt and uncle and how you long to return to the life you knew there."

"That's exactly what I intend to do. I think the simpler life will be better for the children."

"I think it sounds like a wonderful plan."

"But I'd rather we not say anything to the twins about this being a move rather than a visit. I don't want them accidentally telling Otto or my mother."

The next day Clara waited while the teller counted out her money. There was more than an ample amount to purchase train tickets. After that, Clara could write to Otto and let him know where to send her money. He would have a much harder time arguing with her while more than a thousand miles separated them.

"Mrs. Vesper," a man said, approaching from her right. "I was so sorry to hear about your husband's demise."

She gathered her money and put it into her purse. "Thank you." She looked at him through her veil. "Have we met?"

"Oh, I don't suppose we have. I'm the bank manager, Mr. Walker."

"I am pleased to meet you. I was just closing out my old account."

"I do understand, but I hope you will continue to allow us to help with your needs."

Clara didn't want to give away her plans, so she nodded. "Of course. I just want to consolidate everything so I can better understand what I have on hand."

"Well, in that case, you will want to review the contents of your husband's bank box."

"Bank box?" She hadn't known of such a thing, but neither had she known her husband was given over to bad financial decisions and gambling.

"Yes. He has a safe deposit box. You will no doubt have his key. Perhaps among his other keys?"

"Yes, perhaps." Clara hadn't even begun to go through her husband's things. Nor had she really intended to. Since everything apparently belonged to Otto, she didn't know whether this was something he wanted to do himself.

"Well, just bring the key and ask one of the tellers to find me. I will be happy to personally assist you, Mrs. Vesper."

"Thank you. I'll do that."

Clara found herself thinking about the box throughout the day. By the time she had Mr. Lawrence drive her back to the house, she was determined to search for the key.

For the first time since her husband's death, Clara entered his bedroom. The room smelled stale with a hint of tobacco. Adolph had enjoy smoking his pipe by the fire while he read before bed. Clara had often caught the scent of his favorite tobacco from her room, even though the doors were seldom opened.

She went first to his dresser. Atop was a picture of her on their wedding day. The girl in that photo was dressed most impeccably in the latest, most stylish of wedding attire. Clara remembered the exact moment she had posed for that picture. All she had thought of was Curtis and how she would have to forever put him from her mind if she was to accept her new lot in life. Without giving the photograph further consideration, she placed it facedown.

Next she pulled out the top drawer and began to look through the neatly pressed handkerchiefs, gloves, and collars. No sign of a key. Nor was there any key in the remaining dresser drawers. For a moment Clara looked around the room, wondering where else her husband might have put the bank box key. Her gaze fell upon a side table near the bed. She went to it and pulled open the drawer. A gasp escaped her at what she saw there. A revolver.

Clara had no desire to touch the thing. She'd been taught a few things about guns when she was on the ranch. The most important of which was to *"never handle a gun unless you know what you're doing or someone is there to instruct you."* She had neither the knowledge nor the assistance, and so left it alone.

She started to close the drawer, then stopped. Why had her husband felt the need for a gun? She had never once heard him speak of purchasing one. Had someone threatened him? Was it possible he had been murdered because someone had something against him? Perhaps it hadn't been a random robbery. She closed the drawer. There was no sense in contemplating the matter. The police surely had more understanding of the matter than she did.

After lunch Clara decided to investigate her husband's office. She supposed it possible he would have kept the key in his desk with his business things, despite its being a personal item. Her search was rewarded almost immediately. The key was there amid papers, pencils, stamps, and ink pads. The name of the bank was clearly etched at the top.

Clara looked at the clock. There was still time to return to the bank and investigate the contents of the safe deposit box. She hurried into the hall, nearly knocking Perkins off his feet.

"Oh, Perkins, I am so sorry. I'm afraid I am a bit mindless today."

"It is quite all right, madam. Might I be of assistance?"

"Yes. Would you ask Mr. Lawrence to bring the car around? I need to go back to the bank."

"Of course."

Clara hurried upstairs for her black hat and gloves, as well as her purse. She couldn't help but think of the gun in the next room. Perhaps she would have Perkins remove it. There was no telling if it was loaded, but she presumed it was. It was definitely a danger to the children if they should wander in there and find it.

The trip to the bank was slowed by heavy afternoon traffic. The population of the city seemed to have doubled just since morning. Clara wasn't at all sure what was going on, but it seemed that people were everywhere.

"What do you suppose has happened?" Clara asked her driver after several minutes of stalled traffic. Perhaps Hunter's desire for a circus had come to be.

"I haven't any idea, ma'am. Would you like for me to ask someone?"

Clara spied a policeman. "Yes, ask that officer."

The driver nodded. Since traffic hadn't moved in some time, Mr. Lawrence jumped out of the car and made his way to where the police officer stood. Clara watched him speak to the man, and then after a few moments Mr. Lawrence returned.

"Well, what has happened?"

"Apparently, ma'am, Congress has passed the Selective Service Act, authorizing a draft."

"A draft for what?"

"Military service, ma'am. Our army apparently is rather small, and a great many men are needed for the war. The officer said there has been a celebratory spirit of sorts and people are quite excited."

Clara sank back against the seat, shaking her head. They might all die in the war, yet everyone was acting as if they'd just been asked to a grand party. She was glad to be heading west soon and leaving the city. It was bad enough that German submarines lay in wait off the coast, torpedoing passenger ships as well as freighters. It was absolutely terrifying to imagine that those same submarines might threaten the city itself.

The traffic began moving again after some delay, and finally Clara made her way into the bank. The delays had been such that the bank was only minutes from closing. She quickly requested Mr. Walker and breathed a sigh of relief when he appeared.

"You're back so soon. I didn't expect to see you, what with the masses gathering outside."

"It was difficult."

He nodded. "Did you find the key?"

"Yes. I presume this is it." She held up the key.

The man smiled. "Exactly so. Please come with me."

He led her to an area of the bank Clara had never visited. Here he took her key and, in a matter of minutes, seated her at a table with the closed box. "I'll return in just a few minutes. Feel free to leave whatever you like in the box. It will remain in your husband's name unless you wish otherwise."

Clara waited until he'd disappeared out the door before opening the box. To her surprise she found several banded stacks of money and four small books. She picked up the first of the books and opened it. It appeared to be a diary of sorts in her husband's handwriting. How strange. She'd never heard Adolph say even once that he was keeping a journal. She checked and found the other books to be the same. Perhaps their children would one day want to read them and know their father better. She slipped the books in her purse, then took up the money.

For a moment she wondered if she should give the money to Otto. If Adolph had mismanaged their affairs to the degree Otto implied, then this money might help to set things right. On the other hand, something about the entire matter had troubled Clara. Adolph had always been very meticulous with their affairs, and what little she knew of their finances had always seemed solid.

She heard footsteps on the highly polished floor outside the open door and quickly stuffed the money into her purse. She could further contemplate what was to be done once she was in the comfort of her home. For now, all she knew was that there was a gun in her husband's bedside table and a great deal of money no one apparently knew about in his bank box. None of it made sense.

So I purchased train tickets for each of us," Clara told Mim. "I do have some concern that Otto might ask about us at the depot after we've gone, but given the size of the station, I seriously doubt anyone would remember two women with children."

"Perhaps you should forego wearing black," Mim suggested. "That way you won't stand out among the other travelers."

Clara nodded. "I had thought of that as well." She lowered her voice to add, "I hate black."

They were interrupted just then by a very worried-looking Perkins. "Madam, I was just passing the foyer and saw a car arrive. It's your mother."

Clara stiffened. She had hoped they might be able to leave before her mother arrived. "Very well." She looked to Mim. "You should probably return to the nursery. However, I want all of you to join us for dinner at noon."

Mim nodded, not even questioning Clara's instruction. The nanny hurried from the library, leaving Clara and Perkins alone.

Clara tried to think of what she should do. The doorbell chimed, and she shot up from her chair.

"I suppose you'd better let her in. I'll meet her in the formal parlor."

"Very good, madam." Perkins turned to head out of the room, then paused. "Although, I could tell her that you are indisposed."

Clara laughed. "She would never believe it, nor care. No, I'll see her."

While Perkins went to admit her mother, Clara made her way to the parlor and prayed. She found she didn't feel half as brave as she'd hoped to. She had promised Otto she could hold her own with her mother, but now she was honestly concerned as to whether that was true.

She heard her mother before seeing her. Harriet Oberlin was not one to remain silent when she was disturbed.

"You took your sweet time opening the door, Perkins. I won't brook such dereliction of duty in the future. I presume without my son-in-law to keep you all in line, you have simply taken charge of the house, but that has come to an end."

"Yes, madam," Perkins could be heard to reply.

Clara could imagine him shaking his head when her mother wasn't looking. She smiled at the thought and took a seat in an antique throne chair her husband had given her for her last birthday.

"Now where is my daughter? I demand you take me to her immediately."

Perkins opened the door to the parlor and stepped inside. "Mrs. Vesper, your mother has arrived."

She started to instruct him to show her mother in, but instead her mother pushed past him and descended on Clara like a summer storm.

"You would not believe the difficulty I've had getting here. The entire city seems to have gone mad with this war. It was bad enough I couldn't risk sailing here from Florida due to all those intolerable German submarines threatening our shores, but the trains were positively crowded with men going off to be soldiers." She paused and looked down her nose at Clara. "You look terrible."

"Thank you, Mother."

Clara studied her mother for a moment. The older woman was dressed in a pigeon-breasted style reminiscent of the previous decade. The mauve color suited her graying hair and the floor-length hem her sense of propriety. Mother had often spoken out against the newer, shorter fashions. She believed women should keep their limbs concealed beneath their skirts. No doubt she would disapprove of Clara's dress being inches from the floor, despite the black stockings and black heels.

Her mother waved her hand. "I don't know why you chose these garish colors for the main parlor."

Clara shrugged. "I suppose because my husband liked blue and gold."

"Yes, well, he's gone now. Perhaps I will make some appropriate changes." Her mother walked around the room as if already planning what she would do. "This wallpaper will have to go."

"Mother, why are you here?"

Her mother paused and fixed her with a look that suggested complete surprise. "To see you through your time of grief, of course. I have instructed Perkins to have my things moved to the guest room. I intend to stay and see that you are not given over to sorrow."

Clara hadn't figured on her mother planning to stay. "You have your own house, Mother. You needn't install yourself here."

"Nonsense. You will need me. I will arrange for the children

57

to go away to boarding school and for the house to be brought up to date. Honestly, I don't know why your husband allowed everything to fall into such disrepair."

Clara looked around the room, trying to figure out exactly what her mother meant by her statement. Everything was up-to-date, clean, and beautiful.

"I like the way things are, Mother. We needn't change anything. Not only that, but my children are not yet of school age, in case you've forgotten."

The older woman stopped and turned, her expression pinched in obvious discomfort. "It won't do for you to have children underfoot while choosing another husband."

"But I don't intend to choose another husband." Clara got to her feet. "Nor to have one chosen for me."

Her mother's face reddened as she sputtered. "I . . . I . . . well, I never expected such disrespect. You are in mourning, however." She calmed a bit and gave a huff. "I suppose that is the reason for your obvious error in judgment."

Perkins appeared just then. "Mr. Vesper is here to see you, madam."

Before her mother could speak, Clara nodded. "Show him in."

"What in the world is your brother-in-law doing here?"

"He comes here quite regularly." Clara turned as Otto entered the room. "Good morning."

He eyed her mother and then frowned. "I didn't realize your mother had returned."

"I have just arrived, so you needn't remain. As you can see Clara will be in my capable hands, so you may go."

Clara watched in amusement as the two squared off. Otto wasn't about to have Harriet Oberlin order him around. Clara reclaimed her chair and remained silent as they went about haranguing each other.

"I have been here for Clara throughout her marriage to my brother," Otto contended.

"You obviously thought it perfectly fine to interfere in their privacy, but now that my daughter is a widow, it is hardly appropriate for you to be here."

"It is more than appropriate. I have asked Clara to marry me."

Clara wasn't surprised that her mother again turned red in the face. "Marriage to you is out of the question. Imagine the gossip among decent folks."

"If they are in truth decent folks, then they won't be gossiping," Otto countered.

It was a definite point scored for her brother-in-law, as it momentarily silenced Clara's mother. That silence didn't last long, however.

"Decent folks will also not allow for you to marry your brother's wife. I'm appalled you would even suggest such a thing."

"Few people worry about those antiquated notions."

"People of quality upbringing do. Besides, Clara is naïve and needs my guidance. There will be many a man who will try to take advantage of her position and wealth."

Otto looked at Clara as if expecting her to explain. Clara sighed. She wasn't ready yet to explain her financial situation to her mother. Otto didn't seem to realize this, however.

"Your daughter has obviously not seen a need to share the truth with you. You know very little about her position."

"What is that supposed to mean?"

Otto smoothed his mustache. "Just this. My brother was a poor manager of his money, and he died with very little to his name."

Clara noted her mother's stunned expression but continued to remain silent. She would have ample opportunity to explain the details to her mother once Otto was gone.

"I don't believe you. How terrible you are to frighten my daughter. You are exactly the kind of man who would take advantage of her."

The grandfather clock chimed the hour, and Clara got to her feet. "I must interrupt. Perkins is soon to come and announce dinner. You are both welcome to partake, so long as this disagreeable discussion is concluded."

Both Otto and her mother appeared surprised at her announcement. Otto moved to her side. "I am afraid I cannot remain. I have business that must be attended to." He lowered his voice. "Might I return and see you tomorrow?"

"Of course." Clara looked past him to see Perkins standing in the doorway. "Ah, Perkins. I was certain you would soon arrive to announce dinner."

"Yes, madam. Everything has been made ready, and the others are already seated."

"Thank you. I'll be there directly."

He'd no sooner exited than her mother moved to stand beside her. "What others are already seated?"

"Why, Mim and the children. We usually take our meals together."

"Well, that will come to a stop. Children belong in the nursery."

Otto reached for Clara's hand. "I will come to check on you soon, sister." He bowed ever so slightly over her hand, then released her. He looked to her mother. "Good day, Mrs. Oberlin."

"Good day, Mr. Vesper, and you needn't come to check on Clara. I am moving in to stay with her until she is past her mourning and once again settled with a proper husband."

Otto looked as if he might comment on this, but thankfully he said nothing. Clara could see he was quite upset by her mother's words, but surely no more than she. After he was gone, Clara turned to her mother.

"Come, let us join the others."

Her mother began to pull off her gloves. "I haven't even had a chance to freshen up."

"If you prefer, I can have a tray brought to your room."

"No. That won't be necessary."

They crossed the hall and passed from the music room into the dining room. Clara smiled at Hunter and Maddy balanced atop pillows once again. Mim was just helping to push Hunter's chair closer when they entered the room.

"Mama, you need to come see our drawings. Nanny Mim helped us make pictures of animals," Hunter announced.

"How wonderful." Clara crossed to kiss her son atop his head. "I will see them later, but first look who has come to share our meal. Grandmother Oberlin is here."

Hunter frowned and Maddy did likewise. Neither child cared for the overbearing woman. Meanwhile, Clara's mother stared at the gathering as if there were animals seated at the table instead of merely being the topic of the children's drawings.

"Why don't you greet your grandmother," Clara said, smiling at her children.

"Good afternoon, Grandmother." Maddy's words were barely audible.

"Good afternoon." Hunter's voice, though louder, was also filled with obvious displeasure.

"Honestly, Clara. I cannot be expected to dine with these hoydens. It's completely uncalled for."

"Mother, these are my children and I will dine with them whenever I choose. If you do not wish to join us, I will have a tray delivered to your room."

"Clara, I've had just about enough of your disagreeable nature. You have no call to speak to me in such a manner, and I will not tolerate it." Her mother's eyes narrowed. "I am trying to take into account your loss, but your behavior is quite abominable."

Maddy began to tear up. She reached for her mother. Clara immediately took the child in her arms and lifted her from the chair. "It's all right, Maddy. Don't let this ruin your dinner." She whispered the words in her daughter's ear, then turned back to her mother. "You are upsetting my children, Mother."

"That is why they should be in the nursery." She turned and glared at Mim. "Do your duty and take them away from here now."

Mim got to her feet as if to counter this order with words of her own, but Clara spoke up first. "Mim, perhaps you should take the children back to the nursery. I need to speak to my mother, and it would be best if they didn't have to endure it, for it might be quite unpleasant."

"Very well." Mim helped Hunter from the chair. His scowl let Clara know in no uncertain terms how unhappy he was, but she was grateful he remained silent. Coming to Clara, Mim took Maddy in her arms.

"I'll be up to see you very soon," Clara promised the children. Maddy began to weep against Mim's starched collar, but Hunter was already marching from the room. Clara gave Maddy a quick kiss and then let Mim take her away. Once they were gone, Clara sat down and rang for the footman.

A young man appeared shortly, and Clara ignored the fact that her mother was still standing. "Please see to it that dinner is taken up to the nursery for Nanny and the children."

He nodded and started to leave, but Clara's mother demanded his assistance. "Have you lost all knowledge of your training, boy? Seat me at once and then tend to your mistress."

The young man looked shocked but hurried to pull out the chair for the older woman. Once he had her seated, he hurried over to help Clara, but she waved him away. "I'm fine. Go see to the children's food, and then you may serve us."

"I can see I've been away much too long."

"Mother, I am sorry that the children make you nervous. However, in the future, if you wish to dine with me here, I want you to understand that they will be welcome at the table."

Her mother was unconvinced. "Children are useless to anyone until they are old enough to make advantageous marriages. You have clearly lost your wits due to your husband's death. I suppose if my husband were murdered, I might be rather shaken as well." She eyed Clara with a most disagreeable look. "However, I won't abide such nonsense, nor your disregard of my instruction."

The footman returned with their soup, but this didn't stop Clara's mother from continuing. "I am appalled at how the years have changed your once agreeable nature. It is quite alarming. I think perhaps it would behoove me to call for a doctor. You may be in need of a sedative—something to help you relax and regain your composure."

Clara bowed her head and whispered a prayer of blessing for the food. She then silently asked God to help her not to lose her temper. She was determined that her mother would not get the best of her.

Without another word Clara sampled the soup. The warm tomato bisque tasted delicious. She and the children were quite fond of Cook's bisque and had it at least once a week.

"This soup is cold."

Clara looked at her mother. She seemed determined to be disagreeable. Instead of commenting, however, Clara continued to eat. When the footman arrived with thick slices of German rye bread, Clara took a piece, then addressed the matter of her mother's soup.

"Would you please take Mrs. Oberlin's soup away? She says it is cold. Please have another bowl brought to her."

"Yes, ma'am." The young man went to where Clara's mother sat. He first offered her bread, but she waved him away.

"Leave us. The soup is tolerable."

The servant looked to Clara, and only after her nod did he leave the room.

Clara began to butter her bread. No doubt her mother would find something else to criticize or argue about, but Clara didn't intend to be drawn into it. She had learned over the years of dealing with her mother that the woman didn't care at all for what anyone else thought or felt. Instead, Clara silently planned her escape. It would have to be soon.

After dinner, Clara stood and gave her mother a smile. "I'm afraid I must excuse myself. I want to check on the children and then lie down. I'm quite tired."

She didn't wait for her mother to respond, which sent the woman into sputtering comments about Clara's rudeness. It would have done little good to remain and try to calm the older woman. Instead, Clara picked up her pace and all but ran up the stairs.

Just outside the nursery she found Mim speaking to one of the maids. Upon seeing Clara, Mim dismissed the girl.

"Are you all right?" Mim asked.

Clara nodded. "I am, but I have determined we must leave right away. I cannot subject the children to my mother's ill temper. Neither have I any desire to be the center of her attention."

Mim smiled. "I'm sure it's for the best. What can I do?"

"Ready the children's things. They needn't take anything fancy. We'll be living on a ranch, after all. Just bring their play-clothes and perhaps one or two things they might wear for church."

"Perhaps one of the trunks should be packed with toys. I doubt your aunt and uncle would have any on hand."

Clara nodded. "Yes, a few things could be brought along. I'm sure there will be more than enough to amuse them. Still, I imagine Maddy will want her favorite doll, and Hunter will not sleep without his Steiff bear."

"How shall we arrange to have the luggage taken to the station without being noticed by Mrs. Oberlin?"

"I'm sorry to eavesdrop," Perkins said, coming from around the corner. "But perhaps I might be of assistance."

"Oh, Perkins, if you could, that would be wonderful." Clara gave him a smile of gratitude. "Still, I'm afraid Mother will make life quite difficult for you once she realizes the truth."

"You mustn't worry about it, madam. The staff and I are quite capable of handling the situation. Without you here, she will be vexed, of course, but once she understands you do not intend to return, she'll no doubt depart for her own quarters."

Clara frowned. "How did you know that I don't intend to return?"

He shrugged. "It stands to reason."

Clara let go a sigh of relief. "I feel much better knowing you will help to arrange everything. But we must hurry to get it all accomplished without Mother becoming suspicious."

"Consider it already done, madam. The staff and I are quite loyal to you. You've always treated us fairly and with, shall I say, great affection."

Clara put her hand out to stop Perkins from leaving. "What will you and the others do? I mean, when Mr. Vesper sells this house, you will no longer have employment."

"Perhaps if you would be so kind as to leave us letters of reference," he suggested, "we could assume other positions with relative ease."

She nodded. "Of course. I'll go write them as soon as I finish seeing the children. I'll leave them on my desk, and you may distribute them when I'm gone. I'll also write Mr. Vesper a letter, encouraging him to help you all."

"Very good, madam. Now I will take my leave and see what I can arrange."

As he headed down the hall, Clara looked at Mim. "Well, it would seem our adventure awaits."

6

*O*tto paced the small space of his office. Harriet Oberlin was going to be trouble. She already was. The woman was demanding and obnoxious, and he resented her interference. Especially since that interference threatened his own plans for Clara.

"The afternoon mail," Jack Brindleson announced, coming into the room. He put the letters on Otto's desk. "Will you need anything else for the moment?"

Otto stopped in mid-step. "I need a way to rid myself of Clara's mother."

Jack gave an apathetic nod. "That woman would try the patience of Job. I heard she was back in town. News of such a tumultuous storm travels fast."

"Indeed. I've encountered her already. She's installed herself at Clara's, and I know she means to make trouble. Honestly, I cannot stomach the woman, and I don't know how Clara will abide her without giving in to her demands."

"I'm sure it will be a challenge. I've never known Mrs. Vesper to show much backbone. She's always been such a timid little thing."

Otto rubbed his chin. "She told me she could handle her mother, but she will surely fail. Mrs. Oberlin is a woman used to having her own way. No doubt she already has plans for Clara."

"What about the jewelry? Will she interfere in allowing Mrs. Vesper to continue designing the pieces?"

"Her mother knows nothing about Clara's involvement, and I mean to keep it that way."

Jack frowned. "You don't suppose Mrs. Vesper will tell her, do you?"

"I don't think so. It's been my experience that she offers very little information to her mother. For one thing, the old bat won't shut up long enough to let anyone else speak, but I also think Clara enjoys having her secrets."

"Then perhaps we are safe. After all, you have those new pieces to work on. I heard that the wax molds are ready on two of them. They had to remake one of the others. The man working on them carelessly got a tiny portion of his fingerprint set into the wax."

"You fired him, of course." Otto wouldn't brook such nonsense.

"Of course." Jack shrugged. "He seemed unconcerned. Told me he was off to join the army."

"Hello? Mr. Vesper?" a matronly voice called from the outer office.

Otto straightened. "That will be Mrs. Nash to see me." He moved toward the door. "Show her in."

Jack went quickly to the task, and the portly Mrs. Nash soon appeared. The older woman was dressed impeccably in throat-to-floor black bombazine, with a very prominently featured brooch that Clara Vesper had designed some years earlier. She leaned heavily on an ornate silver-handled cane.

"It is so good to see you again, Mrs. Nash. I must say I was delighted to receive your note asking to come to the office." Otto helped her into the leather chair opposite his desk. "Should I have Jack prepare some tea?"

"No. I shan't be here long. I wanted to offer my condolences. I was most distressed to learn of your brother's demise. I'm hoping"—she lowered her voice—"that there might be another piece or two from the Vesper collection which I might purchase."

She fixed him with such a determined look that Otto might have laughed out loud had she been anyone else. However, Mrs. Nash was very wealthy and influential. She was also known as one of the best sources of information. The old busybody knew the details on everyone around her and never hesitated to share them. It gave Otto an idea.

Walking behind his desk, Otto took his seat and smiled. "I will share a secret with you, because I know you will keep it to yourself."

She smiled and touched her gloved hand to her breast. "I am the very soul of discretion."

Otto nodded. "Well, the truth is, I will have several pieces available soon. I intend to have a showing—a gala. You were the first one I thought to invite."

"How marvelous! I am so relieved to learn there will be other pieces available. I think I should want to buy them all. You truly wouldn't need to arrange a party to display them."

He smiled. "Well, I wouldn't want this to get around, but there will be additional pieces for some time to come. I will provide them as I . . . always have." He waited for the idea to sink in.

Mrs. Nash seemed momentarily confused, and then her

expression changed. "Oh my stars! *You* were the designer—not your brother!"

Otto thought for only a second to correct her but decided against it. He'd come this far and might as well see it through.

"My brother was my life," Otto said, hoping his feigned look of sorrow would touch the old woman. "He was far more interested in fame and glory, however. I was content to let him take credit for the designs."

"Oh my. Oh my. This is most exciting."

"Well, as I mentioned, it would be best to keep all of this to yourself. Although I do know there are others who are wise to this situation—workers here know the truth, but they have long been silent on the matter." He ran his finger along his mustache, hoping the lie wouldn't create problems for him with Clara. "But no, I still believe it is better to keep the truth to ourselves . . . for now."

"You can count on me, Mr. Vesper," Mrs. Nash said with a knowing smile. "I have always been able to keep a secret."

"Thank you. In return, I am also happy to give you first rights to the new pieces. They will be costly. We intend to use only the finest gems, and they are much more difficult to get with the war in Europe."

"I completely understand. I will pay whatever is necessary."

Otto couldn't have been more pleased. Not only was he assured of selling each of the new designs for a large sum, but Mrs. Nash would soon have word out on the street that Vesper jewelry was still to be available.

"Well, I must go," Mrs. Nash said, tapping her cane on the floor as if to signal for his help.

Otto hurried around the desk to help the large woman from her chair. "I will be in touch," he told her. "When the pieces are ready, I will be certain to send word."

"Thank you. I'm so relieved."

"And it will be our secret regarding the true designer?" Otto asked as they reached the door.

"But of course, Mr. Vesper." She put her gloved finger to her lips.

Curtis felt like a trapped animal. After a month in bed, he was no closer to being up and around than when he'd started. At least it felt that way. After Paul and Joe had pulled him from the collapsed mine, Curtis had known nothing but pain and misery.

"You have to stop being such a grump," Madeline told him as she entered the room. "Doc said you were a bear to deal with."

"I'm sick of this. He won't take me out of traction or remove the casts. He told me he'd send his father to cheer me up, but I told him not to bother."

"But seeing Pastor Cosgrove might improve your outlook. I know you're hurting and unhappy to be cooped up. But with your back and leg broken, you're lucky to be alive. Fact is, to hear what the doctor told me a month ago, you're lucky to still have that leg."

He shook his head. "I don't know about that. What's the use of having a leg if it doesn't work right? Doc said it might never heal properly."

Going to the window, Madeline paused long enough to give Curtis a look of disapproval. "You're not doing yourself any good wallowing in self-pity. Now, you know full well that you'll recover from this and be back on your feet soon enough. As to why it happened, well, there's no explaining it. God has His reasons, and I'm not about to call Him into account." She opened the window. "There, that breeze will help."

She secured the curtains at the side of the sill. "Doc did say you'd most likely be rid of those casts before the summer heat sets in, so you should be thankful for that."

He sighed. "Sorry. I know you're right, but I'm angry and hurting and . . ." He stopped and shook his head.

"I can help with the latter, but not so much with the anger." Madeline produced a bottle of medicine from her apron pocket. "Doc left this for the pain."

"I don't want it. I can't think straight when I take that stuff."

Madeline nodded and put the bottle on the bedside table. "I guess I can understand that." She pulled up a chair and sat down. "Curtis, I know you and Paul have talked at length about what happened. You know that you have a home with us and we'll see you through this bad time. But I'm worried about you. I'm afraid your anger is going to send you back to the bottle if you aren't careful."

Curtis was surprised by her comment. Madeline had never before brought up the past or his drunken ways. He bit his lower lip and nodded. "I know you're right. I suppose that's why I've fought off taking the medicine. At first I didn't have a choice. The pain was so bad I couldn't think straight even without the medicine clouding my mind. Now it just makes me remember what it felt like when I drank. I don't want to go back to being that man."

She reached over and took hold of his hand. "I know you don't, and I want to do whatever I can to help you avoid that. Maybe it would help if you talked about who you're really mad at. I know it's not yourself, although you naturally have some frustration with your physical limitations. My guess is you're mostly angry at God."

"And why not? All of my life He's taken and taken. I know the Bible says He gives and takes away, but can't He just leave me alone for a while?"

Madeline squeezed his hand, then let it go. "You think you have it so much worse than every other person?"

"Well, you have to admit, I've had it worse than most. My parents died before I was ready to be without them. The only girl I'll ever love was taken away from me. I ended up running with the wrong folks and found myself in prison. I lost my hope and nearly my life."

"God didn't steal those things away from you, Curtis. That much I know."

"If not God, then who? You and Paul keep telling me God is all-powerful and all-knowing. If that's true, then He knew my parents would get sick, and He had the power to make them well. But He didn't. He knew what those losses would do to me. He knew it would send me to drinking and abominable actions, and yet He let it all happen."

"Goodness, Curtis, it seems you can't take responsibility for anything."

He glared at her. "What do you mean?"

"I mean that you were the one who got yourself into that mess with drinking and gambling. You were the one who chose those means of comfort. I'm not about to sit here and let you off the hook for that. Nor am I going to sit here and let you feel sorry for yourself. We all make bad decisions in life, Curtis. We all make mistakes. We are sinful and human." She crossed her arms and fixed him with a stern motherly look. "You are certainly no exception."

"Thanks for reminding me." Curtis let out a heavy sigh. "I know I'm the one who made mistakes and headed down the wrong path. But I didn't kill my folks, and I certainly didn't send Clara into the arms of another man."

"No, and while I do agree that God was able to keep those things from happening, it's not my thought that He was happy to see them happen. Like I said, the devil does a lot of interfering with folks in this world."

"But God could stop the devil from that interfering."

"Yes, you're right. He can. I guess when He doesn't, that's where our faith is forced to grow . . . or die. Curtis, you have to know that God loves you no matter what the world tells you is fair or not fair, right or not right. Either God is worthy of your faith or He isn't. That's something you have to decide."

She got to her feet. "You know I love you. I'll make you as comfortable as possible while you're bound up in that contraption." She motioned to the casts and the rigged-up traction for his leg. "But I won't feel sorry for you. Nor will I stand here and let you feel sorry for yourself. It's true you've lost a lot in life. Your folks and then Clara. It wasn't fair and it wasn't easy to bear, but it is what it is and no amount of sad thoughts will change it. Same goes for your accident at the mine. It was a horrible thing, and I feared we'd lose you altogether." Tears came to her eyes. "I'm grateful to God that won't be the case."

"But the doctor says I might never fully recover," Curtis countered. "He says I'll probably always walk with a limp and have trouble with my back."

Madeline nodded. "You just might. So maybe you ought to work on getting your mind around how you're going to deal with that—if it happens to be true. You've overcome a great deal in a short life, Curtis. I know you have it in you to overcome this as well."

⁂

Madeline walked down the hall, drying her eyes on her apron as she went. She was sad for Curtis and his lot in life, but sympathy wasn't going to help him. She'd been hard on him, but it was all for his own good. Still, she hated causing him even more pain.

Lord, I don't know what else to do. You're going to have to show me how to help him, because I'm running out of ideas.

Three hours later, much to her surprise, the answer came in the form of mail brought back from town by Phil and Joe. Reading through her niece's letter, Madeline could only smile. Clara was coming to the ranch. Coming home, as Madeline saw it.

She couldn't help but glance heavenward. "Thank you."

"Who you thankin' and for what?" Paul asked, coming in behind her.

Madeline turned to him and grinned. "I was thanking God for answering my prayer."

"What prayer was that?"

"Well, what with all the work around here, I was thinking we needed to find a nurse for Curtis. The doctor says he still can't remove the cast, so Curtis will need someone to help him when I'm out working with the lambs."

"I told you I could hire an extra man to help free you up. You don't need to go hiring a nurse."

Her grin widened. "I don't intend to hire a nurse, but I found someone just the same." She held up the letter. "Clara's coming for a visit."

Paul's face showed concern rather than joy. "Don't you think that's askin' for trouble?"

Madeline laughed. "Trouble of the very best kind. She's free from the demands of her mother. A widow with two young children able to make her own choices in life."

"And you figure to help her and Curtis get back to plannin' a life together?"

She nodded. "I do. I can't help but see how this has been God's plan all along. Curtis can't run away, and Clara will help me out of my obligation to care for him. Throwing those two together to work through the past is the perfect answer."

"It could prove dangerous."

Madeline put her hand up to caress her husband's face. "Love always is."

7

"What's this all about?" Otto Vesper demanded. He stormed into Clara's front parlor and stared at Harriet Oberlin in distain. "You've taken me away from very important business."

"Well, this is just as important. I want to know what *you* know about my daughter's disappearance."

Otto frowned and looked around the room. "What do you mean?"

"Come now, surely you were a part of this." Harriet went to a silk-covered chair and took a seat. "Clara is gone. She has taken the children and their nanny and left on some sort of foolish trip."

He couldn't hide his shock. He knew nothing about Clara's plans. "She's gone?"

"I won't brook any nonsense, Mr. Vesper." Harriet fixed him with an intimidating stare. "If you know where she has gone, then I demand you tell me."

"But I don't know. I don't know anything about her leaving. She said nothing to me about it." He turned on Harriet. "This is all your fault. You come here with your insulting, demanding ways and have no doubt caused her great grief. No wonder she left."

Harriet stiffened. "How dare you. She is my daughter and I have every right to be here."

"Perhaps to be here, but not to order her about or impose your will upon her as you did twelve years ago when you forced her to marry my brother."

"Clara has never known her own mind," Harriet countered. "Her choices were always poorly made, and she led such a sheltered life that it was imperative I make good choices for her. Now is no different. The very fact that she has gone proves this."

"Nonsense. My sister-in-law is quite capable of ordering her life and her children's. You stormed in here with your demands, and she simply decided to avoid dealing with you altogether. I cannot say I blame her one bit." He hoped that would be the end of it.

"What is this about your brother leaving Clara with nothing?"

Otto bristled at the change of topic. "I hardly feel it's any of your business."

"Of course it's my business. Now tell me what is going on. I know for a fact your brother made plenty of money selling his jewelry designs. Where has that money gone?"

"He spent it. He loved his gaming and . . . other things." He waited for that to register.

"Clara said nothing."

"Of course she didn't," Vesper countered. "She knew nothing. That was how I wanted it. I told my brother I would continue to bail him out of trouble so long as she never knew."

"That was very . . . considerate of you. But do you mean to tell me she has nothing? Not even this house?"

"The house and all that is in it . . . is mine. However, she is welcome to it for as long as she desires to live here. I have taken great care to see to it that she wants for nothing."

Harriet's tirade slowed as she appeared to take more care in choosing her words. "You said that you asked her to marry you."

"I have, and after a suitable time of mourning we will be married."

She tapped her chin. "You have obviously done well for yourself despite your brother's follies. However, now that he is dead, your income will certainly be compromised without his designs."

Otto gave her a smug smile. "That is where you are wrong, Mrs. Oberlin. The designs were not my brother's doing. He only took credit for them, as he craved fame and glory."

"Then whose designs were they? Yours?" It was obvious Harriet found this bit of news quite intriguing. "Clara never said anything about it."

"Of course she didn't. She knows nothing about it. As I said, it has always been my desire to keep her sheltered from the business dealings and hardships brought about by my brother. You see, Mrs. Oberlin, I have long loved Clara. I love the children as well. And they know me better than they knew their own father. Marriage to me is the right and proper choice. I need only convince Clara."

"Society will be dismayed at the idea of you marrying your brother's widow. It won't seem at all proper, and that will make Clara uneasy."

"Well, perhaps that's where you can help. Both with society and your daughter."

She tilted her head as if trying to better understand his meaning. "And what form would that help take?"

He chuckled. "You have a great many friends and, as I

understand it, have a great deal of sway in society. You could promote my good characteristics and the fact that I have long loved Clara from afar. You could let it be known that Clara and Adolph never loved each other and that the marriage was purely an arranged one. I presume most people know that, but reminding them wouldn't hurt."

"And exactly how am I supposed to do this promoting?"

"For the benefit of society you could mention it when attending summer soirees or when hosting your dinner parties." He paused for a moment and frowned. "Perhaps with Clara it would be best to say nothing. She seems to take a strong dislike to your instruction, since it forced her into a loveless marriage once before."

"And what would I get in return?"

Otto smiled. He knew he had her hooked. Like a fish on the line, now he had only to reel her in. "We can negotiate those terms in the days to come, but for now it would behoove us to find Clara."

She nodded and got to her feet. "I will take it all into consideration. In the meanwhile we should probably hire someone to help us find out where she's gone. I doubt she will be away long, but given her fragile state of mind, she could very well do something foolish."

Vesper stood. "I will arrange it immediately. Now if you'll excuse me, I have business that needs my attention."

༄

Otto was glad to be away from the old biddy. Harriet Oberlin was a decided thorn in his side, but with any luck at all he'd manage to get rid of her. He had in mind one or two gentlemen who would be happy to seek the old lady's attention, and if Otto could just keep her busy with them, then perhaps he could find Clara and marry her without further interference.

When he reached the office, Jack was not there, and no one else was around to tell him where his secretary had gone. He looked around Jack's area, thinking he might have at least left him a note, but found nothing. Nothing turned up in his office either. He thought for a moment he might venture down to the workrooms, where a couple dozen men worked on putting together various pieces of jewelry. Along with their unique Vesper collection, they were still in the business of producing more common pieces. However, he still needed to find the missing money, so the workroom could wait.

Otto made his way to Adolph's office for what must have been the hundredth time. Since his brother's death he had searched without luck for the missing money and papers. Standing in the doorway he looked around the room. They had to be here. No doubt Adolph had hidden them away, but where?

Otto's gaze fell to the polished wood floors. Could there be a loose board somewhere? Perhaps Adolph had a compartment in the floor that he used for hiding those things, which could cause them both a great deal of harm if found.

Moving about the room, Otto inspected every board but found nothing. Once more he began to go through his brother's filing cabinets just in case he had missed something before. With every second his anger increased. How dare his twin jeopardize them in this way?

At the sound of someone in the outer office, Otto gave up his search. "Is that you, Jack?"

He found not only his secretary but also a suit-clad man he didn't recognize, as well as a uniformed police officer. He halted at the door.

"I see we have guests." He forced a smile. "How may I help you gentlemen?"

The suit-clad man stepped forward. "The name's Badeau. William Badeau." He turned to the officer. "Why don't you wait for me in the hall? I'll let you know when I need you." The man nodded and exited the room. Badeau, meanwhile, fixed his gaze on Otto. "I believe we have business to discuss."

Otto studied the man a moment. He had the hard look of a man used to pushing people around and forcing answers to his questions. No doubt he was some sort of law enforcement official.

"I haven't a great deal of time. What is this about?"

"It's about espionage and treason," the man replied. "You see, I'm working for the government to ferret out spies."

"I don't see what that has to do with me."

Badeau's lips curled ever so slightly. "I think it has a great deal to do with you, Mr. Vesper. With your dead brother as well. We have quite a bit of evidence to suggest that your brother was part of a large group supporting Germany. I have a feeling you're a part of that as well."

"While it's true my brother and I do share an ancestry that involves German relatives, we are, or shall I say, I am an American. My brother felt the same way. We were born and raised here. We would in no way compromise our lives by dabbling in Europe's war."

"It's our war now as well, or haven't you been paying attention to the newspapers?" He reached over to Jack's desk and picked up a piece of paper. "And why would you need to have a detailed schedule of ships coming in and out of our harbor?"

"Because we import a great many gemstones and export finished jewelry. The crown heads of Europe can vouch for that, as they are often commissioning pieces. We never use any routine shipping plan, lest thieves take advantage." Otto barely replied in a civil tongue as his ire increased. He knew he needed to remain calm, however. "Why don't you tell me what it is you hope to learn? I'll do my best to assist you in concluding your business here."

This caused Badeau to smile in full. "Our business is just beginning, Mr. Vesper. I have a number of police officers waiting in the hall. We're here to confiscate your business records and any other information we deem questionable." He handed Otto a search warrant.

This wasn't going at all as Otto had hoped. In searching for the missing money and papers, Otto couldn't remember anything of an incriminating nature. Nevertheless, the thought of having strangers go through their offices didn't sit well.

"I must protest," Otto replied. "I have a business to run and people counting on me to fill orders."

"I doubt the delay of jewelry will create that much of a problem. Especially when men are losing their lives in the war." He went to the door and motioned for his men. "Boys, have at it. I want you to fill those boxes we brought with the contents of the filing cabinets and desks." He turned back to Otto. "I presume you have a safe. I'm going to need to see the contents of that as well."

⁓⁊⁊⁊⁊⁊⁓

"But when will we get there?" Hunter asked his mother.

Clara gave him a patient smile. "We should be there by tomorrow. Are you already tired of riding on the train?"

Hunter pressed his nose against the glass. "I like the train, but it all looks the same out there. Just fields and fields and fields. No more cities."

"Well, this is the country," Clara explained. "There are towns, but they are much smaller."

Just then Mim and Maddy returned from a trip to the washroom. Maddy climbed up on the seat next to Clara and picked up her doll. She cradled it like a baby, even though it greatly resembled a girl several years Maddy's senior.

"Was my baby good?" she asked her mother.

Smiling, Clara pushed back Maddy's honey-blond hair. "She was excellent. She didn't cry even once."

Maddy nodded and patted the doll's face. "She's always a good girl."

Mim took the seat facing Clara and smiled. "Just like you are, Miss Maddy."

"I'm good," Hunter declared, frowning at his sister, "but I'm a boy and we need to run."

Clara smiled. "Well, you'll have a chance soon enough. I have some good news to tell you both." Clara waited until Hunter turned to give her his attention. "Tonight we're going to arrive in Bismarck. That's where Nanny Mim is from. We're going to stay the night in a hotel there, and then we'll get back on the train in the morning, and by late afternoon we'll be getting off in Montana."

"That's where Auntie Madeline lives, isn't it, Mama?" Maddy asked.

"She does. The train will take us to the little town, but after that we'll go by wagon or carriage because Auntie Madeline and Uncle Paul live quite far from the station."

Hunter looked concerned. "Don't they drive cars in Montana?"

"Of course they do, but most people in the country still use horses and wagons. I think you'll actually like it, but it will take us longer to get from one place to another."

"Can you ride a horse, Mama?" Hunter asked.

Clara nodded. "I most certainly can. I used to be quite good at it, in fact. I hope to see both of you learning to ride just as well."

Mim smiled at Clara. "I know my folks are going to love getting to meet you all. I'm so glad you decided to stop over in Bismarck."

"It will be pleasant for all of us, Mim. I know Hunter is starting to feel a little cooped up. It's hard for a boy his age to sit for so long at a time."

Hunter nodded. "It's just no fun."

Mim and Clara laughed, but it was Maddy who spoke up. "Nanny Mim says that sometimes you just have to make your own fun. Isn't that right?"

"It is indeed, Miss Maddy," Mim replied.

Hunter clutched his bear and went back to pressing his nose against the window. "Well, I can't make any fun here."

"Don't worry, Hunter. We've not got all that far to go. I promise when we arrive in Bismarck, we will have a very pleasant dinner and perhaps we might even have ice cream for dessert." Clara knew the boy would find that of interest. He didn't disappoint.

"With chocolate on it?" he asked, his eyes wide with hope.

"If they have it available to us, then yes."

Hunter smiled and turned back to the window. "I hope we get there in a few minutes."

Of course it took longer than that, and by the time the train finally pulled into the Bismarck depot, Hunter and Maddy had been sleeping for over an hour.

"Time to wake up," Mim told Hunter while Clara nudged Maddy.

"Are we there?" Hunter asked, yawning.

"We are," Mim replied.

This brought the boy fully awake. He jumped up from the seat and grabbed his bear. "I'm ready to go."

Maddy seemed to catch her brother's enthusiasm and did likewise. "Baby and I are ready too."

Mim helped each of the children into their coats while Clara signaled to one of the porters. She instructed the man regarding their bags and tipped him generously to ensure he would devote his attention to their needs.

Mim and Maddy exited the train first. A porter helped them down the steps and onto the depot platform. Before Clara could say a word, Hunter shot past her and leapt from the train to land with a bounce on the platform.

"Hunter!" Clara looked at the excited boy in disapproval. "You are never to jump off the train like that again. You could get hurt or hurt someone else."

Hunter frowned and lowered his head. "Sorry, Mama. I like to jump."

There was no time to comment further as they were engulfed by Mim's family. Clara thought it all so very nice. Everyone was delighted to have Mim home. Her mother and father were rather quiet, but quite welcoming, while Mim's younger sister, Mary, was boisterous and full of information.

"We managed to secure you a room at the Northwest Hotel," Mary explained. "It's very near the depot, so you needn't go far. Also they have a wonderful place to eat. I think it's the best in town, although we don't get to eat there very often."

Mim kept glancing around, and Clara knew she was looking for her beau. Finally a very tall man with broad shoulders came bounding out from the depot. He saw Mim and took off his hat to wave as he made his way through the crowd.

"I'm so sorry I'm late." He rushed toward Mim but stopped

short of taking hold of her. "You look even prettier than you did five years ago."

"Has it really been five years?" Clara asked. "You haven't seen each other in all that time?"

Mim nodded, her gaze never leaving the man's face. "It was never convenient for me to get home."

The man turned to Clara. "I'm James Wilson. You must be Mrs. Vesper."

"I am. It's very nice to meet you, Mr. Wilson."

"Just call me Jim," he replied. "I'm just Jim."

Clara smiled. "I'm pleased to make your acquaintance, Jim." She turned to Mim. "I wish you would have said something. I would have made certain you came back at least once a year." Clara frowned at the thought that she had never considered Mim's family. She had been so caught up in her own concerns that the needs of her nanny went completely out of her mind. In New York's elite society no one worried about the needs of a mere servant.

"It's all right. She's here now," Mim's father declared. "And I don't know about the rest of you, but my insides are emptier than a preacher's pockets on Saturday night."

Mim laughed, and Clara couldn't help but smile. She took hold of Maddy's hand. "Then I believe we should arrange for our things and head right to dinner because I'm just about that hungry myself."

8

*C*lara marked May twenty-fourth as the start of a new life with their arrival in Montana. As the train slowly chugged to a stop at the depot, Clara felt her previous worries fade away. The tiny Montana town looked much as it had fourteen years earlier. To Clara it was absolutely perfect. Throughout the trip she'd felt she wasn't running away from something, but rather to something. Now she knew that *something* was home and the family she had longed for.

The porter helped Hunter from the steps of the train first, then Maddy, and finally Clara. She looked around the platform eager to find her family. In Chicago she had managed to get a wire off to her aunt and uncle, but there was no telling if it had reached them. If they didn't show up, she supposed she and the children could just spend the night at the hotel. Or maybe she could rent a carriage. Glancing down a little ways from the tiny station she could see the livery, still very much in business.

"Where's Auntie Madeline and Unca Paul?" Maddy asked, gripping her mother's hand tight.

Hunter was running up and down the short platform while the baggage man finished bringing their luggage.

"Clara!"

She turned and saw her aunt and uncle. "Aunt Madeline!" She pulled Maddy along and called to Hunter. "Come along, Hunter, they're here."

Hunter, being his usual self, ran right past Clara to where the older man and woman approached. By the time Clara and Maddy joined them, he was already explaining who he was and why he'd come.

". . . and Mama said you would teach me to ride a horse."

Paul laughed. "I guess I could do that."

Clara threw herself into her aunt's open arms. How good it felt to be held again—to be embraced with genuine affection. A sob escaped Clara, and she tightened her grip.

"There now, what are these tears all about?" her aunt asked.

Clara loosened her hold and met the older woman's eyes. "I've missed you so much. It's just good to be home again."

"Well, what about me?" Paul asked, coming alongside. "Don't I get a hug?"

"A hug and a kiss," Clara said, turning. Her uncle bent down and presented his cheek, and Clara pressed her lips against the leathery skin.

With this done, Paul pulled her into a bear hug and laughed. "It's mighty good to see you again."

He let her go and looked down. Hunter was pulling on his coat. "Did you bring your horse to the train?"

"I brought two of them," Paul replied, reaching down to scoop the boy up in his arms. "You wanna see them? They're hitched to my wagon."

Hunter looked at his mother. "May I see them?"

"Of course," Clara said, laughing. "Maybe you could show

90

Uncle Paul where our bags are." Hunter nodded enthusiastically and pointed.

While they tended to the luggage, Madeline bent to greet Maddy. "So this must be my namesake."

"What's a namesake?" the child asked.

"It means you were named Madeline after me."

Maddy nodded. "Yes, I was, but they call me Maddy. Mama told me you were her favorite person in all the world and she named me Madeline so she would always have you with her."

Madeline straightened and met Clara's teary gaze. "What a lovely sentiment."

"It's true," Clara replied. "Adolph never cared what I called the children, so I told him we would name Hunter after my maiden name and Madeline after you. He was perfectly happy with that so long as their last name was Vesper."

"He had his son to pass along his name and keep the line going," Madeline replied.

"I'm hungry," Maddy interjected.

Aunt Madeline chuckled. "Well, your uncle Paul was just saying the same thing as we drove into town. I reckon we'll have to do something about that. There's a nice little café just across the street where we can get a decent meal."

"Are you sure we can take the time?" Clara asked. "It's already quite late in the day, and if I recall, the trip to the ranch will take a little over an hour. I wouldn't want Uncle Paul to have to drive the team in the dark."

"You forget. This is nearly summer in Montana, and the days are longer. We've had a perfectly beautiful day, and while it's getting a little chilly, it'll stay light for hours yet."

Clara had forgotten that fact. She smiled, remembering the late evenings she'd enjoyed walking outdoors with Curtis. "It's true, I had forgotten."

"So we can get something to eat?" Maddy asked hopefully.

Clara nodded. "Yes. Of course we can. In fact, it will be our treat." She saw her uncle and Hunter returning and bent down. "Why don't you go ask Uncle Paul if he would like to join us for dinner."

Maddy considered it for a moment, her expression quite serious. Then without another word, she turned and marched off to cross the short distance between them. When she'd reached the two, she paused and asked in a loud and clear voice, "Unca Paul, would you like to join us for dinner?"

He crouched down in front of her. "Why, my goodness. I've not been asked out to dinner by a pretty girl in a very long time. Your aunt used to pester me all the time to have dinner at her house when she was but a little older than you."

"I was considerably older than Maddy when we were courting, and if you will remember correctly, you were the one always inviting yourself to have dinner with me and my folks," Madeline interjected.

Maddy didn't concern herself with their conversation but kept her blue-eyed gaze fixed on Paul, waiting for his answer. Paul smiled and lowered his voice as if the rest of them wouldn't be able to overhear him.

"Your auntie doesn't always remember things the way I remember them. Sometime I'll tell you stories about how she used to chase after me all the time."

Maddy's stern expression remained, causing Clara to explain. "Maddy is quite serious about her tasks and is awaiting your answer, as she is very hungry."

Paul laughed and picked Maddy up as he stood. "I would love to have dinner with you, Miss Maddy. Where shall we go?"

"Auntie Madeline said there's a café across the street."

He put his hand up to shield his eyes and gazed out as if trying to spot a storm on the horizon. "Why, there sure enough is, Miss Maddy. I'll bet they have mighty good food."

Maddy nodded, looking rather uncertain at the man who held her. "Auntie Madeline said it was decent."

Paul roared with laughter and hugged the child. "It won't be nearly as good as what your auntie can make, but we'll make do."

"What about our luggage?" Clara asked as Paul started for the café. She glanced around, worried that the bags were nowhere in sight.

"We've already loaded 'em in the wagon," Paul called over his shoulder.

"I guess that takes care of that," Madeline said with a smile. She put her arm around Clara. "It's so good to have you back. How long can you stay? I hope at least the summer."

It was Clara's turn to be serious. "I was hoping forever."

⌒⥾⥾⥾⌒

They enjoyed a lovely dinner and then made the long journey back to the ranch. Clara watched the passing scenery, often spying sights and catching scents that she'd long forgotten. The rolling hills, the distant mountains, sweet scents of meadow flowers and new grass. How she had missed it all.

When the ranch came into sight with the nearby fields full of ewes and lambs, she very nearly broke into tears once again. The bleating of the sheep was like music to her ears, and even the heady smell couldn't lessen her joy.

Paul parked the wagon between the larger of several outbuildings and the log house. He helped everyone from the wagon and then unloaded the bags. Hunter insisted on helping.

"Put them in the west wing rooms that I fixed up earlier, Paul.

Everything is ready for them." Madeline turned and smiled at Clara. "I'd imagine you're all pretty worn out. The children were all but dozing on those last few miles."

"Yes. It's been such a grand adventure for them, but I know they're exhausted. I'll get them cleaned up and put to bed."

"Paul and I will need to check in with the boys. We've been pretty busy with lambing. Your uncle keeps us all on a tight schedule—the sheep too. He's insistent that they finish birthing this week."

"Sounds like the uncle I remember." Clara lifted Maddy and walked toward the house.

Madeline kept step beside them. "Since you were here, we put in a nice little bathroom. Paul rigged up a large reservoir outside and fixed it with a stove for heating. It lets us draw hot water for the bath. We're just as sophisticated as they come—except for the outhouse."

Clara smiled, but her own weariness was beginning to take a toll. "It sounds wonderful."

They entered the front door, and Clara immediately spied her portrait hanging there in the hall. Turning to the right just past the hat tree and pegs for the coats, she smiled to see that so little had changed in the front room. Her aunt had made a very cozy living room with several chairs and a sofa positioned around the large fireplace. Clara could remember many a rainy day spent in that room stitching quilts and learning to crochet and knit.

"It's just as I'd hoped." Her voice was barely a whisper, but Aunt Madeline heard it well enough and gave Clara's arm a squeeze.

The house was a single-story log cabin that had been expanded over the years. Because of that, the house spread out like honey on warm bread. Rooms had been added on and others repurposed, but everything was pretty much as it had been when Clara lived there.

"Would you like me to help get the children ready for bed?" Madeline asked.

Clara shook her head. "No. We'll be just fine. I'll see to them. I know you have things to do. Don't worry about us."

Maddy had already started to doze against Clara's shoulder. Madeline nodded, and when they reached the bedrooms, she smiled to find a bleary-eyed Hunter sitting atop one of the trunks.

"I think Hunter may not stay awake long enough to have a bath."

Clara shifted Maddy. "Perhaps I'll just sponge them off and put them to bed." She noted the two small beds, happy that the children would each have their own. As twins, they had slept together up until last year, but now they enjoyed having their own beds. Although on stormy nights they could often be found curled up together.

"Well, I'll leave you to it, then," Madeline said.

When she'd gone, Clara set to work. She'd never been responsible for bathing or dressing her children. Life in New York had come with its rules, and women of social standing were not to be burdened with the mundane tasks of raising children. It was necessary, of course, to birth them, but then their care and troubles were given over to a nurse or nanny. Now Clara couldn't help feeling that she'd missed out on a great deal.

Once she had the twins washed and dressed in their night-clothes, Clara helped each one into bed, then led them in prayer. She wasn't surprised that they fell asleep almost immediately. Being as quiet as possible, Clara exited the room and made her way across the hall to her old room. Nothing here had changed except the quilt on the bed.

She smiled at the familiarity and found her exhaustion abated. It suddenly seemed important to see and experience everything. Clara left the room and made her way back to the living room. She paused only a moment before crossing the hall to another sitting room, which she thought of as the music room. Clara touched the ornately carved upright piano. Aunt Madeline had tried to teach her to play, but Clara never took to it easily and lost interest.

Through the music room, Clara wandered into the dining room and then the kitchen. She was surprised to see that while much had remained the same, there were some pronounced differences here. Aunt Madeline had a much newer and larger cookstove and a beautiful icebox near the back door. A small kitchen table and chairs for more casual meals stood against one wall, and cabinets and a counter with an enameled sink lined another. Clara went to where the sink was and turned the single faucet. Water came out, and Clara smiled. No doubt this was another of Uncle Paul's creations. The man was ingenious. When Clara had last been with them, she had helped carry in many a pail of water from the pump.

From the kitchen she could make her way into the long hall that connected the east and west wings of the house. Her aunt and uncle's bedroom was at the far end of the east wing, as were two additional bedrooms that used to house their three boys. The west wing bedrooms had been added when those boys had reached their teens. Aunt Madeline had explained this allowed for everyone to have some much-needed privacy. It also allowed Madeline to convert one of the former bedrooms in the east wing to a sewing room.

Walking across the hall to this room, Clara pushed open the door anticipating that everything would be just as it had been fourteen years ago. Instead, she found the sewing machine had been pushed to the far side of the room and a single bed had been added. In that bed was a man whose casted body left no doubt of the injuries he'd suffered.

"Oh, excuse me." Clara hurriedly stepped back and started to pull the door closed, but then her gaze caught sight of the man's face.

She let go of the door. Her hand went to her lips as a gasp escaped. It was Curtis. She had no idea how it could even be possible that he was here, but he was and her heart began to race as words tumbled from her mouth.

"My love. My one and only love."

9

*O*n the evening of the twenty-fourth, Otto was still curs-
ing Badeau and his invasion of the office days after the
man and his thugs had loaded up most of their files and taken
them to an unknown location. *How dare the man come in and
accuse me of being a traitor!* Then Otto chuckled at his own
contradiction. *His accusation is indeed correct, but that doesn't
give him the right to come in and take everything.*

After all, what was he supposed to do now regarding business? He could have the workers continue making jewelry, but
Badeau had taken all of the company papers. Otto had no idea
where they were supposed to ship the inventory once it was
complete. Of course, it was possible that by that time Badeau
would return the files. But given the disagreeable nature of the
man, Otto wasn't about to count on it.

It was nearly eight o'clock. Brindleson had sent word that
they should meet at seven, but so far his secretary hadn't appeared. Otto paced between the three offices trying to figure out
what he should do. He'd just convinced himself to leave when

the door opened and a rather worried-looking Jack slipped inside.

"I think I'm being followed."

Otto frowned. "I'd given you up and was just now going to my sister-in-law's. I haven't yet had a chance to go through my brother's office thoroughly, and it's possible that he kept some of the money and paper work we've been seeking hidden there. If you truly think you're being followed, why don't you come with me? Mrs. Oberlin won't be happy to see either of us, but at least it will throw off whoever is following you."

"But I have no idea if it's our associate's doing or the law. I just know that someone was shadowing my steps." Jack frowned.

"If it's our associate's doing, he won't cause us harm. At least not until we fulfill the jobs we agreed to take on. After that it's anyone's guess as to what he'll do. If it's the law, they won't think twice about us journeying to my brother's house."

"Our associate has had confirmation," Jack said, as though Otto could have somehow forgotten this fact. "That's one reason I sent word to meet me here. The other is to tell you that the submarine will be in position off the coast next Friday morning. He's had proof that the old clothing factory is now a munitions warehouse. Our friend said to tell you that everything must be in place by next Friday. That gives us a week to come up with the money and munitions. And he said to tell you he's losing his patience."

"I know very well the limit of his patience." Otto put on his outer coat. "Stay here or come with me—it's up to you. And if you happen to meet up with our . . . friend . . . assure him that I'm doing everything possible to locate the missing money. If it can't be found, I'll use my own money."

Jack nodded. His pale face betrayed he was still very afraid.

"I'll . . . stay here . . . for a while. Perhaps if they see you leaving, they'll follow you and I might be able to slip out unnoticed."

"Do as you like. Be here first thing Saturday morning and we'll discuss what is to be done."

He didn't wait for Jack to comment but snugged down his hat and made his way outside. At least the street vendors were gone. As well as most of the other workers, shoppers, and a growing number of men in uniform. Otto sensed a movement from somewhere to his right and picked up his pace until he spied a cab. He signaled the driver.

"Where to?" the cabbie asked.

He gave the man Clara's address, then eased back into the seat and tried his best to figure out what he was going to do. He had Mrs. Nash's promise to purchase the new jewelry, and just that morning he'd sent her a note telling her he'd be happy to show her the sketches and if she still wanted the pieces, she would need to make a deposit. A very large one. Otherwise, he would refuse to reserve the pieces. The problem was how to figure the price. With the war preparations that had now engulfed America, people were inclined to spend less. Mrs. Nash had more than ample funds and probably little concern over that "*pesky affair in Europe,*" as he'd once heard her refer to the war. There were others like Mrs. Nash who could very well afford to part with their cash—especially if it was for one of the coveted Vesper Yogo pieces.

Not only that, but Otto felt it only right to increase the price due to the added difficulty of getting gemstones from around the world. No one needed to know that he had most of the needed stones already on hand. The only thing that truly concerned him was whether or not he could get Mrs. Nash to get him the money no later than Tuesday. Even that would make it difficult to procure the necessary explosives.

The driver pulled to a stop in front of Clara's home and opened the door. Otto hastily paid the man and then made his way up the front steps. He had no desire to have to make small talk with Harriet Oberlin, but with any luck she might be out for the evening. After all, there was a new opera debuting in the city.

Otto lifted the knocker and tapped it several times against the door. When Perkins appeared, he didn't seem at all surprised to find Otto.

"Sir?"

"I need admittance to my brother's office. There are important papers I must locate."

"Very good, sir." Perkins stepped back. "Mrs. Vesper said you were to be admitted at all times."

Otto smiled and stepped into the foyer. "Have you heard anything from your mistress?"

"No, sir." The man offered a hint of a smile. "Mrs. Oberlin is quite concerned about her absence, but there has been no word." He cleared his throat and went to the foyer table. He opened the drawer and retrieved an envelope. "She did leave this note for you. I'm afraid Mrs. Oberlin's demands caused it to quite leave my memory."

Otto snatched the paper from him, hoping it would reveal where Clara had gone. Instead he found nothing but a brief request that he was to help the servants find other positions. He crumpled it and glanced toward the stairs. "Is Mrs. Oberlin at home?"

"No, sir. She left earlier this evening to attend the opera."

"Thank goodness. She was the last one in the world I wanted to have to deal with." Perkins assisted him to remove his coat. With that done, Otto handed him his hat. "Hopefully I'll be long gone before she returns."

"Very good, sir. Would you care for any refreshment?"

Otto had always enjoyed the meals he'd shared in this house. The cook was quite talented—much more so than the old woman who cooked for him and cleaned his small apartment.

"Yes. I'm afraid I've been quite busy today and missed partaking of dinner."

"Would you care for a casual meal in the office, or do you prefer a more formal arrangement in the dining room?" Perkins asked.

"The office is fine. There needn't be any big fuss."

"Very good, sir." Perkins turned to tend to the hat and coat.

Otto left the butler in the foyer and made his way to the library. He passed through the chilly room and opened the door to his brother's office. He turned on the lights and found most of the furniture had been covered. The desk and chair in the center of the room were the only exceptions.

As he made his way to the desk, Otto tried to remember anything that Adolph had said about his hiding places. Otto knew there was a safe behind the large gilt-framed painting of a group of hunters on horseback. The only problem was, he didn't know the combination.

It was highly possible, however, that Adolph had left the combination written down somewhere. His brother was never good about remembering details. It was one of the reasons he kept exhaustive notes of their activities. Otto had often cautioned him against such things, but Adolph had assured him that the information was safely concealed. Apparently that was true, because Otto hadn't been able to find the much-needed information in over a month of searching.

He sat down behind the desk and opened up one drawer. He pulled out papers and scanned them. Most were bills that held absolutely no interest to him. Next he found several letters, responses to personal items that Adolph had been trying to purchase. One letter was from a boarding school in Massachusetts that declared that although the twins were younger than they normally accepted, they would be most happy to accommodate them in the fall when school began. Provided Adolph was still of a mind to pay the price they'd previously quoted. Otto wondered if Clara had any idea of his brother's plans.

Finding nothing of interest in the right-hand drawers, Otto moved to the left side of the desk. Here he found writing paper, envelopes, and other necessary things for correspondence. The lower drawer revealed a stack of ledgers that detailed years of household spending.

Letting out an exasperated breath, Otto thumbed through the ledgers just in case there could be any incriminating evidence. Badeau might have his suspicions of their participation in treasonous espionage, but there was no sense in giving the man proof.

For years Otto and Adolph had supported the cause of their ancestral homeland. When the war had first started, they had been approached by a distant relative explaining the money they could earn should they agree to simply furnish information about the ships coming and going and any other news that might pertain to America's clandestine involvement in the war.

Adolph had been hard to convince. He hadn't wanted to participate. He didn't like the idea of involving the jewelry business in affairs of war, but Otto had convinced him that with America standing by idle, it was their duty to help. Germany needed them. Their ancestors and living relatives needed them. Finally his brother had been convinced, believing Otto when he assured him that innocent lives would be saved by giving their assistance. When the *Lusitania* sank, taking with it nearly twelve hundred passengers and crew, Adolph had been horrified. Germany had broken the Cruiser Rules, and innocent lives had been lost. Otto had explained that their sources knew full well that the ship had also carried a great number of munitions for Great Britain's use against the Germans, but Adolph hadn't cared. He was heartsick, and from that point on lost his interest in the war.

Finally Otto opened the center drawer. On top of some papers was a small black book. Inside he found names and addresses of associates and friends. On the very last page he found the combination to the safe. He smiled at his brother's predictable nature and memorized the numbers before shoving the book into his pocket. No sense letting anyone else know how to get into the safe.

He'd only just managed to secure the book out of sight when Perkins arrived with a tray. To Otto's delight the cook had put together a sumptuous feast, including thick slices of roast beef smothered in gravy with long slices of roasted potatoes. Beside this on a separate plate was a large piece of apple pie and next to that a slim silver pot. He couldn't help smiling as Perkins poured him coffee.

"A meal fit for a king. Please give Cook my compliments. I hadn't expected anything quite so grand."

"I will tell her you are pleased. Mrs. Oberlin had ordered the meal prepared for dinner, but that was before the arrival of a Mr. Badeau." He replaced the pot and began moving the dinner plate and silver to the desktop.

"Mr. Badeau was here?" Otto lowered his face lest Perkins see that this news had upset him. He forced himself to keep a calm, steady voice. "I didn't realize he would want to search the house."

Perkins set the plate in front of Otto. "Do you know this gentleman?"

Otto looked up and smiled. "Not well. He came to the offices and demanded to go through all of our papers. He believes my brother to have been a German spy. I told him the entire thing was ludicrous. We were born and raised here, and I told him we were just as much American as he was. He still had his strange notions, however, and took most of our files."

"I am sorry, sir." Perkins finished the task of moving the food from the tray to the desk. "Mrs. Oberlin was quite enraged and refused to allow him admittance. She admonished the staff to refuse him entry if he returned."

"I am surprised that Badeau allowed her to keep him from entering. Legally he has the right and no doubt has a search warrant. With the war going on, sedition won't be tolerated, and since Badeau is convinced of our guilt, I'm certain he will return to storm the place and confiscate whatever he deems usable in his case against us."

Perkins nodded. "I believe Mrs. Oberlin felt the same was possible."

"Well, all I can say is the man is demanding and will no doubt return with a force of men. You should prepare yourself, Perkins, and accept that it will be exactly as they wish." Otto picked up the china cup and savored the rich aroma of the coffee. "We are completely at their mercy."

"Yes, sir."

Perkins exited the room, leaving Otto to consider all that he'd just learned. For once he was grateful for Harriet Oberlin's obnoxious nature. He looked with longing at the food, then decided it would be best to get the safe opened and then get away from the house. He drank the coffee nearly in one gulp, then left the tray and headed for the safe.

He lifted the painting from its hook and set it aside. Quickly recalling the numbers, Otto turned the dial and then opened the safe. Inside were stacks of papers and a small amount of cash. Otto pocketed the cash and then thumbed through the papers. Here he found the deed to the house as well as stocks and bonds, which were, of course, all in his brother's name. No sense in leaving them for someone to find and prove that he'd lied to Clara about her husband's foolish spending.

Otto quickly undid the buttons on his coat and vest, as well as his shirt. He stuffed the papers inside, then redid the buttons. He had barely returned the painting when he heard a commotion that could only be Mrs. Oberlin. Once again he noted the tray of food and decided to forego the pleasure. With Harriet Oberlin in the house, eating would only result in indigestion.

10

*C*urtis could only stare in dumb surprise as Clara came to the narrow bed and carefully sat down beside him. Her eyes filled with tears as she lifted his hand to her lips.

"My poor, sweet love." She kissed his fingers tenderly. "What in the world has happened to you?"

She was here. He wasn't dreaming. His Clara had returned, and she was declaring her love for him. For a moment Curtis very nearly gave in to the race of emotions that coursed through him. He wanted nothing more than to speak her name and feel her in his arms. But then, even as he imagined that wondrous moment, the past came crashing down on him like the posts and rock had at the mine.

The things he'd done were unforgivable. She would never be able to reconcile the fact that he'd given himself to women, drink, and gambling. She would be mortified at the knowledge that he had served time in the penitentiary.

"Oh, Curtis, speak to me. Tell me what happened."

He fought his tender feelings for her and frowned. "What are you doing here?"

She straightened and looked at him oddly. "Didn't Aunt Madeline tell you I was coming?"

"No." He kept his tone curt. "Why are you here?"

She smiled and his heart seemed to flip. "I've come to make a new start . . . a new life in Montana. My mother would say I've run away, but I believe I've come home."

He narrowed his eyes. "Montana isn't your home. You don't belong here. Just look at you."

"Oh, I know I'm a mess, but—"

"You aren't a mess. You're fashionable and beautiful. You wear expensive clothes and no doubt have learned in fourteen years to have equally expensive taste. That isn't something you're going to find out here."

Her smile faded. "I love Montana. Just as I love you."

"Have you forgotten that you have a husband?"

She shook her head. "He's dead. He was shot and killed by an unknown assailant."

Curtis felt like a complete heel. "I'm sorry. Even so, you don't belong here. Montana demands hard work out of its women. You should remember how difficult it was. I know Madeline kept you busy with chores."

"Aren't you . . . happy to see me? You've been on my mind ever since I started this journey." She laughed, but it sounded hollow. "No, you've never been out of my thoughts at all. Even when Adolph proposed and my mother forced me to accept, I thought of you. I thought of you when I took my vows and wished it was you to whom I pledged my life." She flushed and looked away. "I've always thought of you."

A part of him thrilled to hear her declaration, while the stiffness caused by his cast reminded him he might never again leave this bed. Clara deserved so much more than to keep giving her heart to a cripple.

"I'm sorry that you thought so much on me. That must have been very hard on your husband."

She fixed him with a very serious look. "Adolph always knew how I felt. I confessed it to him when my mother first put us together. I reminded him of it when he proposed and again on our wedding day. I told him I loved you—that I'd pledged myself to you and that I would never love another." She squared her shoulders and looked like a soldier about to head into a battle. "He said he didn't care. He didn't love me either."

Her statement nearly broke Curtis's resolve. How terrible it must have been for her to spend twelve years in a loveless marriage. This beautiful woman with her gentle ways and loving heart deserved to be loved above all else. He wanted to say something to offer her comfort. He wanted to tell her the truth—that he still loved her.

"Adolph loved making money. He cared nothing for having a family. In time we learned to have a reasonably amicable relationship. He gave me everything but love, hoping it might be enough to keep me content. I in turn kept his home and hosted his parties. I was everything society demanded I be, but my heart was never his." She let go her hold on Curtis. "I kept hoping he would leave me to myself. I even prayed he might one day release me—divorce me. I didn't even care about the stigma that would follow. I only wanted to come back to Montana—to you."

Curtis didn't know what to say. Here she was finally at his side once again, declaring her love just as he'd always dreamed she might . . . and he couldn't have her. He couldn't impose on her a life of shame. Everyone in the valley knew of his past and the wrongs he'd done. They loved only too well to talk about him behind his back—just loud enough to make certain he knew they would never forget. Or forgive. It hadn't mattered to him . . . until now.

After several long and painful moments of reflection, Curtis finally spoke, keeping his tone serious. "Go home, Clara. Go back to New York. You don't belong here. I'm sorry you've wasted your heart—your life—on forgotten childhood promises."

"Forgotten? Have you truly forgotten what we meant to each other?" Tears streamed down her cheeks.

Curtis bit his tongue to keep from declaring it was all a lie—that he loved her—wanted her more than he wanted his next breath. He had never wanted to be the cause of her tears.

"I can't give you what you want. I can't pretend to feel something I don't feel." He turned away from the look of heartbreak on her face. In that moment he'd never hated himself more.

"What are you saying, Curtis?"

He knew what he had to say and turned back to her with an expression that he prayed was void of the raging emotions within. "I don't love you anymore."

A sob broke from her as Clara jumped to her feet and ran from the room. He heard her crying all the way down the hall. It tore his heart in two. If he could have gotten out of the bed, Curtis knew he would have run after her.

Gritting his teeth, Curtis felt a primal cry rise up inside him. He stuffed it down with reminders of his worthlessness. She was better without him. It was for her own good that she deal with this here and now. Once she realized there was no reason to stay, hopefully she would leave the ranch and go back to New York.

❦

Paul stepped aside as Clara came running and sobbing down the hall. He called to her, but she ran on to her room and slammed the door behind her. Glancing back in the direction

112

she'd come, he saw that Curtis's door was open. Apparently she'd just seen Curtis and his injuries had caused her grief.

Deciding he'd let Madeline help Clara understand what had happened and how Curtis was making good strides in his recovery, Paul went to Curtis. He walked into the room with a smile. "I see you and Clara lost no time getting together. She's grown into a real beauty, hasn't she?"

"Why did you tell her I was here? Better still, why didn't you tell me she was coming?"

Paul thought for a moment that he hadn't heard right. "What did you say?"

"I want to know why you told her I was here. I'm no good for her anymore. You know what I've done—who I was. You know what's going on with me now. I'm busted to pieces and nobody knows if I'll even get out of this bed again. It's cruel to bring her here to me."

Crossing his arms, Paul gave Curtis a stern look. "Before you go reprimanding your elders, you ought to get your facts straight."

Curtis's angry expression softened. "I'm sorry. I didn't mean any disrespect. I'm just . . . just . . . flummoxed. I never thought I'd see her again and never wanted her to see me like this."

Paul pulled up a chair. "Her husband died."

"I know. She told me."

"Did she also tell you that she just up and decided to come here? She didn't give us much of any warning. Sent a letter saying she was planning to come for a visit, but not when she'd get here. We got a telegram barely half an hour before we needed to leave to fetch her."

"That was why you had to go to town?" Curtis asked.

Paul nodded. "It was. We figured Joe could keep track of you and see you were fed and we could fetch Clara."

Curtis shook his head. "I'm sorry for jumping to conclusions. It was just such a shock."

"Well, apparently it was pretty hard on her too. She's sobbing her heart out. What in the world happened? Was she upset by your injuries?"

"No. She was upset because I told her I didn't love her anymore."

"You what?"

"You heard me." Curtis shook his head. "Sorry. I'm just irritated—angry, really."

"I guessed that part," Paul replied sarcastically. "What in the world are you angry about? The woman you've pined away for is back—and she's available."

"But I'm not." Curtis looked away. "I can't expect her to ever overlook what I've done—who I am."

"You're a new creation in Christ, as I recall." Paul once again folded his arms against his chest. "Are you doubting now that God forgave you?"

"I don't doubt He forgave me, but where others are concerned, I know they didn't."

"So what?" Paul frowned. "You don't think for one minute our Clara won't forgive you, do you?"

"It's not that." Curtis drew a ragged breath. He honestly felt close to tears. "Where she's concerned—I can't forgive myself."

"Can't or won't. Seems to me that holding on to the past puts a high wall between you and future plans. I've never known you to be a coward, but it seems to me you're afraid."

"It's not fear driving me," Curtis protested. "It's practicality."

Paul laughed. "Practicality is as good an excuse as any to avoid dealing with your feelings for Clara."

"I'm no good for her. Even if the past didn't matter to her, I'm stuck with this body and these injuries. I don't know if I'll ever walk again. I don't know if I'll ever be able to get out of this bed again."

"And I don't know if I'll wake up tomorrow," Paul countered and started for the door. "But it sure doesn't mean I'm not going to live life to its fullest in the meantime." He stopped just before exiting the room. "I think it's time for some hard thinking, son. You need to figure out what kind of future you really want. You can go on feeling sorry for yourself and wallowing in self-regret, or you can do something more productive."

"Like what?" Curtis asked, sounding quite without hope.

Paul smiled again. "You don't need me to help you figure that out. That's what the Almighty is for."

11

*C*lara rose the next morning, her eyes swollen from weeping late into the night. She hadn't cried this much since she'd had to leave Curtis fourteen years ago. But then, her heart had never been this broken. Not even when she'd waved goodbye to him as her mother's hired carriage took her from the ranch, because she still held hope. Hope that she could change her mother's mind. Hope that she might return to Curtis and his love.

Now that hope was dead, and Clara mourned the loss more than she had her husband's demise. Perhaps this was her punishment for having married one man while always loving another. Perhaps God had been angry at her, even though she had pushed thoughts of Curtis aside to honor her husband. Even though she had resigned herself to never know love again.

She looked at her two precious children as they climbed from their beds. She had always felt they were gifts from God—His consolation.

Without much conversation she dressed Hunter and Maddy. They watched her with odd expressions, knowing that something was wrong but not understanding. She felt horrible and tried to smile.

"We must hurry. Uncle Paul reads from the Bible each morning and then talks about what we've read." She helped Maddy with her shoes. "It's always very interesting."

They were still awkwardly silent, so Clara continued to try to make small talk. "Aunt Madeline always makes a wonderful breakfast. I think you'll really enjoy her cooking."

"Doesn't she have a cook?" Hunter finally asked.

"Or servants?" Maddy added.

"No. There aren't any servants here. On the ranch everybody has to work." She finished with Maddy's shoes and rose. "As you can see, I've dressed quite simply, and that's why I chose these plain clothes for you two. Life on the ranch is hard and dirty. You can't be wearing your good clothes for work." She frowned. The clothes they wore were still fancier than most children would wear for life on the ranch.

"We'll probably get you some others, but these will have to do." She considered the short pants, shirt, and jacket that Hunter wore. "Why don't you just leave the coat here?" Hunter happily complied. He'd never cared for jackets of any kind.

She looked at Maddy with her honey-blond hair flying in all directions. Clara had never been allowed to brush and style it. She picked up the hairbrush and motioned Maddy to turn around. Clara had braided her own hair often enough when she'd stayed on the ranch. There was no reason she couldn't do the same for her daughter. She brushed the tangled hair until it was free of knots, then looked for where she had put Maddy's hair ribbons. Once she located them, she quickly plaited Maddy's hair down the back and secured it with a blue ribbon. Standing back, Clara admired her handiwork with a smile. "There. We're ready."

"I didn't know you could do that, Mama," Hunter said, quite impressed.

Clara squared her shoulders. "I can do a great many things, Hunter. I just wasn't given the chance."

She led the children to the breakfast table and found her aunt and uncle already seated. "I'm sorry we're late. I'll be sure to rise earlier tomorrow." She helped the children into chairs, noting that someone had placed a thick catalogue on each seat to give them a little height.

She took her seat and looked to her uncle. Paul gave a nod and began to read from the Bible about the prodigal son. He only went so far as the point where the prodigal returned before closing the book.

He looked quite thoughtful as he continued. "Sometimes people do things they're ashamed of, but when they come to their heavenly Father and ask forgiveness, they can rest assured that He will forgive and forget. It's hard for us to believe that sometimes, because as human beings we have a hard time forgiving, and forgetting is nigh on to impossible."

"I sometimes forget to wipe my shoes off when they're muddy," Hunter volunteered. "The housekeeper would always get mad."

Paul smiled. "You forgot about it because it wasn't important to you. When God forgives our sins, they aren't important to Him anymore—because they don't exist. He's cast them as far as the east is from the west."

"How far is that?" Maddy asked matter-of-factly.

Chuckling, Paul put the Bible aside. "Well, you remember how far it was from your home in New York to this place?"

"It's real far away," Hunter replied.

"Exactly. God casts your sins even farther away than your train ride here. Now, I think Aunt Madeline is getting hungry, so why don't we pray?"

The children watched as the adults joined hands, and without any instruction they did likewise. Clara was glad they were so willing to fall into the routine. She had worried throughout the trip west that they might have a hard time adjusting, but Mim had assured her that children find it far easier to adapt to change than adults.

Breakfast passed quickly with Hunter and Maddy heartily approving of Aunt Madeline's flapjacks and huckleberry syrup. Clara marveled at how much her children were able to eat before finally telling her they were full. Aunt Madeline instructed Maddy how to help her clear the table, and Paul suggested Hunter come with him to help bring in wood for Aunt Madeline.

Clara gathered up several of the empty plates and brought them to the counter. "Why don't you let me clean up? I know you have a lot of work going on with the lambs."

Madeline smiled. "That would be lovely, Clara. If you don't mind, I'll take Maddy with me. There's a lot to show her. Paul will keep Hunter busy too. We've already discussed it. If it's all right with you."

Nodding, Clara couldn't help wondering if they were doing this because of the terrible time she'd had the evening before. No matter, she was grateful. She wanted nothing more than to have a nice long walk to think things out. Well, that wasn't exactly true. What she really wanted more than anything was to go see Curtis and hear him proclaim that he still loved her.

While she finished gathering dishes, Clara battled with herself about throwing caution to the wind. She should just march down the hallway, open the door to Curtis's room, and demand he stop acting the fool.

"But maybe I'm the fool." She bit her lower lip and fought back tears.

Clara forced Curtis from her mind. She needed to get the

kitchen cleaned up first, and that would be hard to do while having a good cry. She washed up the dishes, wiped down the counter and table, then made her way out the back door. The day was bright and the air crisp. The intense smell of the sheep made her smile. It was funny how country smells had never bothered her as they did her mother.

Clara made her way around the house, passing by the huge garden plot. Aunt Madeline had told her on their trip home from town that she'd only recently planted a few things. She hoped to get even more put in before the shearing commenced. Clara would have to volunteer to help with that. It would be wonderful to teach the children about growing food.

At the far end of the barnyard near the lambing pens, Clara spied five sheepherder wagons. These were houses on wheels in which the shepherd would live while off in summer pastures. Clara had once gone with her aunt during shearing time and had slept in one of the tiny houses. They were small but well organized, with everything a person might need to live alone in the wilds. She knew it wouldn't be too much time after the lambing that the shearing would commence, and then these efficient little homes would be hitched to horses and moved along with the sheep to summer fields.

A little farther away from the house, Clara noted clumps of trees—mostly evergreens and aspen with a few cottonwood thrown in for good measure. She and Curtis had often come here to steal a few private moments to discuss their future. Everything was comfortingly familiar, and yet she knew that fourteen years had changed everything. Especially where she and Curtis were concerned.

Beyond the trees the open fields stretched out to rolling hills covered in new spring grass and sheep. It reminded Clara of the Twenty-third Psalm.

"'The Lord is my shepherd.'" The words offered a small amount of comfort.

Eventually Clara came to a stream where she and Curtis had often walked. She sat down and watched the crystal-clear water as it ran wild over the rocks. Spring thaw had caused the water to climb nearly to the top of the short banks.

Clara sighed and glanced heavenward. She never felt so close to God as she did here in the wide open country. Maybe it was because the city was so noisy or there were too many people. Even in the great churches she'd attended, she hadn't known His presence as she did here.

She remembered how she and Curtis used to pray together. Those times were so special, so intimate. Tears came unbidden as she felt the hopelessness return.

"What am I supposed to do, Lord? I love him so dearly, but he doesn't love me."

For all her years away, Clara had always imagined Curtis pining away for her—feeling as bad and as lonely as she felt. Instead, he had moved on. His heart was no longer hers.

"I can't stay here. Not if he's going to be here. It would hurt far too much to have to face him day in and day out. But where do I go? Even if I took my money and bought a little place nearby, I'd still have to deal with seeing him at church and when visiting Madeline and Paul."

She picked up a smooth stone and turned it over and over in her hand as she contemplated her plight.

"I could go back to Bismarck." The thought intrigued her. She knew Mim and felt confident she would help Clara and the children settle in. Perhaps her parents would even know of a place Clara could purchase.

She wondered if she should write Mim a letter or just show up. It had been terribly hard to get a telegram sent, since the war department had declared that the service would be used primarily for the military. Even so, she might be able to get a telegram through to Mim. Of course, it would require going into town.

Then Clara remembered how happy her aunt and uncle had been at her arrival. They would be heartbroken if she chose to leave.

"But I can't bear the pain of staying." Anger rose up so unexpectedly that Clara jumped to her feet as if to ward it off. But it did no good. She threw the rock into the water, then reached down and picked up a stick and threw it as well. Looking around she picked up several other rocks and threw them one after the other.

"How could you just up and die and leave me to face all this indecision, Adolph?" She shook her head. "Mother forced us to marry and you promised me a life of security, and yet you gambled away your children's inheritance and my home. And then your brother stands ready to make me his wife and continue making my jewelry designs as if nothing ever happened." She spoke on as if Adolph and Otto were her audience.

She began to stomp up and down the bank, shaking her finger in a scolding manner. "You no doubt had your motives, Otto. I've never known you or Adolph to do anything without a reason. It always had to benefit the business, didn't it?

"But what about your children, Adolph? What will their future be? Even if you didn't care about me, you should have cared about them. Mother was certain you were going to provide a life of wealth and ease for all of us."

She shook her fist, imagining her mother had come to join the party. "Mother, you are worse than Adolph or Otto. You didn't care that I had fallen in love with Curtis. You told me it was a foolish, childish infatuation that would pass. You told me I couldn't possibly know my own heart. Well, I did. I still do."

Then why not fight for him?

The thought came from out of nowhere and stopped Clara in her tracks. Tears spilled onto her cheeks. The answer to that was painfully simple.

"Because he doesn't want me anymore."

❧

"I've brought your lunch," Madeline told Curtis. "Although I'm not completely convinced you deserve it."

He looked at her with a raised brow. "If this is about Clara, you can just forget it. I don't want to talk about it."

Madeline put down the tray and then put her hands on her hips. "And if I continue to talk about her, what will you do about it? Get up and leave?" She smiled. "No, you're going to hear me out whether you like it or not. You've hurt our Clara terribly."

"I'm trying to save her from even greater pain," Curtis countered. "I'm sure Paul told you everything. I know the two of you keep no secrets."

"He told me, but it didn't make any more sense to him than it does me. Yes, you have a past that is filled with things you'd rather forget. Yes, you're injured and laid up for a time and you might always have problems with your leg. But that's no reason to throw away true love with both hands."

"It's because I care about her that I don't want her around. If need be, I'll ask the doctor to move me to town. I'm sure Joe and Phil could load me in a wagon and drive me over." He looked at her as if to dare her to say he couldn't go.

Instead Madeline shook her head. She went to the corner of the room and picked up a wood contraption that Paul had made. Since Curtis's arms were free, it seemed the perfect solution for meals. She positioned the platform over his casted body, the legs of the invention coming to rest on either side of Curtis. This would allow him to awkwardly feed himself.

Next she retrieved the tray and set it before him. Curtis reached out and took hold of her arm. "Please understand, Madeline. I want to save her from . . . me. I want to save her from my past and the questionable future I have. Sending her back is the answer."

"And what exactly is it that you think you'd be sending her back to?" Madeline's voice was barely a whisper. "Do you have any idea of what she would face in New York? You know the kind of woman her mother is. She will force Clara to do her will and never take into consideration what Clara needs or wants. Then there's that brother-in-law of hers. Do you know she told me that he intends to marry her?"

Curtis frowned at this news but said nothing. Instead he looked down at the food. Madeline could see that her words had caused him to reconsider the situation, so she pressed on.

"At least here, with you, Clara would have love. She'd have us as well. She wouldn't have to face a questionable future wondering if her mother would force her into another unpleasant arrangement. Curtis, you need to really think about this. I know you love her."

"It's because I love her . . . that I want . . . I want her to forget about me," he murmured less convincingly than he had before.

"So you'll just send her back to New York? Is that it?"

He met her gaze. "No. I don't want her to go back there."

"Then where? She has nobody but us."

"Then I'll go." He sounded so sad and resigned that Madeline might have felt sorry for him if he just weren't so pigheaded.

"And here I thought you were done making poor choices." Madeline shook her head. "I'm going to leave you now and go pray. I'm going to ask the Lord to pound some sense into that thick head of yours."

⌒⫘⌒

That night Clara put her children to bed and smiled as they prayed.

"God bless everybody on the ranch," Hunter began. "Bless the sheep and the dogs too."

"And the chickens and horses," Maddy added.

Hunter nodded. "And help the lambs to get born. Amen."

"Amen," Maddy added.

Clara couldn't help but be proud. She and Mim had long ago taught them to pray aloud before bed and at meals. She wondered if they knew they could talk to God anytime they liked.

She pulled up a chair and placed it between their beds as they climbed in and snuggled down under handmade quilts.

"You are both a treasure to me. You are beyond a doubt the very best God has given me, and I thank Him for you both—all of the time." She sat down and smiled. "I hope you know that you can talk to God anytime you like. He will always listen to your prayers."

Hunter nodded. "Auntie Madeline said we can ask God for anything. I'm going to ask him for a horse of my own. Oh, and a puppy."

Clara cleared her throat. "Well, you can pray to God for other reasons that don't involve asking Him for possessions. You can praise Him too. You can thank Him for all the wonderful things He's given you. You can thank Him for the beauty of the earth."

Maddy yawned. "I thanked Him for letting us come here. It's so much better than our old house."

"How so, Maddy?"

126

She yawned again. "This is a happy house. Our house wasn't happy at all. It was dark and cold and we had to be really quiet."

"And nobody laughed," Hunter added.

"Well, sometimes we did," Maddy countered. "But we had to be very quiet. Here Unca Paul laughs all the time, and he laughs real loud. Auntie Madeline too. It's a happy place, and I don't want to leave."

Clara felt the words pierce her heart. She had never known her children felt this way—that they had realized the misery that resided in their former home. How could she take them away when they'd just found what a home could truly be?

"I'm going to pray we stay here forever," Maddy murmured and closed her eyes.

"I'm still going to ask for a horse and a puppy," Hunter said, sounding as if he might nod off at any moment. "And for us to stay here."

Curtis lay awake long into the night thinking on all that Madeline and Paul had said. Maybe he *was* being pigheaded. He tried to shift his weight, which only caused his skin to itch beneath the cast. The doctor said he'd be able to get the body cast off soon. In truth, the doctor wasn't even sure that the back was broken, but because of the bruising around the spine and numbness in Curtis's legs, he felt immobilization was critical.

He heaved a sigh and stared up at the dark ceiling. The house was so very quiet. He thought of Clara just down the hall. He longed to go to her and apologize. He wanted nothing more than to hold her in his arms and kiss her lips. They'd only ever kissed once, and that had been when he'd proposed and Clara had accepted.

The thought was bittersweet. They had been so young and full of life. Curtis's mother and father had been alive and loved Clara as much as he did. They had even talked of Clara and Curtis living with them after they married. Their house in town was large enough to hold them, since Curtis's older brothers had long ago married and moved away. Curtis had been certain of life then, but now he was certain of nothing.

He tried to pray, but the anger and frustration acted as a barrier between him and the Lord. Curtis knew that until he let that go—until he gave all of his rage and disappointment over to God, nothing would ever be good.

"But it's hard not to be angry, Lord. It's hard not to feel cheated out of all the things a man could want. Hard too to see how you could do anything positive—anything good with this new situation. I always thought that being a believer would mean things would go . . . well . . . maybe not perfect, but surely not this bad."

A Bible verse in Job—one he'd memorized in childhood—came to mind. In spite of himself Curtis had to smile. It seemed God had a sense of humor.

"'Man that is born of a woman is of few days and full of trouble.'"

He'd definitely been full of trouble. His pain had caused him to make bad decisions and seek out people who were damaged and dangerous. He'd yielded his good sense over to actions that hurt others and put him behind bars, where he deserved to be.

He felt some of the fight leave him as another verse came to mind. This one from Psalm 9. "'The LORD also will be a refuge for the oppressed, a refuge in times of trouble.'"

The Scripture comforted him, and a few of the bricks in his wall fell. Curtis drew in a deep breath. "I know you're with me, Lord. I know you have never left me, but sometimes that just makes it all the harder to understand. I prayed for protection—for strength to do what I needed to do in order to be the man you wanted me to be, and yet here I lie."

Hasn't God protected you—given you strength? Hasn't He made provision for all of your needs—given you people to take care of you and to love you?

Curtis closed his eyes, and all he saw was Clara. Had God truly sent her back to him? Why now after all these years? Why now with his future so uncertain?

12

"These buttons are hard to do," Hunter complained as Clara stood watching.

"I know they are, but it's important you be able to dress yourself. You can always ask for help if you first try and can't make it work. However, you must first try." She smiled at him, then looked to Maddy, who was working on her shoes.

Clara knew this new life of doing for themselves was something they weren't accustomed to, but the sooner all of them learned their place and what was expected of them the better. Aunt Madeline and Uncle Paul were extremely busy, and it wouldn't do to add to their workload.

That was why this morning Clara had made certain to get up early. She'd awakened at five-thirty with the skies already growing lighter by the minute. Now it was nearly six-fifteen. They'd have to hurry if they were going to be of any use to Madeline.

Once the children were dressed, Clara showed them how to make their beds and put their nightclothes away. They thought it rather novel, but Clara knew that would pass soon enough.

They made their way to the kitchen, where Clara's aunt was just putting something into the oven.

"Good morning, Auntie Madeline," Hunter said. "We've come to help."

Madeline straightened and gave a smile. "Well, I can see that, and I'm mighty grateful you did, Hunter. Uncle Paul will be back in just a moment, and then you can help him bring in more firewood."

"What can we do to help?" Clara asked, looking at Maddy and then returning her gaze to her aunt.

"Do you still remember how to gather eggs?"

Clara smiled. "Of course I do. Where's the basket?"

Her aunt went to a door on the far side of the kitchen. This had once been nothing more than a canning room pantry, but Madeline had already told Clara about the way her Uncle Paul had expanded the room to include space for the hand-agitated washer complete with wringer and a few lines to hang clothes when the weather was too bad to hang them outside. She had promised to show Clara how to use the washer later that day or the next.

Madeline returned with two baskets. One large and one small. She gave them over to Maddy and Clara. "There should be quite a few eggs to gather. I've been giving the chickens plenty to eat. There are a couple of brooders out there, so don't bother them. After all, we want a batch or two of baby chicks, don't we, Maddy?"

The little girl nodded just as Paul came through the back door with two large pails of water. "Well, here are my girls all together."

"I'm here too," Hunter protested.

Paul put down the pails and eyed Hunter. "You know, Clara, we're gonna have to get that boy some long trousers—made out of canvas. Otherwise, he'll be tearing holes in those fancy britches he has now."

Clara nodded. She didn't want to say anything about Hunter not needing them if they left the area. Still, if they went to Bismarck, he'd need them there as well. "I had thought about that."

"I've got some good material we can use and make him a pair or two to get him through. It's sturdy cloth and will serve the purpose. After that we can order some from Sears and Roebuck," Madeline offered.

"Good enough," Paul replied. He looked at Hunter. "You going to help me with chores today?"

"Yes, sir. Mama said on a ranch everybody has to earn their keep."

Paul laughed. "She's right about that. Come on with me. Now that I've brought your auntie some water, she's gonna want more firewood so she can heat it up."

Hunter left with Paul, while Clara motioned Maddy to follow. "Come on. I'll show you where the chicken coop is." She glanced at her aunt. "Unless you've moved it."

This caused Madeline to laugh. "Not much has moved around here in the last thirty years. Besides, I showed Maddy the chickens yesterday. I'm sure she knows her way." Madeline reached over and took up a mason jar of oats. "Sprinkle these out in the yard for the chickens. They'll leave their nests quick enough and give you very little trouble. Oh, and you can just leave the gate open. I'm sure once they finish off the oats, they'll be anxious to roam around the new grass and look for things to eat."

Clara nodded, taking the jar. Maddy made a beeline for the chicken yard. On the way she caught sight of Hunter with an armload of split logs. It did her heart good to see them learning to have responsibilities. She had never wanted them to grow up spoiled like so many socialite children. She wanted her children to know how to do things for themselves.

They opened the gate to find quite a few of the chickens already roaming the yard. The rooster flew up to the top fence post and gave a loud, clear crow.

Maddy giggled. "Auntie Madeline says he likes to make sure everybody knows he's the boss."

"I'm sure he does. Did she also tell you that roosters can be pretty mean?"

Maddy nodded, growing serious. "She showed me his spurs and told me they were sharp and could cut me, but she also said that usually he didn't bother anybody unless they bothered him."

They went into the coop and began gathering eggs from the individual boxes. Her aunt had certainly been right about the number of eggs. Clara counted at least fifty-two by the time they finished.

Maddy pointed to several boxes toward the back. "That's where the brooders are."

Clara nodded. "It'll be fun when the baby chicks hatch. I remember how much I used to love that."

"Auntie Madeline said some of them could get killed for meat." Maddy frowned. "But she told me that I shouldn't be sad. She said that's the way it is on a ranch."

"Yes. Some animals are used for their meat and some for other things. The sheep are good for providing wool and meat, just as the chickens give us eggs and meat. Isn't it amazing how God created them that way?"

Her daughter nodded and followed Clara back to the house. By now the hens had spread out and were busy pecking and scratching the ground in search of something else to eat. Clara's own stomach rumbled, reminding her that she'd eaten very little the night before. In her turmoil food hadn't appealed.

"Well, there you are. Just in time. I've been frying up the bacon and was just about ready for the eggs."

"I think we counted fifty-two," Clara said, putting her basket up on the counter. She then turned and took Maddy's basket.

"That's just fine. I'm just going to scramble up all but a dozen and then we'll share them with the boys working the sheep. The rest of the eggs we'll use for some cakes."

"How's it going with the lambs?"

"Very nearly done with the lambing, only a few left. We expect the last of them to drop today or tonight." Madeline motioned to a large bowl. "How about you girls wash off the eggs and put them in that bowl?"

"We'd be happy to, wouldn't we, Maddy?"

The little girl nodded. Clara went to the sink and put in the plug before pouring in a little water. Together she and Maddy washed off the eggs and carefully transferred them to the large piece of crockery. There wasn't room for all of them, but very nearly.

Madeline pulled another bowl from the cupboard. "Would you like to help me crack open the eggs, Maddy?"

She nodded, her eyes wide. Madeline showed her how to crack the egg and then open it to let the inside spill into the bowl. Maddy tried several times but always seemed to press too hard, making the shell shatter. Clara smiled, remembering her first time at cracking eggs. As she recalled, her situation had been even harder because they were separating out the whites for meringue.

"I thought it might be good to let the children watch Uncle Paul brand the new lambs and dock their tails." Madeline made quick work of the eggs, then reached for a whisk. "That is if you don't think it too upsetting. I figure the sooner the better in getting used to how things work on a ranch. Especially if you're going to stick around."

Clara looked away so her aunt couldn't see her frown. She hadn't had a chance to discuss the future. "I don't mind at all. I trust you and Uncle Paul to help them understand."

"Good. After breakfast we'll take the children out with us."

Her aunt was true to her word. Once breakfast was completed, she had Paul take Maddy and Hunter while she helped Clara with the cleanup.

"Come on you two," Paul said, reaching out to take each child in hand. "I've got a couple of bums that need your help."

"What are bums?" Hunter asked.

"Lambs that don't have a mama to take care of them."

"But why don't they have a mama?" Maddy questioned.

"Well, in this case I have two ewes—that's mama sheep—and they each had two babies."

"Twins, like us?" Hunter seemed delighted at this news.

Paul nodded. "Yup, just like you and Maddy. Only problem is that the mama sheep is young and these are her first babies, so she won't be able to take care of both. That's where you and Maddy come in. We'll let you two feed and take care of these little lambs." He winked at Clara. "Your mama used to take care of bums for us."

Hunter looked at his mother with an expression of admiration. "Truly?"

Clara remembered those times quite well. "I did, indeed. You're going to have a lot of fun, but it's also a lot of work."

Paul pushed them toward the door. "So we'd best get to it."

It pained Clara to remember those times. Memories used to be such dear friends when she was alone in New York. Now they threatened to torment and torture what little peace of mind she had.

"I know you've got a lot on your mind," Madeline began. "Care to talk to me about it?"

Clara started to say no, but then she realized how much she wanted her aunt's counsel. "Curtis doesn't love me anymore."

"He said that, did he?"

Clara nodded and gathered up the last of the silverware. "He did. He told me our promises and feelings were just those of children. But I don't feel that way, and it really hurts to know he does."

"Why do you suppose he said that?" Madeline moved to the stove to retrieve a large pot of hot water. She poured it into the sink and added some soap.

"I guess so that I would stop caring about him." Clara couldn't imagine why he felt that way.

Madeline nodded. "He's got a lot of worries about the future. Doc didn't know exactly how bad his injuries were and told him he might never walk again. Or at least it might take a long while to regain his full abilities. Curtis is pretty frustrated by that. He doesn't want to be a burden."

"I don't want to be one either."

"And you suppose you are?"

Clara shrugged and put the silverware into the hot soapy water. "I don't intend to be. In fact, I've been trying to figure out what I should do."

Madeline looked at her oddly. "About what?"

"About where the children and I will live and how I'll provide for them."

"You'll live here with us, of course. We have more than enough room and work to go around. Isn't that what you want?"

"I can't stay here and see Curtis every day and know that I feel something for him that he no longer feels for me. It would just be too hard."

Madeline turned with hands on her hips. "Clara, you can't believe that he no longer loves you."

"But he told me that. He was quite serious."

"Of course he was serious," Madeline countered. "You surprised him. He had no idea he would ever see you again, let alone that you still loved him and were available to him again. It was a shock to him all around."

"I can understand that it was a surprise, but why tell me he doesn't care for me anymore?" Clara bit her lip and fought back tears. She didn't want to break down again.

Madeline stopped what she was doing and dried her hands on her apron. She took hold of Clara's shoulders. "A lot of water has gone under the bridge since you were here fourteen years ago. It's not my place to give you all the details of Curtis's life, but it hasn't been easy, and I know he regrets not only losing you, but making some bad choices as well. If I were to venture a guess, I'd say he no longer feels worthy of you."

"But that's ridiculous. I have my regrets as well, and I haven't always made good choices, but I still love him."

"Clara, give him time. Let him heal and see what the doctor says. A man doesn't feel like a man when he's bound to a bed. Don't run away. If you love him—take a stand and fight for your future together."

"But I'm not sure how, and I don't even know if I can bear to see him again."

Madeline let go her hold and turned back to the sink. "Well, you're going to have to see him again. I've got my work cut out for me. Your uncle and I thought we were going to have to hire someone to come care for Curtis while we sheared the sheep. However, I know that your heart is to ease my worries and burdens, so I figure you can nurse Curtis in my absence."

Clara's eyes widened and she shook her head. "I couldn't. I wouldn't know what to do."

Madeline smiled. "You're a bright girl. You'll figure it out."

"But—"

"But nothing. Tomorrow's the Sabbath. Joe is going to sit with Curtis while we go to church. When we get home I'm going to show you all that you'll need to know to take care of Curtis while we're away."

13

*C*hurch services were much as Clara had remembered, although this morning they arrived late and sat at the back of the church instead of the front as they had when Clara was a girl. The same man, Uncle Paul's dear friend Judge Walker, led the congregation in song, and then the same Pastor Cosgrove she'd heard as a child gave the sermon on trusting and obeying the Lord. Clara had to admit it pricked her conscience. She had done nothing but contemplate her aunt's comments since yesterday, and now it seemed the sermon tied right in. The key to happiness, Pastor Cosgrove ensured, was in four simple things. Seeking God. Knowing God. Obeying God. Trusting God.

The service concluded with a hymn that had been chosen for its title: "Trust and Obey." Clara momentarily wondered if the pastor and her aunt had somehow coordinated the topic to make her feel guilty. Clara was more than a little aware that perhaps God had brought her here not for herself, but for Curtis. He needed her.

She considered this as she sang the final stanza. "Then in fellowship sweet we will sit at His feet, or we'll walk by His side in the way. What He says we will do, where He sends we will go. Never fear, only trust and obey. Trust and obey, for there's no other way to be happy in Jesus, but to trust and obey."

The music concluded and they were dismissed. To Clara's surprise they were suddenly in the midst of a crowd. Maddy and Hunter moved to stand closer to her.

"Clara! I thought that was you. Whatever are you doing back here?" a petite blond-haired woman asked.

"Sue? Sue Smith?"

"It's Kaul now. I married Steve. Remember him?"

Clara nodded and smiled. "I guess I didn't realize you had stayed in the area." Just then an older woman joined Sue. Clara immediately recognized her as Betty Smith, Sue's mother.

"Mrs. Smith, how nice to see you again." Clara remembered the children. "These are my little ones, Hunter and Maddy."

"Twins?" Sue asked.

"Yes. Just as their father was."

"Was? Has he passed on?" Betty asked.

"Yes." She didn't want to have to get into the details just yet. "Do you have children, Sue?"

"Two," the woman replied. "Much older than yours. I married Steve right after you left us."

"Well, I never expected to see you back here." The catty voice had to belong to Naomi Carlson. No, Clara reminded herself. It was Bittner now. Her aunt had written long ago of Naomi's unhappy union with the much older Howard Bittner.

Clara turned to find the woman sneering. "I heard your aunt say you're a widow now. But I guess even with your husband dead you must feel pretty lucky to have avoided marriage to a man like Curtis Billingham."

"Naomi, that's hardly called for," Sue interjected. "Curtis has turned his life around."

"Well, it doesn't change the fact that he spent a good many years drinking and . . . womanizing."

Naomi had never been a friend to Clara. She had wanted Curtis for herself, and when he refused to even give her a second look, Naomi had made it her personal duty to malign him at every chance.

"I'm sure we all have things in the past that we'd rather folks forget," Sue's mother declared. "Seems I remember you making a few bad choices, Naomi."

The younger woman turned red. "Well, at least I didn't end up in prison."

The words hit Clara hard. She couldn't imagine Curtis drinking and doing things that fit the image Naomi was painting. Womanizing. Prison. Clara tried to keep her face void of emotion but could tell by Naomi's look of satisfaction that she was doing a poor job.

"Like my mother said, Naomi, we all make mistakes. We're all sinners saved by grace."

"Well, my sins were never as bad as his," Naomi countered.

Just then Aunt Madeline joined them. "I didn't know there was a list of sins to tell us what was bad and what was worse. What book of the Bible did you find that in?"

Naomi frowned. "Some things are just naturally worse than others."

"The outcome and consequences might be," Madeline replied, "but sin is sin. We're all guilty of it, and the outcome for each one of us is death, unless we accept Jesus as our Savior." Sue and her mother nodded in agreement.

"And it seems to me that you're gossiping about Curtis," Madeline added. "Gossips or whisperers are listed right there with murderers in the first book of Romans."

"So are maligners," Clara said, regaining her voice.

"Well, I was only making conversation," Naomi said, acting terribly wronged. "It seems a person can't even speak around some folks." She stormed off in a huff.

"Don't mind her," Sue said, patting Clara's arm. "She's always been jealous of you, probably even more so now with your twins. She's never been able to have children."

It was only then that Clara realized her children were no longer standing with her. "Where are Hunter and Maddy?"

"I sent them out with your uncle once Naomi started to badger you," Madeline answered. "Come on. It's a long ways home, and I'd imagine your uncle is starving."

Clara bid the others goodbye with their promise to come and visit one day after the sheep were sent to summer pasture. Making her way to the wagon she was relieved to see that Naomi was nowhere in sight.

"Clara, do you remember Judge Walker?" her uncle asked.

"I do." Clara smiled and extended her hand. "Your honor, it's good to see you once again."

"No need for calling me 'your honor,'" the man said, taking hold of her hand. "I'm retired now."

Paul laughed. "But he'll always be Judge Walker to folks in this valley."

Clara nodded. "That seems only fitting, Uncle Paul. You'll always be known as a sheep rancher. I suppose those things we do stay with us for a long time." She frowned. Her own words only served to remind her of Curtis's plight.

Once they were well on their way home, Clara decided to just ask her aunt about what was said regarding Curtis. Mindful of the children, however, she chose her words carefully.

"Was Naomi speaking the truth about Curtis?"

Madeline met her gaze. "I think you should ask him about it. It's his story to tell."

144

Clara nodded and eased back. It might be his story to tell, but what if she couldn't get him to speak to her at all?

By the time they reached the house, Clara had managed to work herself up into such a state of agitation that when Hunter jumped from the wagon, she reprimanded him as she had never done before.

"Hunter, I've told you before that you cannot be jumping off things like that. You'll get hurt!" Hunter's eyes welled with tears, and Clara immediately regretted her harsh tone. Uncle Paul helped her from the wagon, and while he assisted the others, Clara took hold of Hunter and brushed the tears from his cheek. "I'm sorry for the way I spoke, Hunter. I was afraid for you. You mustn't keep jumping off things."

He nodded and sniffed. "I'll try to be good, Mama."

She kissed his forehead. "You are good, Hunter. It's just sometimes you make bad choices."

Her words reminded her of Curtis and all that had been said. She walked slowly with her son to the house, and by the time she reached the front porch, Clara was determined to force Curtis to speak to her. After all, it wasn't like he could run away, and knowing men in general, she couldn't imagine he would sit there and let her rant at him without comment. She smiled. It might not be the best way to handle things, but it was going to be done.

They changed their clothes from Sunday best to everyday, and then each went to their various duties. Her aunt and uncle only did what was necessary on the Sabbath, and Clara and the children would do likewise.

Coming into the kitchen, Clara pulled on an apron and went to where her aunt kept the bed tray. "I'm going to take Curtis his lunch," she announced. "I have some things to discuss with him."

Madeline's eyebrows rose slightly, but she said nothing. Instead, she helped Clara set the tray with food. Once that was complete, she looked at her niece with a smile.

"I'll say a prayer for you."

"Thank you. I have a feeling I'm going to need it."

Clara took up the tray and started for the door that led out the back of the kitchen and down the hall. She paused long enough to hear her aunt instruct the children to set the table and knew they would be kept busy for as long as was needed.

When she reached Curtis's open door, she took a deep breath before stepping into the room. She saw that he was busy concentrating on a game of checkers with Joe. She'd only met the man in passing, but he seemed quite friendly and easygoing.

Joe looked up first. "Boy, am I glad to see you. Thought I might starve to death before you folks got back." He stood and stretched.

Curtis cast her only a cursory glance and then looked to Joe. "What about our game?"

Joe leaned down and pushed a checker into place. "There, now you've won." He turned and gave Clara a smile. "That ought to put him in a good mood."

She waited until he'd gone before setting the tray on the bedside table. She took up the checkerboard and checkers and looked around the room.

"They go in the top drawer of that dresser," Curtis said, pointing.

"Thank you." She marched across the room and put the game away. Turning back, she found Curtis watching her. It was now or never. She bolstered her courage.

"I've brought your lunch, but first you're going to answer some questions. I plan to stay here as long as it takes to get my answers, and if you go hungry, then that's just the way it will be."

To her surprise, Curtis actually smiled. "All right. Why don't you close the door and pull up a chair?"

Relief washed over her. She nodded, then closed the door. Curtis's expression showed more peace than it had the last time they'd met. Settling on the wooden chair, Clara tried to think of how to pose her questions. Should she just tell him of her experience at church and go from there? Or should she simply ask him to tell her what happened to him after she left fourteen years ago?

"So, are you going to ask your questions or just sit here keeping me from my lunch?" Curtis asked after several moments of silence.

⁂

Curtis could see that Clara was uncomfortable. He couldn't blame her. He'd been quite cruel to her, and frankly it surprised him that she'd even bothered to return and set herself up for additional pain. And if not for the straightforward words of Madeline and Paul, he might very well have given her more of his anger and grief.

Clara cleared her throat. "I want to know about the past. I want to know what happened to you after I left."

He nodded, never looking away from her beautiful face. "I know, but hearing it won't be easy."

"I don't care. I need to know."

He knew she'd been at church that morning and figured she'd already heard an earful from well-meaning folks who would consider it their duty to let her know just how awful a man he was. He figured Naomi Bittner, in particular, wouldn't miss an opportunity to put in her two cents.

"You look so much like the girl you were fourteen years ago."

He hadn't meant to say the words out loud, but once said they obviously couldn't be taken back.

"And you look like the boy I left behind."

He shook his head. "That innocent young man is gone forever. I'm sure you have an idea of my past. I don't expect you to forgive me for it."

She narrowed her eyes. "How dare you? Do you know me so little that you suppose there is anything I wouldn't forgive of you? I love you. I've never stopped loving you. I know I'm probably a fool to be here telling you this—wearing my heart on my sleeve only for you to hurt me again. But the cost in being here is less than the one I'd face if I didn't try."

He took in her words, and the battle within him stilled. She was right. There would be a price to pay no matter which way he went.

"All right. After your mother took you away, I gave serious thought to coming after you and stealing you away. I kept praying that somehow you would be able to refuse your mother's demands and even prayed that no one would want to marry you." His lips twitched and the corners turned up just a bit. "Of course, all the men in New York would have had to be blind for that to happen."

"Nothing's too big for God," she murmured.

This made Curtis laugh. "Exactly my thoughts." He paused for a moment at the sight of her smile. "Well, losing my folks was hard, but losing you . . ." He left the words unspoken and looked toward the open window. "For the first few weeks I was in a stupor. I tried to make sense of it all, but there was nothing to make sense of. I felt that God had abandoned me just like everyone else." He swallowed the lump in his throat. He hated telling her of his downfall.

"I started drinking. I'd heard enough people say it was a

good way to forget, and God knew I wanted to forget. I begged Him plenty of times to help me forget, but He never did. I only drank at night to begin with. I kept it hidden from Madeline and Paul. They insisted I stay with them for a time, but I couldn't bear it. After a few weeks, I left. I had to. I was so ashamed of what I was becoming." She kept gazing at him with the same expression of acceptance.

"Go on."

"Well, pretty soon it wasn't enough to drink alone. I started drinking in town. I met up with some unsavory fellows who got me a job on a cattle ranch. That only caused me more problems. They took me to Lewistown one weekend and introduced me to . . . women. I kept looking for one that reminded me of you, but of course that wasn't to be found in those hardened souls. I didn't realize then that the things I loved most about you were buried deep or had already died in those working women.

"After a time these friends of mine decided it would be better to rob a bank than to work on a cattle ranch. They figured I would agree, and when I didn't at first, they didn't seem to care all that much. Later on when I kept refusing, they started giving me grief. Finally the ringleader of the group told me I didn't have to go into the bank with them, I just needed to hold the horses while they went in. I thought about it and convinced myself that I wouldn't really be doing anything wrong by holding a bunch of horses. But, of course, it was wrong. Everything about it was wrong, and a man was killed during the robbery. A man who had a family."

Curtis shook his head and looked down at his casted chest. "I'd give just about anything if I could go back and keep it all from happening."

"I know."

Those two words meant more to him than she'd ever know.

"We got ourselves arrested almost immediately. As I sat there in jail with the others, I tried to reason out how I'd come to this. I tried to talk to God, but that was impossible. I held Him responsible for taking my folks and you away, for letting me get caught up in all the ugliness. I blamed Him for everything. It was easier than taking responsibility for my own actions."

"It's easy to blame God when things go bad," she admitted. "I have to say I did some of that myself."

"The judge took pity on me since I was young and it was my first offense. I didn't know it then, but Paul and Madeline put in a good word for me. The judge gave me only five years. The others paid with their life." He shook his head. "But five years was bad enough. I've heard it said that prison is supposed to reform a man, but it didn't do that for me. There was too much time to think—to remember. I sank deeper and deeper. By the time I was released, I went right back to the bottle and never looked back. I can't even tell you what I did during that time. Most of it's a blur and what isn't . . . well . . . I'd never share such things with you. They're just too vile. It's enough to say that I should have died and would have if Paul hadn't found me. He brought me back here, and he and Madeline nursed me back to health physically and spiritually. I only had one minor setback."

"What caused that?" she asked.

He smiled. "I saw your portrait."

She looked momentarily confused. "My portrait?" Then she nodded. "The one in the front hall."

"Yes. I was barely on my feet and wanted to go out on the porch to get some air. Your picture was there and I couldn't help but stop. You were so beautiful and you looked so happy." He shrugged. "It hurt to see you so happy."

"I wasn't happy. The photographer was so put out with me

because he said I looked far too melancholy to photograph. He finally told me to think of something that I loved—something that made me happy. I thought of you and immediately he took the picture. I looked that way because I was remembering you."

Her words humbled him. Here he thought she was enjoying her new life without him. That thought had devastated him so much. "It just goes to show you that things aren't always what they seem."

"That's very true."

"So now you know the truth about my past."

"What I know is just that. It's in the past. You don't stop to think about the fact that I too have done things I regretted. I too have a past. However, my past is very much a part of my future."

"What do you mean?" He could see the emotion playing on her face.

"I have children."

He'd never considered she might have children, but of course it made sense. She had, after all, been married for twelve years. "How many children do you have?"

"Two. They're twins. They're here with me, and they're almost five years old. In fact, their birthday is the twenty-sixth of July." She paused and looked to the window, where a light breeze fluttered the curtains. "I'm definitely not the same girl I was when I left here. Something died in me that day and again the day I married. It was almost more than I could deal with, and after a time I decided to take my life." She looked back to him. "Does that shock you?"

"No," he barely whispered, but the pain in his voice was clear.

Clara bit her lower lip for a moment. Curtis could see she was truly struggling. At that moment he wanted more than anything to take back his denial of loving her. He wanted only to ease her pain.

"I was taking breakfast with my husband when I noticed an article in the paper about a woman who had taken arsenic. Her death had been almost immediate. I nonchalantly asked Adolph where a person would even get such a horrible thing. He didn't realize that I was hoping to take the woman's example for myself."

She drew a deep breath and looked at her hands. "He told me it was easily obtained for killing rats and mice. So I decided on one of my shopping trips I would secure some arsenic for myself."

"What stopped you?"

Clara shrugged. "I believe God did. I purchased the stuff and had it ready to take. I had even planned out how I would do it. Sundays were always our social day. On Mondays Adolph always left early for work, and since we had separate bedrooms, I knew he wouldn't know if I was simply sleeping or dead. I reasoned that I would go to church on Sunday, dine with whomever we were to dine with, and receive anyone who might come to visit us in the afternoon. Then I would feign a headache in the early evening and I would retire."

She finally looked up, meeting his gaze. "I didn't want to live without you. I hadn't wanted to marry Adolph and had tried to run away, but Mother had me watched and kept under lock and key. Adolph was a kind enough man, but he wasn't you, and I knew I would never be happy married to him. When I thought of living twenty or thirty years with him, it was unbearable."

"I know Christians aren't supposed to consider killing themselves, but . . . I . . . it's just that . . ." She fell silent.

Curtis shook his head. "You don't have to justify wanting to end your life to me. I wanted it myself, and I think that's what my actions were all about. I kept hoping someone would just end it for me."

She nodded. "So that was my plan. When evening came I told Adolph I didn't feel well and planned to go right to bed. He didn't care. In fact, he had to go out to meet with his brother regarding some business deal. I was surprised that he would do something like that on the Sabbath, but he was never a religious man and only attended church because it connected him to wealthy people who might buy Vesper jewelry.

"With Adolph out of the house, it made everything all the easier. I went upstairs, told the maid I wouldn't need her anymore, wanted no one to disturb me, and that even in the morning she should just let me sleep and wait until I rang for her. I locked the doors to my room, including the one that adjoined Adolph's, just in case he . . . well . . . just in case. I had thought to dress in something nice and lay myself out like they might at the funeral home, but then I didn't want to shame Adolph by having the stigma of a suicide to deal with and decided I would simply dress for bed, take the arsenic, and appear to have died in my sleep."

"What stopped you?"

She gave a hint of a laugh. "Well, God did. At least that's whom I credit. When I went to where I'd hid the arsenic . . . it was gone."

"Gone? Had someone taken it?"

Shaking her head, Clara shrugged. "I don't know. I don't suppose I ever will. None of the staff said a word about it. In my frustration I tried to imagine how else I might end my life, but with my plan foiled, it took my confidence, and I turned to the Scriptures and prayer for comfort. After that, I believe God gave me a peace of sorts. I knew I would never have the life I'd wanted, but I felt I had to make do with my lot. Also I figured you had probably gone on with your life and found someone else to love. I'd asked about you in my letters to Madeline, but she only replied telling me you had gone away and she had no idea where."

He nodded. "That's true enough. I didn't tell anyone. I just left."

"Shortly after that night I learned I was with child. It hit me hard to realize I might have killed my unborn child in killing myself. I had no problem ending my own life, but the thought of ending an innocent life gave me no end of grief. I later lost that baby, and it only caused me all the more guilt as I worried that my horrible thoughts had somehow caused it to happen."

"But then you had the twins?"

"Years and years later. There were other miscarriages, and my sorrow only deepened. When the twins were born I realized that I had something to live for. For the first time since leaving you, I wanted to live—to go on and make a good life. I decided for their sake to find some way to care about their father, and I did. I never loved him like I love you, and he never loved me. But we learned, in spite of that, to build something that was at least amicable."

"But why would a man marry without love?"

"That's easy," Clara replied. "Money. I didn't learn until years later that Adolph came courting me because of my stepfather. My mother had put it out that I was available for marriage, and Adolph saw an opportunity to better his situation. He wanted my stepfather's backing as he and his brother expanded their jewelry business. My stepfather pitied me, I think. He knew my mother treated me abominably and thought I'd have a better life as Adolph Vesper's wife. He made a deal with Adolph as part of my dowry and we were married. It wasn't until years later when I commented on some of the jewelry designs—pointing out flaws and telling how I would do it differently—that Adolph found value in me. I started designing pieces of jewelry.

I told him about the Yogo sapphires from Montana and how beautiful they were, and he thought them perfect to specialize in. The pieces were a huge success, and now everyone who is anyone either owns or is vying for a piece of the Vesper Yogo collection of jewelry."

"And you designed them?" Curtis never failed to be amazed at her talents.

"I did and I still am. Everyone thought Adolph had created them, and I let him take credit for it. Now that he's dead, his brother still wants to continue the business. He plans for me to continue sending him designs."

"Sending him designs?"

She nodded. "I don't plan to return to New York. I never cared for life in the city, and that city in particular has too many bad memories. I don't want the children growing up spoiled and without the ability to do things for themselves."

Something tugged at his heart, and though he tried to deny his feelings for her, Curtis found it impossible. "I'd like to meet them."

She smiled. "I'd like that too."

14

Clara felt a surge of excitement as she gathered Hunter and Maddy to introduce them to Curtis later that evening. Maybe things would finally be different now. Maybe Curtis could forget about the past and realize there was nothing there that could harm them now. She whispered a prayer that he could finally be free to love her again.

The children were more than a little curious about the man staying in the room down the hall, who Uncle Paul had told them had been hurt during a cave-in at a nearby mine. Hunter in particular wanted to know all the details, despite his mother's warning that they comport themselves in a very well-behaved manner.

Curtis was propped up in bed when Clara entered with Hunter and Maddy on either side. "Curtis, these are my children, Maddy and Hunter. Children, this is Mr. Billingham. He is my dearest friend in the world."

His eyes met hers with a single brow raised in question. Then just as quickly he looked to the children. "Call me Curtis. Mr. Billingham is much too long a name and way too formal for out here in Montana." He smiled. "I'm very pleased to meet you both."

Hunter had no problem in seeking out more information. "Unca Paul said you got buried in a mine. Is that why you're all wrapped up like that?" He pointed to Curtis's chest and then to his leg, which was still in traction.

"It is," he replied. "Come feel. It's as hard as a rock." Curtis knocked on his chest.

This intrigued Hunter, who quickly left Clara's side and made his way to the bed. He stretched as far as possible and mimicked Curtis's action. His face lit up as he looked back at his mother.

"It *is* like a rock, Mama. Did you feel it?"

Clara shook her head. "I haven't had a chance to do that just yet."

"Well, it's real hard." He looked at Curtis with an expression of new admiration. "How do you scratch under that?"

Curtis laughed. "Not very easily, and believe me, it itches like crazy sometimes."

"Can you tell me about getting hurt at the mine?" Hunter asked.

"Well, there was a lot of dirt and rock that fell from the sides and the top. It fell on me and I was knocked unconscious," Curtis said. "But I can tell you some more about it later. I still haven't had a chance to say hello to your sister."

Maddy still stood by Clara and eyed Curtis warily. Clara smiled. "Maddy is a little more reserved."

"I don't mind that at all, but I do hope we can be friends, Miss Maddy," Curtis replied.

The girl took a step forward, fixing him with a steady gaze. "Do you like cookies?" she asked, surprising them all.

"I do," Curtis answered. "Madeline makes the best cookies I've ever eaten. I'm especially fond of her oatmeal cookies."

Maddy nodded and moved another step toward the bed. "Do you like cats?"

Clara and Curtis exchanged a glance before he smiled at the child. "I do. I'm very fond of them—especially kittens."

Again she nodded. "What's your favorite color?"

"Blue. What's yours?"

Maddy seemed to relax a bit. "Yellow, because it's so bright, like the sun."

"Yellow is definitely a beautiful color," Curtis agreed.

For several minutes Maddy said nothing more. Hunter meanwhile tapped Curtis on the arm. "Was there a lot of blood?"

"Hunter, you shouldn't pester Curtis."

Curtis shrugged. "It's all right. He's naturally curious."

Hunter looked back at him. "Was there a lot of blood?"

Curtis chuckled. "I really don't know. I was knocked unconscious." Hunter frowned, and Curtis quickly explained. "I was hit in the head so hard it made me go to sleep."

"I didn't know you could get hit so hard you would go to sleep," Hunter replied, seeming to consider this.

"Well, we mustn't wear him out," Clara said. "Mr. . . . Curtis needs his rest so that he can continue to get well."

"May I come back sometime and talk to you about the mine?" Hunter asked hopefully.

"I guess that would be all right, so long as it's all right with your mother."

Hunter raced back to Clara. "Is it all right?"

Clara smiled. "We shall see. Come along, Maddy."

Maddy had remained at the foot of the bed watching Curtis with great interest. She turned to go at her mother's beckoning, then stopped and turned back ever so slightly. "We can be friends," she told Curtis, then walked in a most sedate manner from the room and down the hall with Hunter racing past her.

Curtis shook his head as if amazed at her having reasoned it all out. "They are beautiful and well-behaved children, Clara."

She nodded, feeling her heart near to bursting with love for Curtis. "I'm glad you think so. I'm hopeful in time that you might even come to . . . care for them."

Curtis frowned. "This doesn't change anything."

"I don't understand."

He shook his head. "You and me. We still can't make a future together."

Clara felt as though he'd slapped her. "But why not? We talked and I thought you understood that I don't hold the past against you. I love you."

She could see that he was uncomfortable. It was as if he were battling within himself.

"I don't know what the future holds for me," Curtis finally said. "I don't even know if I'll ever get out of this bed again. I don't know if I'll ever be able to walk. I can't . . . I won't let you waste your life with a cripple."

For a moment Clara stood silent. She could see he was quite serious about this. No doubt he felt it was all quite logical to refuse her based on this development, but Clara didn't see it that way. She had spent too many years regretting what might have been.

"I think you must have hit your head very hard to be speaking such nonsense. Maybe when you heal up a little more your good sense will return." She headed for the door.

"It's because I've got good sense that my mind is made up. Like we said earlier, we've both changed a great deal. We aren't the same children we were fourteen years ago."

She stopped and fixed him with a look. "No, we're not—I'm not. Therefore I'm not letting anyone bully me ever again. Not my mother, and certainly not you." She slammed his bedroom door behind her and fought back the tears that threatened to flow.

For all the good their talk had done, Clara was still more than aware that Curtis had never said anything about loving her. Maybe he truly no longer felt that way about her. Maybe he didn't mind the idea of their being friends but had no intention of making their relationship more.

If he no longer loves me—if what he said is true—how can I possibly stay? I can't just be friends with him.

⁂

By the first of June Otto was in quite a dither. He'd had to come up with his own money to put in place of the money Adolph had hidden somewhere. It didn't sit well with him to take from his own coffers, but there had been nothing else he could do, since there were deadlines to meet. His associates wouldn't have allowed otherwise. He only hoped he could find the money, and if not, that he could sell off enough of his brother's stocks to make it up.

In the world, things were happening fast. America was training her soldiers with a goal to ship out the first troops within a month. The newspapers carried continued stories of how there were a limited number of men who had actually experienced war and knew how gruesome it could be. Some articles suggested that troops would be sent over without proper training.

Major General John Pershing, nicknamed "Black Jack" Pershing because of the time he spent commanding the black buffalo soldiers of the Tenth Cavalry, was called upon to make the American forces ready for war.

Otto had seen pictures of the man. He was dashingly handsome, causing many a lady to swoon, while his no-nonsense approach to training and refusal to allow for mistakes or excuses caused men to hate him. Otto supposed, given the man's considerable experience in the army, that Pershing would be a force to be reckoned with. But weren't all heroes considered that? Otto smiled, knowing with great confidence that Pershing and his inexperienced army would be no match for the well-trained soldiers of the kaiser.

When the office clock chimed the hour, Otto put away his papers and ledgers. He was anticipating the arrival of Charles Weidel. Otto wasn't looking forward to dealing with the man. Weidel was the man Otto and Adolph answered to regarding their part in helping Germany. Weidel was also the man who had left Otto little choice but to use his own money in place of the funds given to Adolph.

Right on time, Otto heard voices in the outer office and knew Weidel had arrived. Otto pulled on his coat and had just returned to his desk when Jack opened the door to announce Weidel.

"Come on in, Charles. Jack, we're not to be disturbed." His secretary nodded and pulled the door closed behind the stocky man's frame.

"I'm glad you could see me on such short notice," Charles declared. He took the chair opposite the desk without waiting for Otto's invitation. "I've just come from a luncheon with several prominent politicians who are most anxious to increase patrols in the harbor."

"That's unfortunate." Otto knew this would put Weidel in a foul mood.

"Of course I pretended to agree, but then I offered a few suggestions of my own." Weidel took out a handkerchief and blotted his perspiring face. "All of this, of course, means we must move up our schedule."

Otto shook his head. "But that would be almost impossible. I'm already under investigation because of Adolph's death. Badeau and his men are watching me all of the time. I think

162

for now you're going to have to forego using me to benefit the cause. I'm afraid I would only be a liability at this point."

"Nonsense. Badeau is shooting in the dark, and we both know that. If he had anything concrete, he would have already arrested you. No, we must move quickly. Several of our associates have been arrested and charged with all manner of crimes. We need to prove to these people once and for all that we have more power than they have ever imagined."

Otto began to toy with the letter opener on his desk. "What is it you think we should do?"

"We must make a grand show of things. I've talked it over with some of our supporters. It's been decided. One of the confiscated German ships will be moved to the Brooklyn Naval Yards in three days and refitted to transport troops. Our plan is to pack enough explosives in the ship to blow it to kingdom come, along with a good part of the naval yard."

"What? Do you have any idea how difficult that will be? The amount of necessary explosives alone is enough to make such an idea impossible. And talk about a place that is well guarded. They have patrols all over the place."

"That's why it's imperative that we act immediately." The man was unmoved by Otto's concern. "We have our ways, and what I need from you is your assistance in secreting the needed explosives into the city and down to the warehouse. You won't be alone in this endeavor. I have more than a dozen men helping in this effort. That way if any one of you is caught, the others might still make it through."

"I can't possibly see this working, Charles. You know as well as I do that Americans are already running scared, looking for spies behind every tree, seeing submarines not only along the coast but sailing up the Hudson and East Rivers. We can't possibly do this in three days. Three weeks would be too soon."

"I'm no fool, Vesper. Our associates have arranged for it to be fairly easy to get supplies aboard the ship. The original cargo was removed some time ago when the ship was first taken. However, there are a great many things that are needed to transform the ship into the necessary transport for soldiers. This cargo will include our explosives, although no one will realize this but our associates. We have men who are working on the ship already, and they will lay in the explosives and set everything in motion."

"Even if they can pack the entire hold with explosives, how will they ever arrange to set it off once the ship is in the naval yard?"

"That isn't your concern. Your job is to help with the transportation of the explosives." Weidel narrowed his eyes. "You will do this. On the fifteenth of this month, Congress will vote on President Wilson's proposed Espionage Act. If approved, it will make things much more difficult and give the local authorities the rights they've been looking for. Even suspicion will be enough to throw people in jail. We will accomplish this matter, and once it is done, we will send a letter to Washington telling the president that if he moves forward with this nonsense, we will arrange to blow up even more ships."

Otto's throat was so dry he could hardly swallow. "But these things take time. You can't just transport explosives around the state without being subject to inspection."

"Honestly, Vesper, if I didn't know better, I would think you're siding with the enemy." Weidel leaned forward and pounded his fist on the desk. "I didn't come here to invite you to a garden party. If you refuse to cooperate, you will be sorry."

Otto knew it would be necessary to assuage the man's temper. "I assure you, Charles, I have no desire to refuse cooperation. I will happily do my part to lend aid to Germany. However, I don't want to be a liability to our cause. Neither do I want to fail due to a lack of necessary time."

"You didn't lack for time in arranging for your brother to be killed," Weidel countered, his voice low and menacing.

"That was completely different. That involved one man. What you're proposing involves dozens." Otto could see by the man's expression that he wasn't going to change his mind. Otto would have to go along for now and then create something to complicate the matter and interfere in his part. He had no idea of what that might be, but he would have to figure it out in the next few hours. Perhaps killing Weidel would be just as valuable to them as his brother's demise. "Very well. What is it you want me to do?"

Weidel's countenance was no longer the mottled reddish purple it had turned earlier. "Before we get into the exact details," he said, sitting back, "I understand there is a little event you are hosting tonight."

"Yes. I'm introducing a few new pieces of Vesper jewelry. I need to show the public that the Vesper collection has not come to an end." Otto smiled. "It's been of great concern to many women."

"I've also heard it bandied about that you, and not your brother, are responsible for the designs."

Otto pretended for a moment he might deny this. "Well . . . I don't know. . . ." He shrugged. "What can I say? Adolph wasn't the creator, but he was very good at marketing the jewels to those of high finance. He had a way about him, and people trusted him."

"And now they will have to trust you," Weidel said, smiling. "Just as I trust you. Let us hope that our trust in you is not misplaced." He got to his feet. "I plan to be in attendance tonight. In fact, I'm escorting your sister-in-law's mother, Mrs. Oberlin."

This news didn't surprise Otto. Weidel put his business around town, and everyone knew he was wealthy and powerful. What nobody suspected was that he was responsible for much of the sedition going on in the city. Perhaps that was the way to rid himself of the strain Charles had put on him. If the authorities knew that Charles Weidel was suspect in his loyalty, it might very well tie up the old man for some time.

"I will look forward to seeing you tonight. I'm sure by then you'll see the importance of our plans."

Hours later, long after the party to show off the Vesper pieces Otto had rushed his staff to complete, he was still contemplating whether or not supporting Germany was all that important to him. In the beginning he had been certain Germany would win the war. Now he wasn't so sure. When America had remained neutral, there was hope that the kaiser would best the world and then reward those who had been faithful to help. Now there was talk of Germany backing down merely because America had entered the war. Some thought there might even be discussions of peace before the first American troops were sent. At least this was the topic of discussion among the very wealthy that evening.

It seemed to Otto that it would be better for him to play both sides of the field. He went to his bedroom writing table and took up a piece of paper and a pen. Perhaps a nice anonymous letter to Mr. Badeau would lessen the attention focused on the Vesper business and put it on Weidel. With Weidel caught up in a pesky investigation, he'd have little time to torment Otto. With any luck at all, it would postpone activities at the naval yard until much, much later. If they took place at all.

15

*D*r. Cosgrove finished cutting the last few inches of the body cast. The moment had arrived for them to see exactly how well Curtis's back had healed. The doctor removed the top portion.

"Now, I think the easiest way to get you out of the back part of this cast is to have you sit up. I'm going to help you to sit, but we need to take it slowly. We want to make sure that we don't do any injury to the spine. Also, we need to be mindful of your leg." Although the doctor had taken off the traction, the leg was still casted from his foot to the top of his thigh. "Are you ready?"

"As ready as I'll ever be."

Even with the help of the doctor, Curtis found it more difficult than he'd imagined. The body cast had weakened the muscles of his torso, and the cast on his leg made sitting up straight rather painful. He couldn't suppress a moan.

"Just a little more," Cosgrove said. The doctor persisted in his manipulation of Curtis and the cast. "There."

Curtis felt the cast separate from his back. Despite the

discomfort—pain if Curtis was honest—he was grateful to be rid of the plaster prison.

"How does that feel?"

"Better than it was."

Dr. Cosgrove came around behind Curtis and began to run his hand down the center of Curtis's back.

"Your hand is cold."

"Well, at least you can feel it," Dr. Cosgrove said. He momentarily left Curtis to retrieve his medical bag. "I'm going to check and see what else you can feel."

Curtis tried to remain patient as the doctor poked, prodded, and tortured him. "Well, what do you think, Doc?"

"The swelling is gone, as well as the bruising. You have some sores where the cast rubbed, but that's easy enough to fix. I have some salve that Mrs. Sersland can put on you." The doctor came back to face Curtis. "As I told you before, I wasn't certain about the back actually being broken, but the damage done to you indicated the possibility."

The doctor tested the reflexes in Curtis's arms and then touched a needle to each of his fingers. "Can you feel this?"

"Yes, just as I did before." Curtis knew his tone was one of irritation and quickly apologized. "I'm sorry, Doc. I'm just tired of all this." He still wasn't willing to admit he was in more than a little pain.

Cosgrove smiled. "I'm sure you are. You've been in casts for nearly two months now. However, given the extent of your injuries, we had to be careful." He straightened and studied Curtis for a moment. "You don't have to pretend it doesn't hurt."

"I don't intend to give in to it."

"Nor would I want you to. However, you are going to have some discomfort and pain for some time. Maybe always." The doctor put things away and returned to Curtis's bedside. "Let's have you lie back now."

Curtis was glad the doctor insisted on helping him. Otherwise he felt as though he might have simply fallen back against the bed. He was disgusted by the weakness in his abdominal muscles and frustrated by the fiery pain that shot up from his hips.

"I know you were hoping I'd remove the leg cast as well, but the injuries there were much more severe, as you know. We were lucky to save your leg and may yet have to operate."

"So how much longer?"

Dr. Cosgrove smiled. "Well, I'd like to leave it casted at least another two weeks. After that, I'll remove the cast and then we'll see. I know that's a disappointment. However, I do have a bit of good news."

Curtis bit back a snide remark. "What's that?"

"I'm not going to put you back in traction."

"That *is* good news." Curtis felt the gloom lift a bit.

"And I'm going to allow you to sit up in bed for half an hour, three times a day for the first week, and then we'll increase the time to five times a day for the second week and maybe even let you sit in a chair. With the leg elevated, of course."

"Of course," Curtis muttered.

The doctor ignored him. "Then I'll be back and we can see how you're doing." He closed his bag. "If you're just patient for a little while longer, this will soon be behind you."

Curtis nodded. "Is there anything else I need to know?"

Dr. Cosgrove took on a serious expression. "Not at this time. As I told you before, given the damage done to your leg, I'm not sure what to expect when that cast comes off. I'd like to believe you will eventually be able to get back your full use of the leg. However, we will have to wait and see. I don't want you discouraged, by any means, but I do want you to look at this realistically. You may have to go to one of the larger hospitals in the state to set that leg properly. We can only wait and see. Just remember, you're lucky to be alive."

"I don't know how lucky it'll be if I can't walk."

"I feel confident in time you will walk."

Just then Clara appeared at the door. "How's the patient?"

Dr. Cosgrove smiled. "Ornery as ever. But otherwise doing well. As you can see, we've removed the body cast."

Clara came to Curtis's bedside. "I'm sure that feels much better."

"I was just instructing Curtis as to what he can and can't do."

"I'm certain, knowing Curtis as I do, that he doesn't feel there should be any limitations." Clara looked at Curtis with a raised brow. "Am I right?"

The doctor laughed. "I'm sure you are, although Curtis pretends to be the most cooperative of patients." He moved to stand beside Clara. "I want to show you how to help Curtis sit. I want him to sit up in bed three times a day, but no more. If you have some extra pillows that may help."

"I'll get some right away." She disappeared from the room but was back in a flash. She held four pillows in her arms. "Will this be enough?"

"I believe so." The doctor took the pillows and put them behind Curtis at the head of the bed. "Now, Curtis's muscles are quite weak from not being used, so he will definitely need help to sit. Not only that, but the leg cast will make it somewhat difficult." He showed her how to take hold of Curtis. He watched as Clara attempted the job.

Curtis was determined to do as much for himself as possible. The moment Clara touched him he couldn't help but feel a surge of emotion course through him. This wasn't going to be a good situation at all. Madeline was still slated to be gone for another four days, and even if he demanded that Joe or Phil return to help him, he had a feeling no one would listen. A moan escaped him once again as the muscles and nerves contracted.

"I'm so sorry. Did I do something wrong?" Clara asked, looking first to Curtis and then to the doctor.

"He's going to have pain. Back injuries take a long time to heal, and even then they often leave the patient with lifelong pain."

"Well then, I will do all I can to ease it," Clara said, smiling.

Curtis couldn't seem to look away. He wanted nothing more than to reach up and touch her cheek. He drew in a deep breath to steady himself. This was no doubt Madeline's conspiracy with Clara to put them together as much as possible. He grimaced as Clara reached around him to position the pillows.

"There." She looked at the doctor.

He nodded and smiled. "Now help him ease back a bit."

She reached for Curtis and he tensed. Her face was only inches from his, and he could smell the scent of roses in her hair. Thankfully she accomplished the task quickly.

"All right, Curtis. Now that I have you in capable hands, I will let Mrs. Vesper know how to care for your other needs." He turned to Clara. "Why don't you walk me to the door and I'll fill you in. I'm going to need someone to massage his back every morning and evening. He'll also need hot compresses. All of this will require turning him on his side until the cast comes off the leg."

Clara nodded and followed the doctor from the room. Curtis gritted his teeth at the thought of Clara touching him again. It was one thing for her to help him sit up, but massaging him was an entirely different matter. He couldn't allow that.

But what else am I supposed to do? Madeline had gone with

Paul and the others to shear sheep. Even Joe and Phil had gone up to the shearing site to help for a few hours. This left Curtis very much alone with Clara and her children. Even if Curtis wanted to refuse her treatment, he couldn't. Not if he wanted to heal and get back on his feet.

He was still contemplating this when Clara returned. She looked quite happy. "I would imagine you're over the moon."

Curtis met her gaze. "I'm glad to be rid of that body cast. Glad too that Doc says I can spend some time sitting. But you need to know that I won't allow you to give me any kind of intimate treatment like massage. It isn't appropriate."

Clara shook her head. "No, it isn't. I've already considered that. I think we can get Joe or Phil to help with it. Besides, they have stronger hands and will be able to massage your muscles easier than I could." She smiled. "Now, I'm going to go fix your lunch tray. I figure while you're sitting up it will be the perfect time for you to eat. It will be much simpler than before. After lunch, when your half hour of sitting is complete, I'll help you to lie back down. Then when Joe and Phil return, I'll let them know what's to be done."

As Clara exited the room, Maddy appeared. She walked to his bedside and without warning climbed up on the bed beside him. She was no more the hesitant child he'd first met.

"You don't have that cast anymore," she said, pointing to his bare chest.

"No. The doctor took it off." He had a blanket that covered his lower body but allowed for his casted leg to remain out. He pointed. "Just this cast is left."

She nodded. "So when will you be well?"

It surprised him that Maddy was concerned with this, and he couldn't help but question her on the matter. "Why do you ask?"

She shrugged. "We keep praying for you every night. I'm just wondering when God is going to answer."

He couldn't help smiling. "God is already answering. The doctor says I'm much better, and in another two weeks he hopes to take off the leg cast."

"Will you be able to get up then?"

"I hope so, Miss Maddy. I've been in this bed for almost two months."

"That's a long time. Does it hurt?"

"What? Being in bed that long? It's definitely not comfortable."

"No, I mean your leg. Does it hurt?"

Her concern touched him. "It did, but not so much now."

"My father died when he got shot," she said matter-of-factly.

Curtis found it surprising that she should mention such a thing so bluntly. "I'm sorry. You must miss him."

She shook her head. "No. He never came to the nursery. Nanny Mim said he was real busy. I saw him when we went to church, but he always wanted us to stay with Nanny Mim."

"He never played with you and Hunter?" She shook her head. Curtis couldn't help thinking that if Hunter and Maddy were his, he would want to play with them—be with them as much as possible.

"Mama came to the nursery to see us. Sometimes she read to us or we had a tea party. She even played with Hunter and his toy soldiers."

"She loves you a great deal."

Maddy nodded. "She loves you too."

Curtis was taken aback. What could he say? What should he say? He had thought to let the matter lie but found his curiosity wouldn't allow him to. "Did she say that?"

"I heard her say it when she was praying," Maddy replied. "She didn't know I heard her."

"I see. Well, you know it's never good to eavesdrop."

"I know."

She offered no other excuse or comment but merely watched Curtis as if trying to figure out something. Uncertain of what she was thinking, Curtis was careful with his next comment.

"Your mama loves a lot of people. She always has. Did she tell you that she knew me when she was a young girl?"

Maddy nodded. "She told us that you used to go for walks and rides on the horses."

"We did." Curtis felt a sense of relief that she was no longer speaking of love.

"She told God she wants you to walk with her again." Maddy's brow furrowed as she frowned. "She didn't ask God about riding horses."

Curtis vacillated between the amusement he felt at the child's commentary and the discomfort of how much he knew Clara was pining for him. Though if he was honest, it was certainly no more than he was pining for her.

It's your own fault that you're pining. It's your fault that she's pining too.

He sought to change the subject. "So are you having fun here on the ranch, or do you miss the city?"

"I don't miss our old house. Mama's happy here, and I hope we don't ever leave."

I hope you don't either.

The thought came like a punch to the gut. He didn't want them to leave.

"Here we are," Clara said, carrying in a tray. She smiled at Maddy. "Sweetheart, would you bring over that wooden platform so I can put the tray down?"

Maddy hopped off the bed and retrieved the piece. Curtis took it from her and positioned it over his lap. Clara then deposited the tray.

"I hope you enjoy this." She looked the tray over. "Do you see anything that's missing?"

"If it was missing, how could I see it?" Curtis automatically countered.

She laughed and it was like music. Curtis met her gaze. She looked so angelic—so at peace—yet he knew inside her was a turmoil that he had caused. Finally she looked away, leaving Curtis with his guilt and frustration.

"Well, if you think of anything else you need, just ring the bell." She handed him the bell from the nightstand. "Maddy, your lunch is on the table. Hunter is already there, so why don't you go and join him. I'll be there shortly."

Without a word, the little girl did as Clara instructed. Curtis thought to himself just how well behaved the children were. Hunter had a bit of a wild streak, but Curtis figured that was because he needed a father's strong hand to direct him. Maybe once he was out of this bed he could . . .

"I can't think that way," he muttered.

"What was that?" Clara asked.

Curtis hadn't realized he'd spoken aloud. "I'm sorry. I was just thinking about something." He looked down at the tray. "This looks real good."

"I'll be back to check on you."

Curtis nodded and watched her go. He had to admire her trim little figure. She had dressed in a long brown skirt and calico blouse of yellow. She looked very much like she belonged on the ranch instead of among the high society of New York City.

She was definitely happy. That much couldn't be denied. The

children were too. At least they seemed to be. Maddy had said she hoped they'd never leave. And the truth of the matter was that when Curtis wasn't working so hard to guard his feelings, he had to admit that he didn't want them to leave either.

Lord, I don't know what to do with all my thoughts and feelings. I've wanted Clara back in my life for so long. I prayed she'd never marry. I hoped she'd run away and come back to me and then we could marry and no one would ever be able to separate us again. But, Lord, I'm in no position to take a wife and be a father to those children. He shook his head and sighed. *I don't know what to do.*

⚜

While Joe kept company with Curtis, Clara readied the moist towels. She had to admit she was relieved to not be tending to Curtis's back. She hadn't anticipated the way just helping him to sit would make her feel. She hadn't touched him in so very long. Hadn't touched any man, for that matter. She couldn't even remember the last time she and Adolph had embraced. He had never been one to show much affection.

Since the children had been up since five-thirty, Clara sent them to bed for an afternoon nap. Neither one protested, which didn't surprise her, since they had yawned all the way through lunch. Now with them sound asleep and Curtis's half hour of sitting at an end, Clara once again thanked God for sending Joe back to the ranch early.

"You knew what I needed, Lord. Even before I did."

She placed the rolled-up towels on a tray and then pulled a bottle of lotion from her apron pocket and put it there as well. Doing so, she saw how her hand trembled. It was silly to be so apprehensive, but just the idea of being so close to him—even

176

with Joe there—left Clara feeling all jittery. This was the kind of care a wife would give her injured husband.

She entered Curtis's bedroom with the tray and a smile. She saw that Joe had already removed the lunch dishes and had helped him to lie back down. Now both men watched her with an expression of curiosity.

"I'm anxious to know just how this massaging will help," Joe said. "If it's a good thing, I'll let Curtis return the favor once he's up."

Clara laughed. "The doctor said the moist heat will help the muscles relax, and the massage will further the blood flow and help Curtis not to feel so stiff after being in the cast for so long." She looked at Curtis. "I hope this won't be too hot. The doctor said the hotter the better, but I certainly don't want to burn you." She put the tray with the towels and lotion on the bedside table.

"Joe, the doctor said we needed to roll Curtis on his side and prop the casted leg with pillows." Clara reached for some of the extra pillows. "If you'll get him on his side and hold up the leg, I'll position the pillows."

"You can just let Joe do it."

She looked into Curtis's eyes and thought she detected uneasiness. "Well, once I show him what is to be done, of course I will let him see to it."

"I'd feel better if she did show me," Joe added. "I can't say I've ever been much good at doctoring sick folks."

Clara went to Curtis's casted leg. She set the pillows to one side. "All right, Joe. You take hold of his hips. Be careful to keep the blanket over him. No sense in embarrassing us all." She knew from what Madeline had said that Curtis hadn't been able to wear any clothing under the body cast.

"Curtis, you'll need to maneuver yourself to the side using

your arms while Joe pulls you forward. I'll hold your leg so you don't need to worry about injuring yourself." She double-checked to make sure the blanket that covered his hips remained tucked between his legs. This had helped to reduce the chafing and irritation the cast had caused when Curtis was first injured. Aunt Madeline told her they had experimented with all sorts of things, and this, although simple, worked the best.

Curtis grunted agreement, and Joe took his position. Clara nodded. "On the count of three. One—two—three." They moved as one, and once Curtis was on his side, Clara continued holding the casted leg with one hand while she placed the pillows between his blanketed leg and the cast.

Clara came around to where Joe stood and looked down at Curtis. "There, that wasn't so bad . . . was it?" She studied him momentarily for signs of pain.

"No."

"Dr. Cosgrove said some pain is to be expected." She went to retrieve the hot towels. "Joe, the doctor said to drape them over the back like this." She positioned the first towel. "Then press it against the skin." She heard Curtis moan. "Is it too hot?"

"No. Fact is, it feels really good."

Smiling, Clara reached for the next towel and handed it to Joe. "Your turn." He took the towel and placed it just as she had instructed. "The doctor said this will really help you to feel better after being in that body cast."

"Anything would feel better than that."

The towels were finally in place, and Clara turned again to Joe. "We'll keep these in place until they turn cool. Then I'll tell you how the doctor wants you to massage the muscles."

"I think I'll go help myself to a cup of coffee while we wait," Joe replied, heading for the door.

"That's fine. I'll just straighten up the room." She glanced over to see that Curtis had closed his eyes as if sleeping. Clara thought he had never looked so handsome. She hadn't really allowed herself much time to study him since finding him at the ranch. Now she wanted only to memorize every line and detail of his face.

Her survey was halted, however, when she realized Curtis had opened his eyes and was watching her in return. She thought to turn away but decided against it. There was no need to speak, because Clara felt certain her expression betrayed her heart. And she didn't think it her imagination that his did likewise.

"Thanks for all you're doing," Curtis murmured, then closed his eyes again.

Clara refrained from telling him she'd be happy to care for him always. Instead she went to work sweeping up some of the dust and remnants of the cast that had been left behind.

When it was finally time to remove the towels, Clara went reluctantly to retrieve them. She rolled them up and put them back on the tray she'd brought and then took up a bottle of lotion just as Joe returned.

"I do apologize for the scent of this lotion," she began. "But it was all I had on hand. I told the doctor we'd get into town for something else when the shearing was over. He said I could use lard, but I figured this would smell better." She gave a little laugh, hoping it didn't sound forced. She handed the bottle to Joe.

"Rose scented?" he asked, looking at her as if she'd lost her mind. A smile broke his stern expression. "We'll be the sweetest-smelling men on the ranch."

Curtis rolled his eyes, but Clara detected the humor in his expression and relaxed. "Like I said, I'll have someone pick up some lotion that doesn't have such a feminine scent. Aunt Madeline might even have something on hand."

Clara motioned for Joe to stand facing Curtis's back. "The doctor said you should massage him while standing here."

"Exactly how am I supposed to massage him?" Joe looked rather perplexed.

"Well, you use the lotion and rub the muscles starting at the neck and shoulders."

Joe didn't so much as move but continued to stare at Clara with a puzzled expression. She sighed. "Here, I'll show you."

She put a good amount of lotion on her hand, then set the bottle aside and went to work. She started at the top just as the doctor had instructed. Curtis's neck and shoulders were hard and knotted. Clara pressed gently at first, but seeing it was getting her nowhere, she put all of her strength into it. She kneaded the muscles as if kneading bread. She used not only her fingers but the palms of her hands, and after a little time she felt the knots give way.

"My hands aren't as strong as yours," she said, trying not to think of the warmth of Curtis's skin. "When you're kneading the muscles, however, you'll feel the tension ease, and that's how you'll know you're doing it right."

Next she let her hands move down his spine. She pressed gently at the scars. "Am I hurting you?"

"No." His reply was hardly more than a whisper.

Clara swallowed the lump in her throat. This was just as hard to do as she'd worried it would be. Touching him, feeling the warmth of his skin, caused her only to desire all the more to be held in his arms. She silently thanked God that Joe was there and straightened.

"Your turn." She stepped aside to give Joe room to work. She tried not to think about how her heart was racing. She waited as Joe poured lotion in his hands. "Now start where I left off in the middle of his back and be careful of the sores that the cast caused. I have some salve to apply after the massage, but no sense in irritating them with this lotion."

Joe nodded and began to work on Curtis's muscles. Clara could see he was quite capable of the job and breathed a sigh of relief even as she pushed down a sense of desire to be the one tending Curtis.

"Dr. Cosgrove said to do this for at least twenty minutes after the heated towels."

She watched Joe work. Why couldn't Curtis see how much she loved him—wanted to be with him—wanted to be his? Clara shook off the dangerous thoughts and decided to recite Scripture to herself in order to keep her mind on something other than Curtis. The Bible said she should take every thought captive, and for the first time in her life she understood the value of that.

16

*W*ith the coming of July things settled down at the ranch. The sheep bands were now off to the mountain pastures with their particular shepherds, Joe and Phil had managed to cut and bale a bumper crop of hay, and Dr. Cosgrove had removed all but a portion of the cast on Curtis's leg. Clara could see that Curtis was much happier—even more like his old self. She prayed that God was doing a work on his heart where she and the children were concerned, because she never wanted to be separated from him again.

Madeline took up the broom and smiled as Curtis gingerly used crutches to walk from the bed to a nearby chair. "It's mighty good to see you up and around."

"Feels good too," Curtis replied, taking great care to ease onto the chair. "I wasn't too happy to have the doc recast the lower part of my leg, but it's still much better than what I had."

Clara tried not to watch him as she pulled sheets and bedding from the bed. It was washday, and she had already been quite busy helping her aunt with the household laundry. In the weeks since Curtis met the children, Clara had found them more often than not visiting with him when they didn't have chores or something else to keep their attention. They really liked Curtis and often rambled on to her about stories he had told them of when she and he had been much younger. Stories that Clara had thought for certain he'd forgotten.

"Well, it's not going to be long before that last cast comes off too," Madeline declared. "I trust the doctor to know what's best."

"Dr. Cosgrove said he might have to rebreak the tibia," Curtis muttered. "I told him I might have to break his jaw."

Clara emitted a gasp while Madeline broke into laughter. "I'll bet that'll make him think twice about it. Still, if it hasn't healed proper, you sure don't want to leave it as is."

"What I want hasn't been of any concern to much of anyone since I got hurt."

Clara cast him a quick glance. At least she'd intended it to be a quick one. Unfortunately, she found Curtis watching her make the bed. She smiled and couldn't stop herself from speaking. "I know that Aunt Madeline and Uncle Paul have taken your desires, as well as your needs, into consideration. I know I have."

"It's true," Madeline countered as she continued sweeping the room.

"Yes, you both have been very concerned with my . . . needs. A man couldn't ask for better nurses." He fell silent, and Clara went back to work.

"Well, I for one intend to continue to see those needs met," Madeline said, going to the door where she'd left the dustpan. "Doc gave strict instructions about what you could and couldn't do, and I intend to see that you follow them to the letter."

"Now, Madeline . . ."

"Don't you try to sweet-talk me, Curtis Billingham. You and

I both know you can't be trusted to take it easy and slow. If it were up to you, you'd be on your way to join up with the army."

Clara finished plumping the pillows. "Hopefully by the time Curtis gets back on his feet, the war will be over."

"Everybody hopes for that," Madeline said, nodding. "It's already been such a long and destructive one for those who entered it first. I find it hard to even imagine the large numbers of dead and wounded that the newspaper tallies each week." She sobered. "Soon American boys will join those numbers."

"Mama?" Maddy called from the door.

Clara turned. "What is it, Maddy?"

"You need to come quick."

"What have you two found this time?"

Maddy was ever her calm, almost stoic, self. "We didn't find anything. Hunter jumped out of the tree and hurt his arm."

Clara's hand went to her mouth. She tried her best to remain calm for the sake of her daughter. She hurried to the door. "Show me where he is."

Now Maddy seemed to sense the urgency and picked up her pace. By the time they stepped out onto the porch, they were very nearly running.

Hunter's anguished cries could be heard even before Clara could see him. She'd never heard him cry like that and it tore at her heart. She followed Maddy to where she'd left her brother in a grove of trees and found Hunter holding his right arm. His shoulder looked strangely positioned.

"Oh, my poor baby, what have you done?"

Hunter's reply was ragged. "I . . . I . . . disobeyed. I . . . jumped . . . out of the tree." Having declared this, he began to wail.

Clara knew she couldn't very well chastise him now. She needed to get him to town so Dr. Cosgrove could take a look at his arm and shoulder. She scooped her son up and started for the house. She found Madeline waiting for her on the porch as they approached.

"Hunter jumped out of the tree, and I think he may have broken his arm." She panted under the weight of the child. "And dislocated his shoulder."

"I'll have Joe hitch the wagon so we can take him in to see Dr. Cosgrove." Madeline hurried off the porch and disappeared around the side of the house.

"Will he have to have a cast like Curtis?" Maddy asked, rubbing her right arm as if in sympathy.

"I don't know, Maddy." Clara continued to try to calm her son. "Hunter, you're all right now, and no matter what, the doctor is going to know what to do to help you feel better."

"It hurts real bad, Mama," he replied.

His sobs were abating with the shock of what had happened, and now the pain would no doubt be his focus. Clara was close to tears herself, but she kept doing her best to keep them from coming. She needed to be strong for her children. They'd led such a sheltered life, and this was the first time either of them had really faced any danger or injury.

"Is he all right?"

Clara startled at Curtis's voice. She looked up to find him at the front door. "You shouldn't be out of your room. You know what the doctor said."

He grimaced. "I wanted to know if Hunter was all right."

She nodded, finding his concern touching. "I think he may have broken his arm and hurt his shoulder."

"I fell out of the tree," Hunter offered, looking up.

"No he didn't," Maddy countered. "He jumped."

Hunter nodded, looking quite contrite. "I jumped and then I fell."

Curtis gave him a smile. "Well, that's because you didn't have me to show you how to properly climb and get back down out of a tree. Once we get your arm mended and my leg healed, I'll show you how it's done."

"No!" Clara said before she could think. She felt rather embarrassed at how she'd raised her voice. "I just meant that I don't think I want either of them climbing trees."

Curtis seemed to have anticipated her response. "Mamas worry too much. She'll come around in time." He winked and smiled at her in the old way—in the way she'd not seen since coming back to the ranch. It caused her heart to flutter and her breath to catch.

Just then Madeline came back around the house, this time driving the wagon. Joe was seated at the back and jumped down as the wagon came to a stop. He reached out for Hunter without so much as asking. Clara let him take her son, then she helped Maddy into the back of the wagon. Once the child was settled, Clara climbed up herself. She arranged her skirt, then held out her arms.

"Now, don't you fret none, Hunter," Joe said, smiling as he handed the boy back to her. "Dr. Cosgrove has had a lot of experience patching folks up. He'll have you fixed up in no time."

Clara leaned back against the wagon side and sighed as Madeline put the team into motion. As they drove away from the house, Clara found that Curtis was still watching them. How she wished that he might be going with them. He had always known how to make her feel better. How to calm her worries.

Pray. God is your refuge—not Curtis.

Clara felt her concerns ebb. God truly was her refuge. He alone had been there for her the past fourteen years. She'd been so panicked that she hadn't even thought to pray.

"Forgive me, Lord," she murmured.

⊙⊶⊱⊰⊷⊙

Curtis heard the wagon return. He had prayed that Hunter's injuries would be minimal. Clara had been so pale standing there holding her son. Maybe she'd never seen either of them hurt before. Given that they'd lived in a wealthy household in the city, he figured that was a great possibility. He smiled at the thought that he'd broken his arm at the age of five. With a doctor for a father, Curtis had simply borne his father's repairs with impatience and then headed out again to attempt something he probably shouldn't have been doing in the first place.

Hunter soon appeared, arm in a sling and a smile on his face. "Curtis, I got a sprained wrist and a hurt shoulder."

"His shoulder was dislocated and Dr. Cosgrove put it back in place. He said Hunter was to do nothing for the next five days," Clara said, entering the room after her son.

"I asked Mama if we could move my bed in here so I could be sick with you."

Curtis met Clara with a questioning gaze. She shrugged. "I told him he'd have to ask you," she replied.

"I for one," Madeline said, coming into the room behind her niece, "think it would be a good idea. That way we have just one sick room instead of two."

"So can I stay here?" Hunter asked.

There was no way Curtis was going to tell the boy no, even though he wasn't at all sure he wanted him there. Since having the ability to get up and walk short distances, Curtis had seen less and less of Clara. She still came in occasionally, but Joe now helped him with his exercises to strengthen his leg and back, and Madeline often reverted to bringing his meals. If Hunter were to reside here as well, no doubt Clara would come more often. Curtis knew it could prove danger-ous and thought to refuse, but instead acceptance came out of his mouth.

"I don't see why not," he answered, hoping it wasn't a mis-take.

Hunter nodded enthusiastically. "I knew you'd say yes. We can play checkers and you can read stories to me."

"Well, you need to keep in mind that Curtis is still healing," Clara said.

Curtis wondered if she too worried about the additional time they'd be together. He hated that he no longer knew what to do. A part of him saw hope in his healing, while another knew that healing his body wasn't going to change the past. He thought she was wonderful to claim indifference to the man he'd once been, but he knew how his actions could damage her reputation and that of the children.

Madeline took hold of Hunter's good arm. "I'll have Joe and Phil come in and move things around and bring his bed in. Meanwhile, Hunter, why don't you come with me and show Uncle Paul your sling."

They left before Curtis could say anything. Even Clara seemed surprised by their hasty departure. Silence engulfed them as Clara seemed to look right through him.

"Are you all right?"

She slumped against the wall and let out a long breath. "I think so. I feel quite overwhelmed."

"Was that the first time something had happened to one of them?"

She nodded. "It's my fault for not watching them closer."

"Clara, they're kids. They're going to get hurt. We got hurt and we survived. Hunter and Maddy will do the same."

"But some children don't survive. You and I both know that.

189

I suppose I never really considered the dangers of ranch life before bringing them here."

Even though she was conversing with him, Curtis felt she was lost somewhere deep in her thoughts. He knew seeing her son injured had taken its toll, but he hoped she wouldn't turn into one of those mothers who never let her children out of her sight.

"Clara, you can't keep them locked up in a box. Everything has turned out all right." He looked at her standing there. She seemed so frail—so needy. He longed to go to her and pull her into his arms and promise her nothing bad would ever happen again. But, of course, he couldn't guarantee that, and he didn't dare let her think there was something more between them than what there was. They were just old friends living under the same roof. Two people who had once loved each other enough to plan a life together. Two people who were still in love.

The thought slammed into him like a wild horse against a fence. No matter how hard he worked to convince himself that he didn't love Clara, his heart refused to listen. *I can't love her,* he told himself sternly. He lowered his gaze to the floor and sighed as the truth washed over him. *I can't* not *love her.*

✁✁

For the next couple of days, Curtis continued to mull over his feelings for Clara and pray. He talked it out over and over with God, apologizing for his bad attitude and anger toward Him and seeking direction for what he should do. Now that he was on the mend and could see hope—the real possibility of getting back on his feet—Curtis found himself feeling less inclined to put Clara away from him. Whenever she came to tend to Hunter, he tried his best to be good-natured. He even started conversations, which he'd been hesitant to do before.

"And Curtis told me about breaking his arm when he was five," Hunter told his mother that morning when she came to bring them lunch. "He fell off a horse."

"I actually got bucked off," Curtis corrected.

Hunter's eyes were wide in the retelling. "The horse started jumping up and down and went all over the place." He tried to bob to one side but winced.

Clara looked over her shoulder at Curtis. "Been filling his head with wild tales, eh?"

"They're true tales. I've had a bit of a wild past, that much I admit to." He met her gaze, knowing she would realize he was speaking about more than his childhood.

She nodded and quickly turned away. "We all have our regrets."

"Curtis told me he'd teach me to ride a horse when he gets well, and Unca Paul said maybe for our birthday he'd take us out for a ride. If my arm's all better."

Clara said nothing but turned away from her son's animated face to serve Curtis his lunch. He could see the idea wasn't sitting well with her.

"When is your birthday, Hunter?" he asked.

"July the twenty-sixth. Maddy was born first, but I was the boy and Mama said that was important too."

"You both have your importance," Clara said, stepping back. "Each person is important to God."

"Your mama is right," Curtis said, picking up a piece of cold fried chicken. "And since we aren't able to go to the Fourth of July picnic in town, I think we should plan up a big birthday party for you and Maddy. What do you think?"

"I think it sounds great," Hunter declared. "We never had a birthday party."

"Well then, I think it's about time." Curtis smiled up at Clara.

She smiled back, no longer looking fearful. "Hunter and I will start thinking up ideas for the party."

"What party?" Maddy asked from the doorway.

"Hey, just the gal we need," Curtis called out. "Your brother and I figure to plan a birthday party for you two. We're going to need your ideas."

Maddy walked across the room to where Clara stood. She looked up at her mother and then to Curtis. "We're going to need a big cake, 'cause Auntie Madeline told me Unca Paul really likes cake."

Curtis laughed. "He does. I think he could eat a whole cake by himself."

Maddy frowned and looked momentarily perplexed before saying, "Then maybe we need two cakes."

As Curtis and Hunter ate, the trio continued to discuss ideas for a birthday party. After lunch, Curtis wasn't surprised when the twins nodded off. Hunter and Maddy had rambled on and on about the party, and it wasn't long before Maddy curled up at the foot of her brother's bed and closed her eyes. It was only a minute or two later when Hunter too fell asleep.

Clara showed up at the door with a couple of books and a newspaper shortly after that. She handed these things to Curtis, then turned toward Hunter's bed. "Paul thought you might want to read when the opportunity presented itself."

She smiled with great tenderness as she covered each of her children with a quilt. "Maddy has missed having Hunter in her room. They've never slept apart until now. Used to be you couldn't even get them to sleep in separate beds." She straightened and met Curtis's eyes. "I hope you don't mind."

He shook his head. "No. I don't mind. I kind of like having them around." She nodded, then hurried from the room.

Curtis knew his heart was changing where Clara and the

children were concerned. He wasn't at all sure how the future was going to play out, but he was starting to allow himself to think about the possibilities.

Picking up the newspaper, he thumbed through the pages. Seemed Montana's own Jeannette Rankin had been condemned for being the only person in Congress to vote against entering the war. The woman was the first to hold such a high position in the government, and people loved to find fault.

Curtis turned the page and scanned the story of an eastern railroad facing bankruptcy, and then his eye caught sight of a tiny article in the corner. He might not have noticed it at all but for the title.

"Vesper Genius"

He read the brief announcement that the real creator of the Vesper collection of jewelry was not Adolph Vesper, as originally thought, but rather his brother, Otto. The twin had displayed several new pieces as proof of this and gave the public the promise of more. Curtis lowered the paper, wondering if Paul had seen the notice.

"What kind of game is Vesper up to?"

He put the paper aside and wondered if Clara knew her brother-in-law was taking credit for her creations. Perhaps she was aware of it and didn't care, but there was an equal chance she knew nothing about it and Vesper was taking advantage of her absence.

For several long minutes Curtis pondered what, if anything, he should do about this news. Clara had made it clear that she hoped to remain in Montana. Perhaps this was her arrangement. She'd create jewelry here and send the designs east for her brother-in-law to develop and sell. It made sense, but his claiming the glory didn't. Clara deserved to have people know that it was her creativity that had designed such beautiful pieces.

"But if I tell her and she didn't know, she might want to return to New York."

He barely whispered the words, but it caused Maddy to stir and roll over. Curtis decided it might be better if he contemplated the matter later. Maybe after supper he could get a chance to speak with Paul alone, and together they could figure out if they should tell Clara.

17

"ontana!" Harriet Oberlin stormed around the room, huffing and puffing. "I should have thought of that. She used to spend her summers in that wretched place with her father's sister and her husband. They have a ranch there where they raise sheep." The final word was delivered with much disdain. "Sheep—of all things. They couldn't even have a respectable cattle ranch. It's an abominable place in the middle of nowhere."

Otto nodded, marveling at the various colors Harriet Oberlin's face had turned. "So my man tells me."

Harriet seemed to momentarily run out of steam. She pulled a handkerchief from her sleeve. "It was quite useful for ridding myself of Clara each summer." She dabbed her forehead, then tucked the lace-edged cloth back where it had been. She blew out a breath, and Otto steeled himself for another onslaught of Oberlin temper.

"Well, there's nothing to be done but for me to bring her back." Harriet shook her head, looking thoroughly disgusted. "I dread even thinking about the trip out there. It's such a miserably long train ride, and then one must go by wagon because a carriage never holds up on that rough terrain."

"Perhaps things have changed in the last fourteen years. Hasn't it been at least that long since you were last there?"

"Yes, but Montana is such a backward state."

Otto chuckled. "Not so backward. They are after all the first state to elect a woman to Congress. That in and of itself is an amazing feat, given women don't even have the right to vote in elections."

Harriet *harrumphed* and shook her finger at him. "This isn't about that ninny; it's about Clara and getting her back. Clara has never known what's good for her. She's like a child who requires constant guidance. I'm sure she drove your brother half mad."

Otto didn't believe Clara was all that helpless, and he knew full well his brother considered her an asset, even if he didn't love her. Not only that, but she'd made her way with two children clear across the country without the benefit of her mother's help and apparently was just fine. He thought for a moment of throwing that in Harriet's reddened face, then decided against it. Better to put his anger at Harriet—and Clara, for that matter—aside.

"When will you go?"

Harriet tapped her chin. "Well, I have quite a few engagements this week, but I could see my way to going next week." She muttered something incoherent and shook her head. "I had hoped to never make that trip again."

"I don't suppose if we sent her a letter requesting she return—"

"Ha! She'd never obey. She didn't stay here when she knew it was expected of her. Why would you ever imagine she'd come at our beck and call? No, I'll have to go get her. You might even consider joining me. It may well take us both."

Otto thought about it a moment. It might be a good way to remove himself from all the espionage and Weidel's demands. Ever since the foiled attempt to blow up the naval yards, thanks to Otto sending an anonymous tip to the authorities, Weidel had been almost impossible to deal with. Otto feared he might even suspect him of causing the problem.

"I'll see what my schedule will allow," Otto told the woman. "For now, however, I must return to my office. I have a meeting at one." He glanced at the clock on the mantel. "I'll telephone you later and let you know if I can accompany you."

Harriet nodded. "Well, just keep in mind that you were the one who wanted to marry her. You have just as much at stake here as I do."

"Indeed I do, but as I also told you, it will be worth your time and trouble to assist me in making this marriage happen." He ran his finger along his mustache. "I don't think you'll be sorry."

"You've been rather vague on how this is to benefit me," Harriet said, her gray eyes narrowing. "However, I suppose we can work out those details on our trip west."

Otto considered that statement all the way back to the office. He had no intention of giving Clara's mother anything more than he absolutely had to give. However, she was a menace—and the sooner he rid himself of her interference the better.

He entered his office to find his lawyer, John Bradley, waiting with a cup of coffee. "Sorry, the traffic was quite tangled." He looked at Jack. "See that we aren't disturbed."

"Should I bring you coffee?"

Otto shook his head. "Just leave us be." He turned to the awaiting man. "Come on, John. I have a great deal to discuss."

He led the way, then stood back at the door to allow the thin man a chance to enter first. The man was neither tall nor

distinguished in appearance, but there was a look about him
that left no doubt he was capable and used to getting his way.

"Have a seat." Otto closed the door, then divested himself
of his hat. It was quite warm and so, without thought as to
what the older man might think, he took off his coat as well.

If Bradley was offended, he said nothing and merely sank
into the offered chair. Otto had known the man for over thirty
years, and this wouldn't be the first time he'd sought John to
help him on some underhanded deal.

Otto opened his desk drawer and pulled out a file folder.
Inside he revealed the deed to Clara's house, the stocks and
bonds he'd taken from his brother's safe, and a copy of his
brother's will.

"I find the business in desperate straits due to my brother's
foolish choices and this infernal war. Imagine the government
shutting down the mining of gemstones in order to put those
men to work mining metals. It's oppression of the worst kind in
a country that prides itself on freedom." He pushed the papers
toward John. "I had to let most of my workers go. It seems our
business is less than necessary for the war efforts. Never mind
that my creditors continue to want their pay."

"And that's where I come in?" John asked in an almost
amused tone.

Otto glared and slammed his hand down on the desk. "I've
been striving to straighten out the mess, but unfortunately there
is still much to be done and it's going to take a bit of discretion."

"And what is it you think I can do?"

"As you might remember, my brother's will left me nothing
of importance. He left everything to Clara and the children.
And while Clara knows this about the will, I've already made
it clear to her that Adolph died without a penny of his own."

Otto swallowed hard, fearing that his lawyer would figure out this was not the whole truth.

John chuckled. "You mentioned that once before. She must be quite naïve to believe you. Good thing too. In this day and age of women asserting themselves, demanding the vote and wanting to stick their noses into every aspect of man's business, I'm surprised she trusts you at all."

"She is too concerned about her children to worry overmuch about whether I'm telling the truth or not. What I need from you is to arrange all the proper papers to prove my case. I managed some time ago to get into my brother's safe. I have the house deed here, and you already have the corporate papers. These stocks and bonds I need to have sold, even if you do so pretending to be acting on Clara's behalf."

"That's easy enough—for the right price. There will be plenty of palms to grease. There is just one matter that I won't be able to risk altering."

"What's that?"

"The trust your brother set aside for his children."

Otto frowned. "I didn't even know he had a trust for them."

Bradley nodded. "He told me that when they were born he arranged it, should anything happen to him. I offered to oversee it, but Adolph told me he was content to have it handled elsewhere." He held up his hand. "Before you ask me who is handling it, I don't know."

"Does Clara know anything about this?"

"I have no way of knowing, but I would venture a guess that she does not. After all, when you told her that her husband died without anything left to his name, she surely would have asked about the trust."

"I suppose you're right on that account." Otto had never

heard his brother mention the trust, and certainly Clara had never commented on it.

"Unfortunately, as I mentioned, the trust wasn't set up by me. However, as I understand it, Mrs. Vesper will handle the funds and have access to use them for the benefit of her children until the twins reach their majority. It's quite a hefty sum of money, but it won't be possible for us to touch."

This news didn't sit well with Otto. "How much money are we talking about?"

"Over one million dollars."

Otto narrowed his gaze. "Where in the world did my brother get that kind of money without my knowing?" He picked up a pencil and broke it in two. "Why did you never say anything about this?"

The lawyer shrugged. "There was never any need. Your brother's affairs were his own, just as you had yours. I certainly didn't make him privy to all of your doings. I only mention this now because you want all of these other changes. I figured if you knew about the trust, you'd expect it changed as well, but it can't be done."

"I've never known you to find anything that couldn't be done. However, I'll worry about it later. Clara and I intend to marry after a decent time of mourning, so perhaps there won't be any need to worry ourselves over the trust. After all, once we're married, I will be able to control her business affairs."

John got to his feet and gathered up the file documents. "I'll get right to work on all of this. It should be easy enough to draw up papers showing that your brother signed over his ownership in the business, as well as the house. I have his signature on file as well as a good forger in my employ. The rest will take a little more doing. I'll need to pay for witnesses and the proper recording of said documents with falsified dates."

He paused and rubbed his chin. "If you'll write out a draft for say . . . hmmm, one thousand dollars, I will be on my way."

"One thousand dollars?" Otto shook his head. "You need one thousand dollars to bribe officials to make these changes?"

John smiled and shook his head. "Five hundred is for my services . . . and silence." He smiled in a self-confident manner. "The rest will be used for bribes and incidentals."

Otto sighed. "Very well. I'll have Jack write out a draft, but it will very nearly clean me out." He got to his feet and crossed to the door. "I'll expect a quick turnaround—otherwise, I'll be hard-pressed to pay my remaining salaries and rents."

"There's a war on," the lawyer said with a shrug. "Nothing but war efforts moves fast these days."

"Well, you need to find a way to make it move fast."

"Perhaps that check will need to be made out for fifteen hundred." Bradley looked him in the eye and didn't back down.

Otto knew the lawyer had him right where he wanted him. "Very well. I want this resolved by the end of the week."

Jack wrote out the draft at Otto's instructions, then turned the check over to Otto for his signature. It grieved him to part with so much money, but he knew in a very short time he would have the money from the stocks and bonds to help cushion the blow.

He handed the check to Bradley. "Oh, and one more thing— you must keep this strictly between the three of us. I may be accompanying Harriet Oberlin to Montana. That's where Clara and the children are at present, and Mrs. Oberlin wants me to aid her in bringing them back to New York. Jack will be able to handle matters in my absence—if I do decide to go. However, I don't want anyone else to know where I've gone."

Bradley looked skeptical. "This hardly seems a wise time to travel."

"I know that, but it may be necessary."

"Very well. I will keep that in mind." The two men shook hands. "I will endeavor to see you again before the close of business on Friday."

Once Bradley had gone, Jack rose from his desk. "When do you figure to leave?"

Otto shrugged. "Like I said, I don't know for sure that I will go. I'll keep you informed, but it won't happen before next week. I have too many things to do before I can leave."

The office's outer door opened and a very angry Charles Weidel came into the room. "Vesper, I need to speak with you. Now!"

He didn't wait for permission but pushed his way past Otto and headed into the office. Jack looked at Otto in question.

"See that we aren't disturbed." Otto started for the office, then stopped. "But first, bring us some coffee and add a healthy splash of whiskey."

He left the door open and went to take a seat at his desk. "What's got you so riled up, Charles?"

"This infernal war and a government who sees spies behind every bush."

Otto nodded. "Jack is bringing us coffee, but why don't you go ahead and explain. Jack knows to keep his mouth shut."

"I wish that were true of everyone."

"And just what is that supposed to mean?" Otto frowned, hoping—almost praying—that Weidel wasn't wise to his actions.

"There is a traitor in our organization. That much is clear."

Jack appeared with two coffees. "Will there be anything else?" he asked, putting the cups on the desk.

"No. Leave us," Weidel ordered as if this were his secretary rather than Otto's.

Otto decided to allow for the command. "Just close the door behind you, Jack."

Jack made a hasty exit, and Otto waited until the door was shut tight before turning back to Weidel. "What has happened to make you suspect a traitor?" He picked up his cup and sampled the strong brew. The coffee wasn't all that hot, but the whiskey warmed him all the same. Pity it wasn't a cold day.

"Because all of my efforts are failing. At every point I'm met with complication and interference. I've barely managed to keep myself from coming up suspect. If not for my strong political allies, I might well find myself hauled in for questioning."

Otto gave a casual smile. "Now, why would anyone consider a staunch American such as yourself a possible threat? You've done much for this state, and your friendship with James Gerard, our esteemed ambassador to Germany, is well known."

"Yes, but Gerard has resigned and will no doubt retire to that Montana ranch of his. You know he married the daughter of that Marcus Daly fellow. They called Daly the Copper King because of his vast holdings in various mines. No doubt they will benefit greatly from this war."

"I wasn't aware of Mrs. Gerard's background. Even so, it can only help. Gerard is known to be American through and through, and tying him to the West and ranch life will make him seem ever more the faithful citizen living out the dreams of his forefathers. So you see, your close friendship with him will hold you in good stead. They once questioned his loyalty as well and it proved a moot point. No doubt it will be the same if they try to implicate you, and you can always call upon Gerard to speak on your behalf."

"I hope you're right." Weidel looked most uncomfortable. "The fact is, however, our own associates are quite distressed with me. Perhaps they will believe me to have turned coat." He nursed his drink a moment.

"I'm sure our associates are smart enough to realize the game you must play. You have access to men that are critical to our cause—even if those same men fail to realize how they are helping us. It isn't easy to have a foot in both worlds, but we definitely need for you to continue doing so."

⁂

"So will you teach me how to dig up sapphires?" Hunter asked Curtis over a game of checkers.

"I don't know if I'll ever be returning to the mine." Curtis moved his piece, then straightened. "In fact, I'm thinking I'll probably give it up altogether."

Hunter frowned. "Why?"

Curtis leaned back against the chair. "I don't know if I'll ever be up to such work. The doctor told me it will be a long while before we'll know for sure if I'll be able to walk properly. It may also be a long time before my back stops hurting me."

"I heard you tell Mama that you wanted to join the soldiers going to war." Hunter looked at him as if expecting him to deny it.

"I did want to join them. As an American I feel it is our duty to serve our country when called upon. This war is going to require a great many men to fight."

"I don't want you to go. You might get shot like my father."

Curtis had never heard the boy speak of his father before now. He dared the same question he'd posed to Maddy. "Do you miss him?"

Hunter frowned. "Father didn't come play with me, and he was quite cross when we were too noisy. I don't miss him, and now he's never going to come back. I don't want you to go away and never come back."

Maddy's attitude about her father's lack of interest in their lives came to mind. Curtis had thought perhaps this was due to her being a daughter rather than a son. He had figured that perhaps Vesper had at least given something of himself to Hunter, but apparently not.

"I'd like a father like you," Hunter said with a smile. "Even when you're hurt you tell me stories and play games with me. You'd be a good father."

His comments so stunned Curtis that for several seconds he couldn't reply. After all, what could he say to the boy?

Maddy saved him from having to comment as she came bounding into the room. "Mama said to tell you she's bringing you some cookies and milk." She climbed up on Curtis's empty bed and smoothed out her new calico skirt. "Auntie Madeline made this for me. Do you like it?"

Curtis smiled. "I like it very much, Miss Maddy. The blue matches your eyes."

She nodded. "I like it too. It feels better than my other dresses. Auntie Madeline and Mama are making me some more dresses like this so I won't tear my city clothes."

Hunter, not to be outdone, chimed in. "They made me these pants that go all the way down to my shoes just like a grown-up man."

"Ranch clothes are pretty different from city clothes." Curtis could tell that the children were more comfortable in their new clothes than they had been in their finery.

"Mama said that's 'cause you have to work in them," Hunter replied. "They gotta be strong and bend every which-a-way."

"Auntie Madeline made me two aprons," Maddy interjected. "That way I won't get stuff on my dress."

"Well, it sounds to me like you two plan on sticking around." Curtis hoped that was true. He had come to accept the truth of how much he wanted to play a part in this family.

Maddy jumped off the bed when her mother appeared with a tray of milk and cookies. Clara smiled at her children and placed the tray at the foot of the bed. "I'm sure you boys could use some refreshment."

Curtis chuckled. "Yes, we worked up quite an appetite playing checkers." He leaned forward and made a final move with the checkers. "Crown me. And I just won the game."

Hunter looked at the board and frowned. "One of these days I'm going to win."

"You're getting better all the time," Curtis assured. "Why don't we clear the game away and we can have our milk and cookies here."

Hunter did his best, and with Curtis's help, they made quick work out of it. Clara stood watching them, her expression tender. Curtis thought she was more beautiful than ever, and his desire to be with her had taken over his concerns about his physical problems. Even the past no longer seemed like an insurmountable obstacle. There was something about her that gave him hope. The only thing that really worried him was Clara herself. She'd stopped saying anything about her love for him.

With the table cleared, Clara brought the tray over and placed it between her son and Curtis. "We just made these cookies this morning, didn't we, Maddy?"

The girl nodded. "It wasn't hard at all, but I couldn't take the pans out of the oven. Mama was afraid I'd get burned."

Curtis picked up a cookie and held it up as if inspecting it. "You'll be old enough to do that before you know it. Say, I believe these are some of the finest cookies I've ever had. This one is perfectly round." He bit into it and savored the flavor.

Maddy continued to watch him as if trying to gauge his pleasure or displeasure. Curtis swallowed and nodded. "This is the best cookie I've ever eaten."

Maddy smiled and looked up at her mother. "Can we go make some more?"

Clara shook her head. "No. Remember I told you we're going to help Aunt Madeline in the garden. In fact, we'd best get out there or she'll have done all the work." She moved to the door and smiled at her son. "Hunter, when you finish you need to lie down and rest."

"Does Curtis have to take a nap too?"

Curtis lifted a brow and gave her a questioning smile. She shrugged, the smile leaving her face. "I wouldn't be surprised if he wasn't tired, but it's not my job to tell him what he's feeling. He has to figure that out for himself."

Curtis was taken aback at her tone. What had changed her mood? One minute everything had been light and friendly, and the next she looked . . . well . . . she looked sad.

After she'd gone, Curtis continued to try to figure out what was wrong. He finished his cookie and chased it down with some milk. Was she worried about him getting enough rest or concerned that he was in pain? He sighed and drew the glass to his lips as Hunter sighed too. Curtis glanced over to find Hunter was doing his best to mimic his actions. It made Curtis only too aware that children were easily influenced.

"I'm sure glad they thought to bring us cookies and milk." Curtis picked up another cookie. "Your mama is a good woman."

Hunter nodded and picked up a second cookie as well. "She smells good too."

Curtis laughed. "Is that what you like best about her?"

"No. I like it when she plays with me or reads me a book.

She does different voices sometimes." He giggled. "She read us *The Wonderful Wizard of Oz*. That was my favorite, and she made all sorts of voices for the people. Have you read it?"

Curtis shook his head. "I haven't. Maybe we could talk your mama into reading it to us while we're getting well."

"I'll ask her, but I don't think she brought the book." Hunter didn't wait for Curtis to start eating his second cookie. With his mouth full, he added, "Mama doesn't make me eat liver. I don't like liver." The boy's face was scrunched up at the very thought.

"I don't like it either," Curtis replied.

Hunter smiled and nodded. "Then we're just alike."

18

The day of the twins' birthday arrived and the atmosphere at the ranch was one of celebration. Throughout the day the adults bestowed little birthday surprises, much to Hunter and Maddy's delight.

Clara had surprised them first thing with the announcement that they wouldn't be required to do chores that day. Hunter asked if this extended to not having to wash up as well, but that idea was rejected. Next Clara served them a breakfast of their favorites. Pancakes rolled up with sugared berries and topped with whipped cream.

After breakfast they begged to go to the barn to feed their lambs, declaring that it wasn't work—it was fun. So Paul took them out and helped with that bit of fun. When that was completed, Paul and Madeline took them fishing, something Maddy wasn't at all sure she wanted to do until Madeline told her that inevitably they would end up in the water themselves and Uncle Paul would teach them how to swim. This intrigued her enough to go along quite willingly.

With all of them gone, Clara set up an outdoor picnic for

their lunch. Madeline had made them a large chocolate cake, and together with Clara's help they had created a meal of the children's favorites. Corn on the cob, fresh tomatoes, fried chicken, and sweet pickles were to accompany the birthday cake, and Clara knew it would more than meet with Maddy and Hunter's approval.

And, of course, there were the gifts. Shortly after their arrival at the ranch, Clara had written to Perkins, requesting that he locate a box of children's books she had purchased prior to Adolph's death. She enclosed cash and asked him to please mail the books as soon as possible, being careful not to allow anyone to know where she had gone. She knew she could trust the man, and only a few days ago the box had arrived, brought from town by the sheriff, who was coming out that way to pay Paul and Madeline a visit.

Perkins had written her an interesting letter, telling her that her mother had taken herself back to her own house a few weeks after Clara's departure. She had ranted and raved at the staff, confident that they knew where Clara and the children had gone. She had even threatened them with losing their positions, but many of them had already accepted jobs elsewhere and weren't concerned. Since then he'd seen nothing of her or Mr. Vesper. Clara knew that could either be good or bad.

Seeing that it was almost time for the children to return, she gathered up the gifts she and her aunt had wrapped and brought them out to the table. After that she asked Phil and Joe to let Curtis know it was time for the party. She had done her best to avoid him ever since the doctor removed his remaining cast. With him back on his feet, even though he had far to go before being fully recovered, Clara felt there was no need for her to spend time with him. In fact, she had come up with the idea that perhaps Curtis again needed to see what it was like to be without her. Absence might make the heart grow fonder. Or maybe it would help him to finally figure out what he wanted where she was concerned.

With this new plan in mind, Clara turned any Curtis-related duties over to her aunt, explaining that it would be better for her to do household and ranching chores. To her surprise, Aunt Madeline had agreed. Her aunt's reaction had also disappointed Clara, although she would have never admitted it. A part of her had almost hoped her aunt would insist Clara continue caring for Curtis. At least that would make it her aunt's command and not Clara's desire. But Madeline had cheerfully taken on the arrangement, and Clara was relegated to housework. She told herself this was how she wanted it. She even advised the children not to visit Curtis as much, as he needed to focus on healing. She didn't tell them that she hoped the separation might also help him realize that he didn't want to spend the rest of his life without them being a part of it.

She had Hunter's bed moved back to his shared room with Maddy once his arm had healed, much to the boy's disappointment. She eased his misery and her own by reading her children bedtime Bible stories. Of course, that did nothing to assuage her loneliness when she was back in her own room.

Clara caught sight of Curtis stepping out onto the porch. Joe was right behind him, offering support if needed. The doctor had given Curtis strict limitations, including the need to use a cane, which Curtis hadn't liked at all. She noticed, however, that he leaned pretty heavily on the cane when stepping on his left leg.

Then without warning he looked up and met her gaze. Clara felt his eyes burn through hers as if searching for something deep within. She braced herself. It wasn't like she hadn't seen him at all during the last week, but seeing him only served to remind her of what she couldn't have. Her longing for what might have been had eaten at her, and the more Curtis recovered, the worse she felt. She was lonely. Lonely in a house of people. Lonely for a man who swore he cared nothing about her.

I was so sure he would change his mind about us.

"Hey there, Curtis. You're getting along pretty good," Phil declared as he brought another chair for the party.

"Doing my best," Curtis said, giving in to allow Joe to help him down the stairs.

Clara tried her best to ignore him. "Phil, just put that chair at the head of the table. We'll let Uncle Paul sit there."

Phil nodded and did as she directed. Clara heard the un-mistakable sound of her children. "They're coming back from fishing," she announced and stepped to the table.

"Mama! Mama!" It was Maddy who came bounding around the house first. Her hair was wet and her clothes damp. "We learned to swim. Unca Paul taught us." She lowered her voice. "We swam in our underclothes."

Hunter soon joined her, carrying a string of fish. There was a look of great pride on his face. "I caught some fish. Look. Auntie Madeline says we can eat them for supper."

"Well, I must say, you two have had a grand birthday." Clara surveyed the fish. "They look delicious."

Hunter wrinkled his nose. "They smell bad, but Auntie says they'll smell mighty good when she's done with them."

Clara laughed as her aunt and uncle joined them. They looked tired but happy, and Clara knew better than to suggest they rest. She pointed to the table. "We're ready for a celebration."

Hunter spied the cake and gifts. "Are those for us? Yippee!" He gave a yell such as Clara had never heard come out of him.

"I'm afraid my children are becoming as wild as this coun-try," Clara mused.

"Nothing wrong with that." She turned abruptly at the sound of Curtis's voice. He stood only inches away and offered her a sheepish smile. "At least it never hurt me any."

"Nor me," Paul declared. "I think a fellow needs to keep a little bit of wild tucked inside himself." He grinned and winked at Madeline. "Never can tell when he might need it."

Madeline laughed and rolled her eyes heavenward. "The good Lord overdosed your uncle when He gave out wild ways. I'm still not sure what He was thinking."

Paul grabbed her up and whirled her in a circle. "He knew I was going to need it to keep up with you."

Joe came forward and took the string of fish from Hunter. "How about I take care of these?"

Hunter nodded with great enthusiasm. "I'm gonna need my hands to open presents."

The adults laughed, but Hunter and his sister were clearly preoccupied with the promise of presents to open. Clara couldn't stand to make them wait any longer. "You may each open one gift now and the rest after lunch and cake."

"Do we get to pick?" Hunter asked.

Paul hugged Madeline close, then let her go. "I'll tell you what. I'll pick out the present, 'cause I know what's in a couple of 'em." He went to the table and took up two of the larger boxes. These hadn't been wrapped, but they held Hunter and Maddy's interest due to their size.

Handing them over to the twins, Paul smiled. "Now, this might seem like a strange present, but I'm thinking that after you see the rest of your gifts, you'll be mighty glad for this one."

Maddy was first to open the top of the box. She grew serious and reached inside to pull out a pair of boots. She looked at Paul and then to her mother.

Clara couldn't help but laugh at the puzzled expression on her daughter's face. It was only a second later that Hunter's expression matched.

"Boots?"

Paul nodded. "Like I said, don't be too disappointed."

The children seemed to take it in stride, but Clara could see they were more than a little curious about their other gifts. She also knew her aunt and uncle's plans and felt confident the children would be delighted with the gift once they were made aware of how it fit into their lives.

Everyone gathered around the table, and Paul blessed the meal and prayed a special birthday blessing on the children. Clara dabbed at the tears in her eyes, hoping that no one saw. They were so blessed to be here, and she never wanted to leave, but staying was growing harder each day. She knew her aunt understood. They'd had plenty of conversations about it. Aunt Madeline encouraged Clara to keep taking her desires back to the Lord, but nothing ever seemed to change. Curtis showed no signs of a change of heart. Oh, he was friendlier and smiled more, but he never offered her anything more. Certainly he gave no indication of love.

The merry little party continued, and after everyone had eaten their fill the twins were finally given the go-ahead to open the rest of their gifts. Again Paul was the one to hand them out.

Hunter was first to get the next present open. This one was even more puzzling than the first. He held up a canteen. "What is it?"

"It's to fill with water for drinking," Aunt Madeline told him.

His face scrunched. "Can't I just use a glass?"

Everyone laughed, except the children. Maddy now had her canteen in hand and was posing the same questioning look her brother had only moments before.

"You won't always have a chance to have a glass with you," Madeline explained.

Before they could ponder it any further, Paul handed them another present. The twins quickly opened this new offering and found knitted caps. A red one for Maddy and a dark green one for Hunter.

"Your auntie made those," Paul declared. "You're soon gonna need them to keep warm."

The twins asked no questions this time and instead simply looked to the remaining presents. Paul obliged them and handed them one more.

"This is the last one from your auntie and me."

The children opened the small package and found two small pairs of leather gloves. They looked up at Paul for explanation.

He laughed. "Seems kind of confusing, but I think you'll be happy when I tell you what you're going to need all of these for."

The children looked at each other, then back to Paul. He completely held their attention. "Your auntie and I are going to take you and your mama camping up in the mountains."

The children's eyes grew wide as saucers. They had heard stories about camping out in the mountains—about wild animals and nights spent under the stars. Both had begged to go. Clara could see the joy in her aunt and uncle's faces when the children leapt up, mindless of dropping the gloves, and went to wrap themselves around the older couple.

"When can we go?" Hunter asked but gave no time for a response. "Can we go today?"

Maddy wasn't to be outdone. "Are we going to ride horses?"

Paul hoisted each of them up. "We are going to ride horses, Miss Maddy, and we are going to head out next week." The children hugged his neck in delight.

"Yippee!" Hunter declared. He looked at his mother. "Did you hear that, Mama?"

"I did," she said. "I've known about it for some time now."

"And you didn't tell us?" Maddy asked in disbelief.

"Well, it would hardly have been a surprise if I had." She smiled. "I'm glad you're excited and happy."

"Can Curtis come too?" Hunter asked innocently.

Clara glanced at Curtis and found him watching her. She quickly looked away and was glad her aunt responded to Hunter's question.

"Curtis can't go along because he's still getting well. He can't ride a horse just yet, and hiking around on the mountain would give his leg a lot of trouble. He'll be able to go someday, but just not this time." Paul and Madeline exchanged a smile.

Hunter let out a laugh as Paul tickled him. "Thank you, Unca Paul. It's the best birthday ever."

"It is," Maddy said, giggling and wiggling like her brother as the tickles came her way.

Paul put the children down and pointed to the table. "I don't know who the rest of those presents are from, but I suspect you ought to get to opening them."

The children made quick work of it, discovering much to their delight that their mother had given them books. They asked in unison if she would read to them.

"I promise to read to you tonight—at bedtime."

"Meanwhile," Phil said, stepping up, "Joe and I have asked your mama if we can give you a birthday present too."

Maddy and Hunter looked at the men in awe. "You got us something?"

Joe laughed and looked at Phil. He nodded and squatted down. "We're going to take you for a horseback ride. Would you like that?"

The twins nodded with only the tiniest glance at their mother. "Can we go on a real long ride?" Hunter asked.

"It'll be long enough," Phil assured. "Since you two aren't used to riding all that much, we don't want to go too long. We'll do a little every day to get you used to riding so you won't get too tired on the ride up the mountain."

Their response again came in unison. "Thank you! Thank you!"

Maddy and Hunter began to dance around in delight. Clara had never seen them so pleased. In New York, living in grand style, their birthdays had consisted of expensive gifts that were seldom played with and a small cake served in the nursery with only Clara and Nanny Mim for company. She had thought prior to Adolph's death that she would throw a large social event for their fifth birthday and invite all of the most important people to attend. She knew it would have pleased Adolph to rub elbows with the wealthy who purchased his . . . her designs. But that kind of party could never have made her children as happy as this simple family affair.

Love . . . the true love of family and friends had transformed her children from sullen and cautious to joyous. They even looked healthier, and it did her heart good, but at the same time she feared what it would do to them if she took them away.

"I got you something too, but you have to share it," Curtis said, hobbling forward. "Actually, I had Paul pick it up for me when he was in town."

"Oh, that's right. I pert near forgot," Paul said. He took off for the barn without another word of explanation. It was only a few seconds, however, when he came back with a bundle of something in his arms.

"What is it?" Maddy asked. She strained on tiptoe to see.

Paul bent low, and as he did, a wet nose poked up through the blanket.

"A puppy!" Hunter shouted and gave a twirl. "A real live puppy. Not just a stuffed one."

Maddy had her arms out to take the black-and-white pup in hand. She hugged him close to her and began to cry. Paul looked startled and glanced at Clara. She had tears of her own and smiled.

"He's our very own," Maddy murmured. The puppy yipped and then wiggled around to lick the tears from Maddy's face. She was so surprised at this that she began to giggle. "Thank you, Curtis. I love you." She beamed him a smile just before burying her face in the pup's furry coat.

Clara stiffened at her daughter's exclamation of love. She couldn't help shooting a look at Curtis. He looked at Maddy with such tenderness—dare she hope—love?

"I want to hold him too," Hunter said, holding his arms out. He looked back at Curtis. "What's his name?"

"That's up to you and Maddy. He's yours now." He seemed to sense Clara was watching him and turned to meet her gaze.

Clara couldn't seem to look away. He had delighted her children. He had befriended them and cared about their needs and desires. He had already been much more of a father to them than Adolph ever had been. He smiled at her as if he knew her thoughts, all while the children danced around with the puppy, calling out possible names. Clara knew she ought to feel joyful, but she didn't. She bit her lip and turned away, blinking back tears.

"Why don't we take him to the barn," Uncle Paul suggested. "I'll show you where his bed is, and you can figure out his name while I show you how to feed and water him."

"Can't he sleep with us in the house?" Maddy asked, looking up with such a hopeful expression that Clara thought her uncle just might agree to it.

"Well, maybe after he learns to do his business outside," her uncle countered, leading them toward the barn.

Madeline laughed when Maddy asked what his business was. "He's got his hands full now," her aunt mused.

"We're gonna go saddle up the horses," Phil told Clara. "Although I'm bettin' it's gonna be hard to get them away from that pup." He and Joe moved off toward the barn.

"I think I'll go rest," Curtis said. For most of the party he'd been quiet, and while the children had opened their gifts, he stood off away from the others. Now he looked almost as if he'd lost his last friend, but for the life of her, Clara couldn't figure out why he should be sad. He had no reason to be sad. Only moments ago he was smiling.

Maybe he feels alone.

If he did, then he deserved it. Maybe if he knew what she was feeling—what he'd forced upon her—he'd realize how foolish he was being.

"I think he's pining," Madeline said in a whisper.

Clara hadn't realized her aunt was still there. "If he is, it's his own fault. He's a fool to sit there and bemoan what might have been when he could still have what he wants."

"Maybe he needs to be told again." Madeline smiled. "He's got a particularly thick head. After all, getting hit with that beam at the mine didn't kill him." She took off after Curtis. "Hold on, I'll help you up the steps."

Clara felt a surge of anger mixed with desire. She wanted nothing more than for Curtis to declare his love. She wanted him to tell her that he wanted . . . needed to spend the rest of his life with her and the children. She wanted him to say a lot of things, and none of them were going to be said if she just stood there.

Picking up a couple of dishes, Clara's irritation grew. She stacked the dirty plates, being none too careful. It wasn't fair that one man's stubborn, nonsensical attitude should ruin the lives of three . . . no . . . four people. She reached for two more plates and accidentally knocked over an empty glass. It startled her and made her slam the dishes down harder than she'd intended.

"You feeling all right, Clara?" Her aunt had returned and eyed her with a curious expression.

She untied her apron. "I'll be back to help you clean up shortly. I need to have words with Mr. Billingham."

"Don't worry with these," her aunt said, chuckling. "I can manage. I only hope you can."

Clara stalked into the house with more determination than she'd ever mustered in her life. She threw her apron aside, not caring where it landed, and marched down the hall to find Curtis.

His door was open, so she didn't bother to knock. "I want to talk to you," she said, coming to stand directly in front of the chair he'd just taken.

"Something wrong?" he asked, his tone guarded.

"Something has been wrong for the past fourteen years. Now you have the chance to put it right, but you're too pigheaded to let go of your worries. So you have a past—who cares? Yes, you were sinful. You sinned and did wrong in the eyes of the Lord and everybody else. But you asked forgiveness and repented. You chose not to do those things anymore. That means you've been redeemed. You're a new creation in Christ."

She bent slightly and shook her finger at his surprised face. "You aren't the only sinner in this house. You aren't the only one who had to seek forgiveness for wrongdoing. We are all sinners. All of us. You didn't corner the market on it, as they would say in New York." She straightened and began to pace.

"I've taken all of this I can bear. I'm so heartbroken and lonely that I decided today I might as well take the children and go. I don't know where exactly, but seeing you day in and day out and knowing you don't love me—it's more than I can bear.

"I was lonely in New York. I was lonely all of my married life, but that was nothing compared to the loneliness I have found here in this house—a place I had hoped would be a refuge." She drew a deep breath and came to a stop just inches from him. "If loneliness could kill a person, and I'm not convinced that it can't—I'd be dead." She was panting and suddenly realized there was nothing more she could say.

Without a word Curtis reached out and took hold of her arm. She wasn't at all sure what he was doing until he had pulled her down to sit on his good leg.

"I *am* pigheaded. And I know exactly how bad it feels to be lonely—to long for something—someone." He reached up to stroke her cheek. "You don't have to be lonely anymore, Clara." He pulled her face to meet his. Their lips had almost touched when Clara stunned him and pulled away.

She put her hand on his chest. "Wait just a minute. I'm not about to kiss a man who doesn't love me. You said you didn't love me anymore." She stared into his eyes, daring him to deny it.

He gave her a sheepish grin and shrugged. "I guess being a liar is just another of those sins I need to repent of." He pulled her close again, cupping her chin with his warm fingers. "I love you, Clara. I've never stopped, and I never will."

Clara eased against him as their lips met in a kiss that seemed to wash away fourteen years of sorrow in a moment's time. She wrapped her arms around his neck, afraid to end the kiss in case it was all just a dream. Nothing would ever come between them again.

"Where in the world is everyone?" A boisterous female voice called from somewhere down the hall. "Clara! Where are you? I demand you come here this moment."

Clara sat up straight, pushing away from Curtis as if she'd been caught redhanded robbing the cookie jar. She felt the blood drain from her face. "It's my mother."

19

*C*lara hurried from Curtis's room, slamming the door behind her. She all but ran down the hall and happened upon her mother just as Harriet had begun to investigate the empty dining room.

"Mother, what in the world are you doing here?" She stopped at the edge of the table.

Harriet Oberlin, dressed in a very dusty green traveling suit, turned and looked at her daughter. "What do you suppose I'm doing here? I've come to retrieve you. How dare you run off and leave me to worry! I cannot tell you how it grieved me to find you gone."

"It was important for me . . . and the children to leave New York." Her mother glared at her, but Clara quietly stood her ground.

"Utter foolishness," Harriet spluttered. "You simply made another of your poor choices, which is exactly why I've come to take you home. If left to your own devices, you would no doubt bring harm to yourself or the children."

"The children and I are doing quite well right here." Clara

put her hands on her hips. "And I have no intention of ever leaving Montana again."

Her mother turned a mottled red. "How dare you speak to me like that! I am your mother."

"Yes, you are." Clara felt emboldened from her previous confrontation with Curtis. "But you are not my keeper."

"I should have hired someone to be," her mother countered. "You have no consideration for others. I have worried myself half sick over you and the children. Poor Otto has been terrified that harm might have befallen you. He's the one who hired someone to find you."

"No doubt you would have done the same had he not." Clara shook her head and drew a deep breath. She was no longer afraid of her mother. "I am sorry for the worry I caused, but not sorry for my actions. This is where I belong. It is where the children belong as well."

"Nonsense. You belong in your beautiful house in New York City. You belong in opulence and luxury. I didn't raise you to be a poor ranch hand. You have a place in society and a name to uphold. Honestly, you live like a pauper here."

"I would soon enough live like a pauper there. None of those so-called friends in society would give me a second thought if they knew my husband had gambled away our home. Otto is the one who holds title to everything I had in New York."

Her mother smiled and nodded. "But that's the good news. Otto still plans to marry you. He told me so and explained how he has loved you from the first moment he saw you. You always complained that I had saddled you in a loveless marriage. Well, now you can have the love you desire. Although in time you are certain to realize that love holds little importance in such things. Marriage is more of a business arrangement."

"Not for me." Clara could see growing frustration in her

mother's expression. "Otto may well love me, but I do not love him, and I will not marry another man whom I do not love. Marriage is not a business arrangement to me. It is a covenant between two people and God. It is a covenant of love."

"Bah! Don't speak to me of God and covenants." Her mother stormed past her into the hall. "Where is your aunt? I'm sure she's filled your head with all this religious nonsense. It's time I give her a piece of my mind for leading you to such ridiculous beliefs."

"My aunt was outside when you arrived. I'm surprised you didn't cross her path coming into the house. However, she has not taught me ridiculous beliefs, Mother," Clara challenged.

Her mother turned and eyed her in stern consternation. "I must say I am shocked beyond my senses. This is so much worse than I had imagined." She took up a fan that hung at her waist and began to fan herself in a most furious manner. "You have lost all of your comportment. Years of work have been undone in a few short weeks. I hate to think of what I'll need to do in order to set things right again."

"You needn't do anything." Clara squared her shoulders. "Why don't you return to New York and explain to Otto that I am quite happily situated here." She walked to the open front door. "I see your transportation and your maid are still awaiting you." The sight of her mother's maid almost made Clara giggle. The poor woman looked positively aghast at her surroundings. "If I'm not mistaken, that looks to be the town liveryman holding the reins to the wagon. I'm certain he will want to get back before darkness sets in, and while our daylight won't be gone for some time, it would be best for you to go now."

"I'm not going anywhere. My maid and I will take up residence here, and when I leave, you will be at my side. And until you come to your senses, I will stay right here and dog your every step. I will not leave you to be further influenced by these people."

She moved past Clara, muttering something more, but the words were inaudible. It took a moment before Clara realized what her mother was doing as she opened each and every door to the various rooms. She was headed down the hall toward Curtis's room before Clara could even think of what might happen when her mother discovered him here in the house.

"Mother, you have no right to do this. This is Madeline and Paul's home. You can't just go about sticking your nose into their business."

Her mother whirled around and pointed her now closed fan at Clara. "*You* are my business, and they have usurped my authority in taking you in and turning your thoughts against me."

"My aunt and uncle have never spoken ill of you even once. In fact, all those years you sent me to spend my summers here, they never spoke out against you."

"Hah! I don't believe you. Your father's sister never had any use for me. She hates me and the feeling is mutual."

Her words stunned Clara. "Mother, that is entirely uncalled for. Aunt Madeline doesn't hate you at all."

Her mother continued down the hall until she came to Curtis's room. Clara knew she couldn't prevent her mother from opening the door and drawing him into their argument, so she pushed past her mother and opened the door for her.

Curtis still sat in the same chair Clara had left him in. He wore a frown—almost a scowl at the sight of Clara's mother.

"Mrs. Oberlin," he said, nodding. "You needn't have come all this way. I assure you I could hear you just fine from the front room."

Her mother pulled up short and stared at the man in surprise. "Who are you?"

226

"This is Curtis Billingham, Mother." Clara went to stand beside him. "The man I intend to marry. The man I should have married years ago."

Her mother's eyes widened and her face began to change colors. Clara wasn't at all sure the woman was even breathing anymore until a roar came from her mother's throat.

"You are quite mad." She pointed her finger at Curtis. "This is your doing. You have corrupted my daughter's mind. Hopefully, that's all you have dallied with."

"Mother!" Clara couldn't believe her mother's crass remark.

Curtis got to his feet without the aid of his cane. "Madam, I believe you should stop now before I decide to stop you myself."

"This is outrageous." She pointed again at Curtis. "I will not be spoken to in such a manner. Not even by some worthless Montana cowboy. I know all about you and how you tried to convince my daughter to give up a good life in New York to stay here with you."

"Mother, please stop."

The woman turned on Clara. "And you, you are the worst of hussies to come out here with your husband barely in the ground and take up again with this . . . this . . . reprobate."

"What in the world is all this yelling about?" Madeline asked, coming into the room. She looked at Harriet and nodded. "I might have known."

Clara watched her mother whirl on her heel.

"If I am yelling, it is because I am beyond enraged. What kind of place is this that a single man and widowed woman would live under one roof? It is a corruption of the flesh." She shook her finger at Madeline. "You who always spout Bible verses and talk about spiritual matters as if it came from God's mouth to your ear." She gave a harsh laugh. "I should have known it was all a façade to mask the wickedness that went on."

227

Madeline's eyes narrowed. "Harriet, I'm going to forget you said that. As a Christian woman I am called upon to forgive you . . . and I will . . . perhaps later . . . after prayer."

Clara might have smiled had the situation not been so grave. She could sense that Curtis was about to do something and put her hand on his arm. They exchanged a glance, and Clara shook her head, hoping it would dissuade him from making matters worse.

"I care not one whit about your forgiveness," Clara's mother countered. "I came to take my daughter home, but she is already heavily influenced by your . . . your . . ." She threw her hand up and pushed past Madeline. "I intend to share my daughter's room in order to keep her from further misconduct. Be so good as to have the driver deliver my bags accordingly and find my maid a room. I'm not leaving here without my daughter . . . and grandchildren."

Madeline followed Clara's mother out of the room. It was clear from their voices that they were headed for the front of the house, and Clara hurried after them. She had no intention of following them, however. She hurried into her bedroom and dropped to the floor. Reaching under the bed she pulled out a small valise. This is where she kept the money and diaries she'd taken from the bank box. If the case were to remain here, she was certain her mother would find it and confiscate the contents.

She hurried back to Curtis's room and found him at the door. He was clearly about to come in search of her or the others.

"Wait, Curtis. I need for you to keep this for me." Clara came into the room and glanced over her shoulder to make certain she wouldn't be overheard. "It's important my mother not find this. It has money that Adolph left in the bank along with his diaries. Mother won't care at all about the books, but she will demand the money if she knows it exists."

She looked around the room, then went to the far side of the bed. "May I hide it here . . . under the bed?"

Curtis nodded and very slowly walked back to his chair. Clara gave him a weak smile and nod before dropping to her knees with the valise. She tucked it under the bed, then sighed.

"Thank you." She rose and let go another sigh. "I'm so glad Joe and Phil took the children riding. I would have hated for them to witness my mother's behavior."

Reaching out, Curtis took hold of Clara's arm. She found him smiling at her. "What do you find amusing about this?" she asked.

He shook his head. "I'm not amused. I'm curious."

She hadn't expected that declaration. "What in the world are you curious about?"

"What you said."

Shaking her head, Clara tried to recall what she might have said that had him so interested. "I don't understand. What did I say?"

"You told your mother I was the man you intended to marry." His grin broadened. "I just wondered why you said that."

Clara felt rather sheepish. She hadn't meant to make such a declaration and presume upon Curtis's earlier kiss, but now that it had been said, it was too late to take it back. So instead she shrugged a little. "It sounded like a good idea at the time."

Curtis threw back his head and laughed, causing Clara to put her hand over his mouth. "Curtis . . . stop laughing. My mother will hear you."

He pulled her hand away from his face and held it close to his heart. His expression grew quite serious as he gazed into her eyes. "I don't much care what your mother hears or doesn't hear. I don't care what she says or does, so long as it doesn't hurt or involve you. I love you, and I'm going to do what I should have done fourteen years ago."

"What's that?"

He gave her a lazy grin. "I'm going to marry you, of course."

❧

Paul came into the house through the back door. He could hear the shrill voice of a woman who was quite distressed. He hurried through the house to find the source and was completely surprised to find Harriet Oberlin shaking her finger only inches from his wife's face.

"You are to blame for all this talk of love. It's all a part of that ridiculous religious nonsense."

"It isn't nonsense, Harriet. It's the very heart of who we are—who God is. Clara is happy for the first time in fourteen years, and I won't let you interfere with her or the children."

"Those are my grandchildren!" Harriet caught sight of Paul. "You have subjected innocent children to examples of wanton lust and allowed my daughter to become a harlot."

Smack!

Paul hadn't expected his wife's actions, but when she slapped Harriet Oberlin across the face, he couldn't help but duck his head to hide his grin. He had always known Madeline could be a real ball of fire when the occasion called for it, and God knew she was justified this time around.

Harriet grabbed her cheek, her eyes wide in disbelief. Madeline was now the one who pointed her finger. "Your heart has always been filled with ugly, selfish thoughts. You believe everyone capable of the basest actions, because you practice them yourself. I have always tried to treat you with Christian charity, but, Harriet Oberlin, you have exhausted my supply."

She didn't give the woman a chance to reply. "If you can't keep such evil thoughts to yourself, you won't be welcome in this house. This is a home of decent, Christian folk, and I won't allow for Satan to get a foothold through you."

Paul felt it was time to put in his two cents. "Madeline is right. You have hurt a lot of folks over the years, and that isn't something we take kindly to, especially when it comes to a girl so sweet as our Clara. You can stay with us for a few days, but only if you refrain from speaking ill of our family."

Harriet finally found her voice. "You two have always hated me. You've never understood that I did what was best for Clara. My Clara. She isn't yours. She is my child and I know what's best for her."

"Do you?" Paul asked softly. "Do you really suppose that taking her from a home where people love and admire her and forcing her into a life without love is what's best?"

"Emotions are useless to people. The sooner Clara comes to realize that, the better off she'll be. Her childish infatuation with that cowboy was better ended before she got hurt. Now I find she's back here again, panting at his heel." Harriet shook her head. "I will not allow her to throw her life away, nor that of my grandchildren. Those children deserve to be brought up in proper society, and if need be, I'll take them back to New York without Clara."

Paul narrowed his eyes. He'd had about as much of this woman as he could stomach. "I think it might be better after all if you were to take a room in town."

Harriet opened her mouth to counter and then appeared to think better of it. She turned and stormed out of the house and down the porch steps, muttering all the way. Paul put his arm around his wife and pulled her close.

"You don't think she'd really try to take the children from Clara, do you?" Madeline asked, looking at Paul. There was real worry in her expression.

"She better hadn't try."

20

he next afternoon Clara sat at the kitchen table sketching out the details of several pieces of jewelry while Madeline rolled out dough for pies. Clara found that her creativity had returned now that Curtis once again loved her.

"I can't believe how many of those designs you've turned out," Madeline said, smiling.

"I had all sorts of ideas, but no heart for it." Clara carefully added the position and type of stones that were to be used on this latest creation. The image of an iris was to be a brooch, and Clara wanted the details to be exact. They were to use Yogo sapphires not only in the cornflower blue but also ones of a deep violet hue. The latter were rarer, quite beautiful, and perfect for this design.

"I don't know how you come up with your ideas." Her aunt glanced over her shoulder. "Nor do I understand how you decide the placement of the stones and which stone to use."

"That's a little trickier," Clara admitted. "The light is critical. If the gem isn't set in such a way to take in the light properly, then the stone will look dull. Adolph taught me a great deal when it came to stone placement."

"But to see it in your head and then put it down on paper and then make it into jewelry . . . well, it amazes me."

"Another aspect is that most of the Yogos aren't that big. So I have to create designs that will show them off to their best advantage, even when they are small."

"I suppose you know that they won't be mining sapphires now that we're at war," her aunt said, turning back to the dough.

"I had seen that in the local paper. I know, however, that Otto has a great many stones on hand. He and Adolph were quite insistent that they procure as many stones as possible. Since Yogo Gulch is the only place in the world where these stones can be found, they always feared their supply would eventually play out. I'm sure Otto will be able to make a great many pieces of jewelry before the war is over."

The sound of someone knocking at the door caused both women to abandon their duties and go in search of the source. Clara peered out the window to find her mother pacing back and forth on the porch as if she were searching for something.

"Oh no. It's Mother." Clara shook her head. "I had hoped she'd forget all this nonsense."

"I'll ask her to leave if you like."

"No. If I don't see her, she'll just keep coming back to hound us." Clara untied her apron and turned to face her aunt Madeline. "I know you're busy with the pies, but would you do me a favor and take the children elsewhere? I don't want them to witness my mother's tirades, and I have no reason to believe she'll behave herself. Maybe Joe and Phil could take them riding again. I know they're very disappointed that my mother's appearance might keep us from going camping. If the boys could take them for a ride, then you wouldn't have to leave the pies."

"The pies will wait." Madeline wiped her hands on a dish towel. "But it'll be hard to tear them away from that puppy. I know they're still trying to figure out a name."

An anxious sense of dread settled on the room. "Please pray for me."

Madeline came to Clara and took hold of her shoulders. "Are you sure you'll be all right without me?"

Clara nodded with a smile that she didn't really feel. "Curtis is here. I'm sure if Mother gets too outrageous in her comments or tone, he'll come to my defense." She wasn't entirely sure Curtis could manage to do much, but it comforted her just to know he was there.

Madeline looked hesitant but nodded. "All right. I'll see to the children, and then I'll return to make sure you have someone at your side in case Harriet decides to push you around."

Another knock sounded and Clara stiffened. "I'd better answer it."

Madeline hugged her close. "Don't worry. I'll keep the children out of sight, and I'll be praying the whole time."

Clara squared her shoulders. She had to be strong. Her mother only respected strength, and when a person showed weakness, Harriet Oberlin would run right over them. "Thank you for protecting them."

She waited until Madeline was headed back to the kitchen before opening the door. On the opposite side of the screen door Clara saw her mother.

"Good afternoon, Mother."

Harriet jerked her head back to meet her daughter's gaze. "I was beginning to think everyone had gone off with the sheep. I want to speak with you, Clara. Alone."

Clara nodded and opened the screen door. But instead of ushering her mother into the house, she pointed to the chairs on the front porch. "Have a seat."

"Why can't we speak inside?"

"You said you wanted to be alone. This is as private as I can make it. Remember, this house has several other people living within." Clara went to take her seat in a large wooden rocker that she had come to love.

Her mother remained standing for a moment as if uncertain that the porch would be acceptable to her needs. Finally, she took a seat in a straight-backed chair. She folded her gloved hands on her lap and raised her face to eye Clara in a most serious manner.

"I have come to try to reason with you, Clara. I realize I was quite angry yesterday."

"Yes, you were." Clara knew her mother was doing all within her power to remain calm. It wasn't like Harriet Oberlin to yield to anyone—especially her daughter. That could only mean she wanted Clara's cooperation enough to humble herself to get it . . . which would only make her all the more dangerous.

"I suppose it was because I felt you were being led astray. You are only a few months a widow, and that doesn't allow for sensible decisions. I know, because I have buried two husbands. It's a time of great turmoil, and decisions are often complicated by grief."

Clara held up her hand. "Mother, before you continue, I want you to understand something. While I did not wish death upon Adolph, neither did I love him. I never came to care about him in the fashion you told me would happen. Not even after twelve years of marriage and the birth of our children. Adolph knew this and understood. I never played him false. The fact is also that he didn't love me. We held nothing in common but the children, and even there, Adolph wasn't inclined to become involved." She drew a deep breath, surprised that her mother had allowed her to state her mind uninterrupted. Clara took the opportunity to continue.

"I am sorry that Adolph had to die in such a violent manner. He didn't deserve that—no one does. However, when I buried him I felt only relief. Relief that I would no longer have to live a lie. Relief that I could now live my life the way I wanted to, rather than the way others wanted me to. I don't intend to give up that freedom now."

Her mother leaned forward as if she might get up, then settled back once again. It was clear she was fighting her nature to control the situation. "That's well enough for you, but have you considered the children? They deserve better than this." She waved her gloved hand at the landscape before them.

Clara smiled. "The only place better than this will be heaven itself. My children are laughing and happy for the first time in their young lives. They've begged me to never leave this place. That hardly sounds like deprived children."

"But children never know what is good for them. That's why I insist you reconsider. You are acting out of the shock that came in losing your husband. Whether you loved him or not, he was your companion for over twelve years."

It was obvious her mother wasn't going to let go of her belief that Clara's emotions were making her decisions. Perhaps they were—emotions of comfort and peace of heart might very well be guiding her choices, but her mother would never understand that. There had to be a way to convince her otherwise, but even as that thought came to mind, Clara shook her head. Her mother wasn't here to be convinced. She was here to wear down Clara's resolve.

"Mother, I am going to share something with you and then

we will put this matter behind us. Adolph and I were very rarely together. We appeared in public together, which you know was only on rare occasions, with exception to Sunday church services. We only entertained occasionally, usually when a new collection of jewelry was available. And while I don't wish to give you ammunition to further suggest Aunt Madeline has influenced me to be crude and vulgar, Adolph and I only shared a marriage bed perhaps twice a year." Her mother's mouth dropped open.

Clara had never actually seen her mother at a complete loss for words, so she pressed on, hoping to be allowed to speak her mind in full. "Furthermore, the children didn't even know Adolph. They, of course, knew he was their father, but they had no relationship with him. Adolph was from that old school of thought, like you. He believed children were to be kept silent and in the nursery. They were proof of manhood and the promise of one's name being carried on into the future. Adolph didn't love his children. He loved his business. He knew more about the cut of a stone or the setting of a piece of jewelry than he did his children."

"But that's to be expected," her mother protested. "It is necessary for a man to be committed to his business."

"Be that as it may, Mother, I am not in mourning or shock or any other debilitating condition. Neither are the children. For the first time in their lives, they know what it is to be loved and valued. They have the love of an aunt and uncle and . . ." She hesitated to include Curtis.

"That man? That ruffian you propose to marry?"

Clara nodded. "Yes, Curtis loves them. He will be a father to them in every way that Adolph wasn't."

"And what will you do to provide for them? How will your Curtis make his living? Working for your aunt and uncle? Tending sheep?"

"Sheep ranching is an honorable and much-needed profession. And we may or may not remain here. Curtis has some land of his own, and I know Uncle Paul has offered to stake him with a herd. And I have the money Adolph left me, and I could arrange to have a house built."

Too late the words were out of her mouth. There was no taking them back, and given her mother's widened eyes and expression of interest, Clara prepared herself for her questions.

"What money? I thought Otto said he left you penniless."

"I had very little knowledge of Adolph's business or personal affairs. I assumed the house was his, as well as the furnishings. That, however, is apparently not the case. The money I have was a small amount he left me in our bank. I assure you it isn't enough for you to get excited about."

"Still, it is enough to build a house," her mother countered. "That's no small amount. I think you're lying to me."

Clara let go a heavy sigh. "Mother, I have lied to you on many occasions in my life. Usually in order to keep the peace. I repent of that here and now and hope you will forgive me. However, my affairs are no longer your concern."

"Of course they are." The older woman got to her feet. "You need someone wiser than yourself to make important decisions. That is why I am here. You have obviously given little thought to the children and their comfort, their schooling, or their social standing. A ranch may well be entertaining, but it is hardly a place that offers them safety. Danger lurks all around." She glanced over her shoulder as if expecting to see just such a threat approaching.

Clara looked in the same general direction and found only the bored-looking livery driver, who waited patiently in the rented wagon.

"Where are my grandchildren?" her mother questioned. "I demand to see them."

"I'm sorry, they aren't available to visit at this time. They have gone off with Aunt Madeline." Clara smiled. "She is very good with children and loves to show them new things."

"She's a menace. She corrupted you and now she'll do the same with them—if I let her."

"If you let her? Honestly, Mother, the choice is not yours to make."

Harriet leaned closer and shook her finger as she had often done throughout Clara's life. "The choice will be mine if I arrange for a court to say as much."

It was Clara's turn to look surprised. She knew from the way she'd gasped and started at her mother's comment that she couldn't very well deny the effect. Perhaps it was better to play on the words rather than avoid them.

"You would do such an underhanded thing? You would spend money to steal children from the bosom of their mother? What kind of monster are you?"

Harriet straightened and narrowed her eyes. "You are talking quite out of your head. A good judge would see you as unfit—a mentally unstable woman to be put away in an asylum so that she couldn't harm herself or anyone else."

Clara rose. She didn't want to stoop to her mother's level of ugly threats, but she felt she had no choice. She leaned in until their faces were only inches apart. "If you ever try to do such an indecent thing to my family, I will make certain it will be the last you ever see of any of us. Do you understand?"

Her mother seemed momentarily taken aback. She held Clara's gaze for a moment, then lifted her chin in defiance of her daughter's comment. "That is just one more piece of evidence I can use against you."

"You need to leave now, Mother. And I would suggest you go back to New York, because if you come here again, I will let Uncle Paul deal with you. I won't speak to you again on this matter . . . or any other." Clara turned to go, but her mother grabbed hold of her arm and forced her to take a step back.

"I will see this matter through. If I have to enlist the help of others, I will do so. Mark my words, Clara, you haven't seen the last of me." She dropped her hold and stalked off down the porch steps. The driver jumped from the seat at her approach and helped her into the wagon.

All the while Clara could only stare after her mother's retreating form. The threat was very real, and Clara knew her mother would find a way to hurt her. Harriet Oberlin had never brooked defiance. She would make Clara pay—of that Clara was certain.

❦

It was the sixth of August when Otto received a letter from Harriet Oberlin. He found the letter waiting on a silver tray in the foyer of his home when he returned from work that evening. With great trepidation he opened it in the privacy of his sitting room and read the words he had feared to find. Clara had refused to return to New York. He read on.

Furthermore she has made clear her intentions to marry a worthless ranch hand employed by her aunt and uncle. It's appalling to see the conditions in which they live and the obvious threat to the welfare of my grandchildren. I have threatened to have Clara declared unfit and mentally unstable in order to take charge of my grandchildren. This, of course, did not bode well with her, and she has become quite defiant in her behavior—a sure sign of insanity.

*You will also find it of interest to know that Clara stated
she has money. She said this money was left in their bank
account by Adolph. She wouldn't reveal the amount, but
at one point declared it enough to build a house. I thought
perhaps you knew nothing of this.*

Money enough to build a house. It had to be the missing
money he'd been searching for since the death of his brother.
Otto read on.

*I feel you should come at once to protect your inter-
ests. Given that your brother's money was truly owed to
you, the money Clara has is no doubt yours as well. I feel
certain that if you come and join with me in the threat
to remove her children, Clara will yield and return home
to marry you.*

He wasn't at all sure what he was to do. Badeau and his men
had made it impossible for him to leave town with Harriet. He
had all but purchased his train ticket when Badeau arrived and
served him with orders to give a deposition regarding what he
knew of his brother's traitorous affairs. Now, however, the one
who would surely protest his exit would be Charles Weidel.
Weidel was feeling the noose tighten around his neck as one
confederate after another had been caught and killed. Only a
couple of men had been taken alive, and they were only too
happy to share what they knew, which thankfully wasn't much.
The road, however, was very quickly leading to Weidel, and
he had vowed he would not be taken. He had a strong phobia
about being locked in a cell, and Otto had the distinct impres-
sion the man might very well take his own life before he'd let
the police incarcerate him.

"That could very well take care of my problems at this end," Otto mused aloud.

But how was he going to handle the situation with Clara? He needed her. He needed her to continue creating the jewelry designs, something she was not likely to do for long if she stayed in Montana, even if he offered to pay her handsomely. No, she'd obtain the trust and have no need to make money. And even if she wanted to continue designing, she'd expect control, which would mean Otto would have none. She would control everything, and he'd have to answer to her or make his own designs. Otto shook his head. He couldn't go back to only creating standard pieces. They brought a profit, of course, but they weren't going to bring in anywhere near the amount of money the Vesper Yogo collection had. Not only that, but now that he knew about the trust fund his brother had left to the children, he wanted that as well. That money would assure him an easy life, but he had no chance of getting his hands on it if Clara married this cowboy.

He crumpled the letter and threw it into the fireplace. He really had no choice. He had to go to Montana and help Harriet. He had to force Clara to marry him, and as Harriet had already figured out, the key to her cooperation would be the children.

"Sir, would you like your dinner to be served here in the sitting room or in the dining room?" the butler asked from the doorway.

Otto headed toward the man. "Neither. Bring it to my office. I have some letters to write."

Otto didn't wait for the man's response but passed by him and headed down the hall. Without giving it a second thought, Otto pulled out some stationery. He would write an anonymous but full account of all that he knew Weidel to be involved with. He would detail all of the planned attacks of the past. He would write in the names of all the confederates who had already been captured, as well as others, while carefully omitting his own. Weidel had been quite careful about not letting one man know about another. It was, as he said, safer for no one to know what anyone else was doing. That way, if caught, they couldn't identify any of their confederates, nor attest to their plans. Of course, Otto had made it his business to know who else was involved and what they were doing. He and Adolph had devised a plan to learn as much information as possible and keep an accurate record, just in case they needed the information to protect themselves. The only problem was, Otto had no idea of where those accounts had been hidden. If only he had his brother's journals, he could copy off the information to exclude his own participation, then take it to Badeau as a way of showing his own innocence. He could simply explain that he had been driven to investigate the matter himself and had found his brother's diaries.

"Of course someone is bound to accuse me." Otto rubbed his mustache and smiled as an idea came to mind. "They could accuse me, but I could just plead innocent and tell the authorities that my brother had posed as me." There were definite benefits to being an identical twin.

Otto smiled to himself. It was the perfect solution. He and Adolph were often mistaken for each other. It would work. It had to. He refocused on the paper and picked up his pen. He would seek Badeau's help. He wouldn't write an anonymous letter at all. He would tell the man all that he could and explain that once Badeau had accused him, Otto had made it his job to learn the truth. He would say that his knowledge had come from the journals and that Weidel was threatening his very life if he didn't join them in their efforts. He would plead with Badeau to protect him and in turn offer his services in any way possible to rid the city of traitors. Surely that would be enough. With his full cooperation and willingness to give up information and people, Badeau would have to believe Otto innocent of taking any part in the espionage.

Otto frowned, knowing there was still one small problem. The journals. He most desperately needed to keep the originals out of the hands of the authorities or else he would be condemned along with the others.

21

I wonder if you would mind my taking a look at your husband's diaries?" Curtis asked as he and Clara finished their lunch. He had thought about the books ever since Clara had hidden them and the money in his room.

Clara shook her head. "Not at all. But I am curious as to why you would want to."

He smiled. "It may sound a little crazy, but I'd like to see you through his eyes. I'd like to know his mind. I mean, how could a man be married to you and not cherish you completely?"

Her face flushed red and she looked at the table. Curtis smiled at her embarrassment. "If I've overstepped proper bounds, then I apologize."

"No, it's not that at all." She looked up and met his gaze. "Read them if you like. I have no issue with it. I only kept and brought them because I thought maybe one day the children would want to know about their father."

He nodded, knowing her heart. "Thank you. I appreciate the trust you've put in me."

Clara got to her feet, laughing. "I've always put my trust in you. It's easy to trust someone when you love them."

She reached for a plate, but Curtis gently took her wrist and pulled her close. "I'm so sorry for ever doubting that love."

"You should be." She still smiled, but there was a hint of reproof in her tone. "It better never happen again."

He shook his head. "It won't. I promise." He drew her hand to his lips and kissed each of her fingers. "You know we haven't talked about when we should marry."

"No, we haven't. I suppose I've been so upset by Mother's threats and this strange lull of silence from her that I've not given it much thought."

He could hear the fear in her voice. "You know you don't have to worry about her. I won't let anything happen to the children, and I know Madeline and Paul won't either."

"They've been so good to keep the children busy. I haven't been myself, and I know they sense my uneasiness."

"I hope you don't mind, but I'd like to talk to the children about us getting married." Curtis had given this a great deal of thought. "I want to make certain it's all right with them."

"I'm sure it will be. They already adore you." She sighed. "Just as I do. But feel free to talk to them as you wish. I want there to be no secrets about this."

"Neither do I. In fact, I want to make everything so clear and unhidden that none of the area gossips will have any ground to accuse us of acting inappropriately."

"There's nothing inappropriate about this," Clara countered, but a hint of worry edged her voice. "Still, perhaps we should marry right away. Today even. I don't want anyone to think badly of Madeline and Paul."

"Anyone who knows them or you will know nothing inappropriate has happened, nor will it. I value you too much to dishonor you, despite what people think of me and my past."

She put her hand to his cheek. "I know you are completely honorable. And those people who think badly of you and refuse to forgive or forget your past are of no concern to me."

"They will be if your mother starts asking about me around town. There are plenty of gossips, as you well know, who will be only too happy to tell her every ugly detail of my life."

Clara sighed and retook her seat. "And that will give her all the more ammunition to take the children from me." Her expression grew worried. "I can't just keep running away from her, but I don't know what to do. She has money and powerful friends. She's always gotten what she wanted and usually at great cost to others."

"Well, she won't get the children. Nor is she going to take you away. I won't let it happen, Clara. You need to just trust me on that. Your uncle has some powerful friends too, but more important, we have the power and defense of the Lord. I can't say that I've always understood His ways. There are so many things that remain a mystery to me, but I do know that He is on the side of right."

Clara wrung her hands together. "This is just so hard. I knew my mother was a determined woman. I knew she could be ruthless and inconsiderate of other people's feelings. I just never expected her to be so cruel as to want to rob me of my children. I never thought she'd threaten such a thing." Tears came to her eyes. "I suppose I was naïve in that and so much more."

"Well, we still don't need to be afraid. God will help us through this matter. We need to trust Him and pray fervently." He smiled. "I've done a lot of praying lately."

Clara wiped her eyes. "I know you're right. Aunt Madeline

said the same thing. I just start thinking about all the harm Mother could do."

"The Bible tells us to take those thoughts to Him. Why don't we do that right now? We haven't prayed together in a long time."

"You're right. The Bible says there is great power in our prayers when we pray with others." Clara bowed her head. "Dear Lord, show us the way to overcome the obstacles others have put in our path. Show Curtis and me when we should marry. Help me to deal effectively with my mother, but not to dishonor her."

She fell silent and Curtis continued. "Lord, we need you now more than ever. You've been so good to bring Clara back to me and to bring me back from the pits of self-pity and sin. You alone hold the answers we need, and we trust you to show us what we need to do in order to keep the children safe. Help us, Lord, to know your will in all of this."

An hour later, Curtis sat in his room reading Second Corinthians chapter ten verse five aloud as a reminder to himself. He hadn't wanted to say anything to Clara, but he wasn't entirely without his own concerns. Her mother was an unrelenting tyrant when it came to ordering people about. She didn't care about feelings or motives; she only cared about herself. However, Curtis realized he'd fallen victim to the very thing he'd warned Clara about and that had sent him to the Bible.

"'Casting down imaginations, and every high thing that exalteth itself against the knowledge of God, and bringing into captivity every thought to the obedience of Christ.'"

He glanced toward the ceiling. "Every thought. That's not gonna be easy, but I definitely see the value in it."

He read the Bible for a few more minutes, then remembered the diaries of Adolph Vesper. How strange for a man like Clara's husband to keep detailed journals. Given his love of business and absence as a husband and father, it seemed unlikely that he would leave a record of his thoughts and feelings.

Curtis opened the small case, catching sight of the banded stacks of paper bills. There was a considerable amount of money. No doubt Clara was right to hide it from her mother. He reached into the case and pulled out the first journal. Taking it back with him to his chair, Curtis settled in to read. His leg ached, so he took a moment to prop it up on the ottoman before he opened the book.

Scanning the first few lines, Curtis quickly realized the contents of this journal dealt with numerous business dealings. At least that's how it appeared at first. The further he read, however, the darker and more sinister the content grew.

Otto has imposed his will upon me once again. There is no refusing him as his threats grow more devious by the day. I find it impossible to leave our associates and their plans of treachery and espionage.

Curtis continued reading as Adolph gave an account of activities that had resulted in destruction of property and loss of life. Many of the pages were simple yet detailed lists of activities that had been performed. To Curtis it was clear these were events that had been planned out by German sympathizers.

This is done in hopes of forcing America's hand to come into the war in support of Germany. Promises have been made by emissaries of the kaiser. They have made it clear that with our support and investment in their cause, we will be richly rewarded when Germany wins the war. I have told Otto the foolishness of this. First of all, as Americans we owe allegiance to our country. Otto believes our allegiance is for sale to the highest bidder.

There were additional dates and events listed for several pages and then another page of scrawled writing that clearly told of Adolph's regret in his participation.

It's just as I told Otto after the sinking of the Lusitania—*the loss of all those precious souls; life must matter for more than this. We have become puppets of a regime that cares nothing about the loss of life. Otto has threatened me once again, and I know he will see his threats through if I do not comply, but I do not see how I can agree to what he is asking—demanding.*

Curtis shook his head, realizing the truth. Adolph and his brother were involved in treason against America. They were operating with others to mastermind the sinking of ships, both civilian cargo and passenger liners as well as military. They had helped to finance and arrange bombings and destruction of property. They had helped subversives to escape local authorities and had given information to others who would take back this new knowledge to their king.

Glancing at the door, Curtis wondered if Clara had any idea of her husband and brother-in-law's guilt. He scanned yet another page of details. This one had a list of supplies and monies that had been donated for the cause. He turned the page and saw several lines of writing.

I told Otto today that I cannot go on participating in this treason and plan to give myself up to the authorities.

I know my life has been forfeited. I will no doubt meet my end very soon. I fear that most likely it will come at the hand of my own brother. He believes me a coward and a disgrace. I told him I would rather be dead than go on as a spy, and he told me that if I held to this decision, he would see to my death personally. I do not fear death. I face it without sorrow for myself, but I fear for Clara and the children. They don't deserve the fate that awaits them as the wife and children of a traitor. Poor Clara. She has suffered her fate in silence all these years. My deepest regret is that I had no love to give her. If I should be killed and anyone lays hold of this journal, I want it known that she had no knowledge of my treachery. She is completely innocent of any wrongdoing.

It was dated April 3, 1917, and was clearly the last entry made by Adolph Vesper, as the rest of the book was blank. Curious, Curtis went to retrieve the other three books. He found that the first of the journals showed dates set in 1915. The first was a notation in January.

I have agreed under some duress to help in aiding Germany in their war efforts. Otto demanded I participate, and after he explained the reasons, I was of a more co-operative nature. Germany has a right to their cause, and as one with ancestors who came from that country and relatives who still live there, I agreed to comply and do what I could to help. My first order of business is to make detailed accounts of all shipping. Others will help with this by bringing me information. The lists will be compiled as far into the future as possible and then turned over to Otto, who will in turn take them to Charles Weidel.

Weidel is a powerful American with deep pockets and ties to the Fatherland.

The journal continued much as the first with a detailed list of donations given by various sympathetic Americans. There was also a list of information that Vesper had compiled on the ships and their dates of sailing. This went on for several pages, intermingled with comments about the results of some of their dealings. It wasn't until Curtis read the entries dated May 10, 1915, however, that he truly understood the impact of this espionage.

My heart is grieved beyond words, and yet I cannot tell a soul of how I feel at the knowledge that information I gave aided in the sinking of the Lusitania. *This ship carried munitions and cargo bound to aid Great Britain in their fight against the kaiser and his allies. It also carried nearly 2,000 souls—most of whom were lost. How can I bear my guilt? I made my feelings known to Otto and he actually laughed. He told me I was foolish to even care, reminding me that the ship was in violation of agreements that passenger liners would not carry troops or munitions. Somehow in his mind the presence of such things makes it acceptable that so many human lives were taken.*

After that declaration, Curtis found newspaper articles folded between the pages. Many were about the *Lusitania*, but after a few pages there were others that told of additional ships being sunk and of plots being uncovered to place Americans in peril.

Curtis glanced through the other journals and found more of the same. The comments given by Adolph betrayed his growing desire to be rid of his responsibilities, as well as the impossibility of leaving because of his brother's demands and threats.

A knock sounded on his bedroom door. Curtis quickly closed the journal, placed all four books back in the case, and set it beside his chair. "Come in."

"Look who's come to check up on you." Clara smiled and stepped aside for Dr. Cosgrove. "I told him you were behaving yourself and following orders, but he wanted to see for himself."

Curtis tried to clear his mind of what he'd just learned and smiled. "Good to see you, Doc."

"I hope you can still say that after I examine that leg." Cosgrove crossed the room and put his medical bag on the quilt-covered bed. "I see you've propped it up. Is it causing you pain?"

"Yes, but nothing I can't manage."

"I'll leave you to examine your patient," Clara announced, exiting the room.

When the door closed behind her, the doctor motioned Curtis to the bed. "I need you to disrobe so that I can examine your back as well as the leg. I want to make certain you are healing and haven't developed any new issues."

Curtis thought the doctor would never conclude with his poking and prodding. At one point he made Curtis walk back and forth across the room. First with the aid of his cane and then without.

"You are obviously in a great deal of pain, and that limp seems even more pronounced. I am still of a mind that we may need to send you to Billings, where a surgeon can rebreak and set the leg properly." He held up his hand, seeming to know Curtis would protest. "We'll give it another month or so and see how it goes. After that, we'll have to make a decision. The last thing you want, however, is to be crippled."

The news wasn't exactly what he'd hoped for, but Curtis held back his complaints. There was no sense in protesting what wasn't yet reality. After the doctor had gone, Curtis dressed and waited for Clara to appear. He knew she'd want to know all the news, but what the doctor had told him paled in comparison to what Curtis had read in her husband's journals. He knew the authorities needed to see these. No doubt Clara's brother-in-law was still quite active in the espionage.

At the sound of Clara's light knock, Curtis bolstered his courage. She deserved to know the truth, but at the same time Curtis longed to protect her.

"Come in."

Clara opened the door with a look of expectation. "So what did the doctor say?"

Curtis hobbled to the chair. "He's still worried the leg hasn't healed properly, but everything else checked out just fine." He sank into the chair. "We'll know for sure in another month or so."

Clara came to stand in front of him. "That is good news. I knew it would be. And I feel certain that in another month, you'll be much better."

"I hope so." Curtis frowned. "Clara, sit down for a minute."

Her expression changed to one of worry. "Is there something you haven't told me? Did the doctor have other concerns?"

"No. It's about your husband's journals."

Clara sat on the edge of the bed and waited for him to continue. Curtis wasn't exactly sure how to break the news to her. For a moment, he struggled to find the right words.

"It would seem that the journals were of a business nature more than a personal one."

"Somehow that doesn't surprise me," Clara replied, looking notably relieved. "He always loved his jewelry making far more than anything or anyone else."

256

"But this isn't about the jewelry, Clara. It's about something far more sinister."

She frowned. "Such as?"

"Treason." Curtis could see the confusion on her face. "Your husband and his brother were spies for Germany. Otto is most likely still working to give information to the enemy."

"I know the entire city was on edge looking for traitors, but I would never have believed Adolph capable of that."

"But it's true, and it's all detailed in those books." He saw the disbelief in her eyes give way to acceptance.

"So what should we do?"

"The authorities need to have the journals. There are dated accounts of information given, as well as lists of people who supported the cause of aiding Germany. Your husband listed donations and the activities of a great many people, and the government will want this information in order to bring those people to task for what they've done. That includes your brother-in-law."

"I can't imagine Otto acting in such a way either. He always seemed so . . . well . . . so patriotic." Clara shook her head. "Are you certain he's involved?"

"Yes. In fact, Adolph spoke of Otto's threats to him. Adolph feared for you and the children and what might happen if the truth were discovered. He even spoke of . . ." For a moment Curtis wrestled with whether or not it would do any good to tell Clara the truth of Adolph's fears.

"Spoke of what?" Clara insisted, as if she could read his mind. She squared her shoulders. "I can handle whatever the truth is."

"He feared he was going to lose his life," Curtis replied. "And he was afraid that Otto would be the one to take it."

22

"We've had a long talk," Clara announced to her aunt and uncle after dinner.

They looked somewhat puzzled, and Curtis thought to add an explanation, but Clara continued. "Curtis and I—we had a long talk. We want to be married right away."

Curtis smiled, knowing Clara had waited until the children had left the room before making the announcement. She hadn't yet spoken to the children about the idea, because Curtis wanted to speak to them first and get their approval.

Paul slapped Curtis on the back. "It's about time you came to your senses and married our Clara."

Curtis smiled and nodded at Madeline. "I suppose even pigheaded folk manage to do the right thing now and again."

"They do if they're smart." Madeline fixed him with a smile. "I couldn't be happier. You two have always belonged to each other."

"I agree," Clara replied.

"Do the children know?" Madeline asked.

Clara shook her head. "No. We wanted to tell you first.

259

Curtis plans to talk to them afterward." She glanced toward the window. "With it raining they'll be glad for the diversion."

"I've never seen anybody enjoy the great outdoors like those two do," Paul said, scratching his chin. "Does a body good to see children healthy and happy."

"Well, they are, thanks to you and Aunt Madeline. They love it here. Oh, and it was so kind of you to set up that table on the porch for them," Clara said. "I know they've enjoyed working on that wooden jigsaw puzzle you brought from town."

"Judge Walker had it from when his children were young."

Clara nodded. "The children have always loved puzzles."

"So when are you going to talk to the children, Curtis?" Madeline asked.

Curtis rubbed his leg. The rain and chill made his leg feel stiff. "I'll go talk to them about all of this in a minute, but first I was wondering something. Do you suppose the preacher would marry us after services this Sunday?"

"That's just a few days from now," Madeline said, looking rather concerned. "It would be hard to make a wedding dress and arrange—"

"We don't want to arrange much of anything," Clara interrupted. "And I don't need a special dress. I've had all of that. My stepfather spent more money on my wedding to Adolph than I care to remember. Curtis and I just want to get married and be done with it. We already feel married in our hearts, so the pomp and circumstance is unnecessary."

Madeline smiled. "Of course. I don't know why I thought you'd want it any other way."

"I have to go into town tomorrow anyway. I could stop and talk to Pastor Cosgrove," Paul offered. "I'm sure Doc has let him know that Curtis is pretty much all healed up, so I know Pastor will be expecting you back in church."

Curtis nodded. "Thank you. That would be very helpful." He looked over at Clara. She had pinned her hair up in waves of curls much as she had for the portrait that hung in the hall. Her happiness in being here—in their love—had taken years of sorrow from her features, and Curtis could almost convince himself that the years had never separated them. Almost.

He still had a great deal of anger toward her mother for the way she'd separated them to begin with, but even more so for the way she continued to try to run her daughter's life.

"So what are your plans after you two get hitched?" Paul asked.

Clara spoke up before Curtis could. "There's something else you need to know before we get to that." She glanced toward the hall and lowered her voice. "There's been a development of something rather distasteful."

Madeline exchanged a look with her husband, then settled back in her chair and gave a nod. "Go on."

"Before I came here I went to the bank where Adolph had set up an account for my personal use. I had hoped there would be enough money for me to buy tickets and bring the children west. What I learned was that there was a bank box with a great deal of money and four books that appeared to be journals. I assumed these to be diaries Adolph had kept, so I brought them along with the money thinking the children might one day want to read them and know more about their father."

"Diaries?" Paul asked. "What kind of man has time to keep diaries?"

"The kind that wants to make a record of his underhanded dealings," Curtis interjected. He looked at Clara and saw her nod of encouragement. "It seems the Vesper brothers were involved in more than the production of jewelry. They were knee-deep in espionage as well."

261

"They were working for the Germans?" Paul asked.

Curtis nodded. "Clara let me read the journals, and that's what I learned. It seems Adolph was less happy with the arrangement than his brother, Otto, but that both had signed on to lend aid to Germany prior to America getting into the war. From what I was able to read, they even played a role in the *Lusitania*'s tragic end."

"Oh my!" Madeline's hand went to her mouth. "All those lost souls."

"Exactly. And from what I gathered that was only the beginning of many other ships being sunk, both civilian and military." Curtis shook his head. "It seemed that the *Lusitania* haunted Adolph. He wanted out, but no one wanted to let him out. He feared for his life . . . even believing that his brother would arrange his death."

"How terrible," Madeline said, looking at Clara. "That must have come as quite a shock. I know you said that Otto had been quite kind to you and the children."

"Yes. He said a great many things that I no longer trust," Clara admitted. "Knowing this, I've written a letter to the lawyer who handled Adolph's private affairs. I hadn't thought to confer with him after Otto told me Adolph was penniless. Now I want to know the truth about Adolph's financial situation and whether he truly had signed everything over to Otto."

"The fact is, now that we know what Otto and Adolph were involved in, and have proof of their activities," Curtis continued, "we need to get that proof into the hands of the authorities."

"What will you do?" Madeline asked. "Surely you don't mean to go back to New York City, do you, Clara?"

"No. I most assuredly do not. Curtis feels that we can talk to the sheriff and get his advice. He can most likely arrange for the journals to get placed in the right hands."

"That makes sense," Paul said, nodding.

Curtis leaned forward. "Maybe when you go in to talk to the pastor, you could also encourage the sheriff to join him in coming to meet with us."

"We'll invite them for supper tomorrow," Madeline declared. "I've never known either man to turn down a good meal."

Paul chuckled. "That's the truth."

"I appreciate all that you're doing for me . . . for us," Clara said, letting go a heavy sigh. "This has really weighed on my heart."

"What about your mother?" Madeline asked with a frown. "Do you think she knows anything about all of this treason business?"

Clara shook her head. "I seriously doubt it. It's never been Mother's style to interest herself in the affairs of government. She's easily bored with anything that doesn't pertain to her social circle. Frankly, I'm amazed she came here herself instead of hiring someone else. She hates Montana."

"Good." Paul stood and stretched. "I'm just as happy for her to go on hating it. Maybe that way she'll leave us be."

"I hope so, Uncle Paul. With all the threats she's made toward me and the children, I would be just as happy to never see her again." Clara lowered her head. "I know that sounds horrible, but I can't help it."

"You aren't the only one who finds her attitude appalling." Madeline reached over and patted Clara's hand. "Now, don't give it a second thought. Besides, she may have already caught the train for home. We might be fussing over nothing."

Paul gave Clara a reassuring smile. "Once you and Curtis are married, she won't have anything to say about it anyway. Now, if you'll excuse me, I need to get back to work. Work doesn't wait even when it's raining."

"Are you sure there isn't something I could do to help?" Curtis asked, wishing he could be of more use than he'd been these past months.

"No. You know the doctor said you needed to take it easy for the next few weeks and see how your leg does. I promised him we'd keep you idle except for having you do those exercises." Paul glanced toward the hall. "Besides, you already have a job to do."

Curtis got to his feet. "Yes. Yes, I do. I'm going to go speak with the children right now. I have a feeling they're going to have all sorts of ideas about our future."

Laughing, Clara rose too. "I'm sure they will. I'll be helping Aunt Madeline with the dishes. Once you finish your talk, would you have them come in? They still need to finish cleaning their rooms and get a bath before bed."

"I'll do that."

Curtis left the ladies and made his way down the hall. He paused for a moment at Clara's portrait. This time, however, the picture made him smile. She had been thinking of him then, even as she did now.

Out on the porch Curtis found Hunter and Maddy quite absorbed in their puzzle. Their puppy slept at Maddy's feet, obviously worn out from play. The rain had stopped, but none of them seemed to notice.

"So how's it going?"

Maddy looked up with a frown. "Unca Paul said it's a picture of two people riding a horse, but so far we can't find the right pieces to make horses or people." The puppy perked up at the sound of her voice.

Curtis squatted down and gave the pup a few strokes. "So did you two settle on a name for this fella?"

"Yup," Hunter said, looking over the table. "We're going to call him Blessing."

"Blessing?" Curtis found the name to be a surprise. The last time he'd heard them bandying names about they were more along the line of Spot, King, and Beau.

"Mama said that he was a blessing, so I told Hunter we should call him that," Maddy said, leaning back. "I think it's a good name."

Curtis chuckled and straightened up. "I do too. But if you don't mind, I'd like to talk to you both about something else. It shouldn't take long, but I'd like you to come and sit with me so we can discuss this matter thoroughly. It's really important."

"Are you going to marry Mama?" Maddy asked, fixing him with an expression that demanded an answer.

Curtis was surprised by her blunt question. "Well, I just might. But it depends on you two."

The children got up and followed Curtis to where they could all sit together on the porch. Blessing looked up, yawned, then lowered his head again. It was obvious that the discussion was of no interest to him.

Hunter was the first to speak. "Why does it depend on us?"

"Because I want to know if it's all right with you that I marry your mother."

"It's all right with me," Hunter replied with a shrug. "So long as we don't have to go back to the city. I don't ever want to leave here."

Maddy nodded. "Can we stay?"

"We would definitely stay in Montana. I don't know if we'd remain here at the ranch. I know Paul and Madeline would probably like that, but we might want to start a ranch of our own."

"Or mine for sapphires," Hunter threw out. "I'd like that."

"Well, we will have to see about that. I've still got a long way to go before the doctor will let me go back to doing any kind of hard work. But we can worry about that later."

"But you will get well, won't you?" Maddy asked.

"Of course I will. But the doctor might have to operate on my leg and put me back in a cast. It wouldn't be for long, though." Curtis could see she was mulling this over, while Hunter already looked bored.

"I have something else to ask you. This is pretty important to me, and I hope it is to you as well." Curtis leaned forward. "I want to know if it's all right for me not just to marry your mother but to be your new father as well."

For a minute neither child spoke. Instead they looked at each other as if communicating mentally. Maddy gave a nod and looked most seriously back at Curtis.

"Can we call you Daddy?"

Curtis grinned. "I'd like that a lot."

She got up off her chair and came to Curtis. She held out her arms to be picked up, so he obliged. Settling her on his good leg, Curtis waited for her to speak. Instead, Hunter was the one to pose his question.

"And will you still play with us, or will you go away like our other father?"

"I will play with you whenever possible. It's my hope that I can teach you how to do a lot of things like hunt and work with your hands. And if we ranch, I'd like to have you help me with the sheep. After all, it's a big job to run a sheep ranch, and if we move to have our own place, I'll need your help."

"I like helping," Hunter declared.

Maddy placed her head against Curtis's chest. "I'm glad you're going to be our daddy, 'cause I like you a whole lot."

Curtis wrapped his arm around her. "And I like you, Miss

Maddy. In fact, I love you. I love you too, Hunter. I think we were always meant to be a family."

Sunday morning was even more chaotic than usual. Pastor Cosgrove had agreed to marry them after the services and to keep it a secret until that time. Clara had spent most of the night tossing and turning, hoping and praying her mother wouldn't cause a scene. Clara had specifically decided against telling her mother about the wedding in hopes that everything would be said and done by the time she found out.

After a hurried breakfast, Clara helped the children into their Sunday clothes. She hadn't seen Curtis or her uncle since the night before. Madeline told her it was to keep with the tradition that the bride and groom shouldn't see each other before the wedding.

"We aren't superstitious," she had said earlier, "but sometimes traditions should be observed."

Clara didn't mind the traditions. In fact, she rather liked them. However, she would have felt more confident had she been able to see and speak with Curtis. He always seemed to know just how to calm her worried mind. Now as she worked out the tangles in Maddy's hair, she could only pray they were making the right decision in their rush to marry.

"Ow, Mama. That's too hard."

Clara looked down to find Maddy rubbing her head. "I'm so sorry. My mind wasn't on my work. I'll be gentler, I promise." She ran the brush through her daughter's long blond hair. "Better?"

Maddy nodded but said nothing more. Clara had just

managed to finish dressing Maddy's hair with a bow when Madeline showed up.

"Do you need any help?"

"No, I think we're doing all right. Is everyone ready to go?" Clara asked. She hurried over to Hunter and gave his hair a quick brushing. "I keep thinking I'm forgetting something."

"Perhaps your shoes?" Madeline asked with a grin.

Clara stopped in her tracks and looked down at her stockinged feet. She nodded. "I suppose that would be sensible." She hurried back to her bedroom to retrieve her shoes.

Madeline ushered the children out to the wagon with Clara bringing up the rear. She tried not to show how nervous she felt. She had wanted to marry Curtis Billingham all of her life, and now that it was about to happen, Clara couldn't help feeling anxious.

"I don't know what I'll do if Mother interferes."

"What was that?" Madeline asked, helping Maddy and Hunter into the back of the wagon.

Clara shook her head. "I'm just worried that Mother will do something to stop us from getting married."

Madeline climbed into the wagon and took up the reins. "She wouldn't dare. Besides, I've never known Harriet to go willingly into a church except for being seen by all the right people. None of whom will be here for your wedding." Madeline threw Clara a smile. "Now, climb up here and let's get going." Once Clara was seated, Madeline snapped the lines and the horses put the wagon in motion.

When they finally arrived at the church, Clara thought she might very well embarrass herself by losing her breakfast. She tried to pray to settle her nerves, but she couldn't shake the feeling that something would once again come between her and Curtis getting married.

"Now stop fretting," Madeline said as they helped the children from the wagon.

Once Hunter's and Maddy's feet hit the ground they were off and running to find Curtis and Uncle Paul. Clara was just as glad to have them go. She didn't want them to see her in such an uneasy state. She drew in several deep breaths, all the while glancing toward the main part of town, where the tiny hotel housed her mother. At least Clara presumed she was still there. It wouldn't be like her mother to give up the fight without at least one final salvo.

With Madeline at her side, Clara walked into the church. She could see their regular pew and almost immediately sensed Curtis's gaze. She looked past a rather burly man to find Curtis was indeed watching for her. She smiled, feeling her nerves settle a bit. He had a way of giving her strength just by being there.

Hunter was already seated beside him, and Clara took her place between her children. Madeline sat on the other side of Maddy, and Paul appeared at her side to take his place. He gave Clara a wink and a smile, making her feel much better. She leaned over to thank him, but just then Judge Walker took to the pulpit and instructed the congregation to open their hymnals.

As they started to sing "Blest Be the Tie That Binds," Clara began to relax. In a very short time she would be married. Her children would finally have a father who loved them. They would be a real family. She couldn't let the threat of her mother's gloom ruin the day she'd waited fourteen years to fulfill.

After another hymn and then Scripture read by Pastor Cosgrove, the congregation took their seats. Curtis reached across Hunter and gave her hand a squeeze. Clara took hold of his hand for a moment and held it tight. She needed to feel his nearness.

Pastor Cosgrove began to speak, but Clara found it impossible to pay attention. Once Curtis pulled his hand away to open his Bible, she found her mind wandering. She thought back to her husband's journals and espionage. The sheriff hadn't been able to meet with them the day before, but he sent word that he'd meet with them soon.

She wondered what would happen when Otto learned the truth. She imagined the police, or perhaps soldiers, showing up to take him from his New York office to jail. He would be outraged, no doubt. The thought that he could have arranged Adolph's death haunted her even more. Was it possible he had done such a horrendous thing to his own twin brother?

The sermon concluded with the congregation rising to sing once again. Mrs. Cosgrove, the pastor's wife, boomed out the notes to "Take the Name of Jesus with You." Clara tried to sing, but the words stuck in her throat. In a few short minutes she would step forward and take her wedding vows.

Dear Lord, don't let me faint.

The final notes faded. Everyone was waiting to be dismissed, but instead Pastor Cosgrove smiled and asked them to retake their seats.

"Today we have a very special service to add on. A wedding."

Excited murmurs passed through the crowd. Clara bit her lip and forced her lungs to keep taking in air. She hadn't been this nervous when she'd married Adolph. Of course, she'd been so consumed with sadness that it overpowered any other emotion.

"I'm happy to announce that I will be joining Curtis Billingham and Clara Vesper in marriage. Clara and Curtis, will you step forward with your witnesses?"

Clara heard a muffled shriek. It had to be her mother. She wanted to turn around and look, but Curtis reached out to take hold of her. She let him pull her to her feet. There was a disruption at the back of the room, leaving Clara more certain than ever that her mother was about to make a scene.

"I demand that this wedding be stopped," her mother declared loudly.

"Madam, might I inquire as to your name?" Pastor Cosgrove asked.

"I am Clara's mother, Harriet Oberlin."

Clara couldn't help but turn to see her mother marching down the aisle. She was clothed in a gray walking suit with a black-and-gray hat perched atop her head. She had all the grace of an approaching tornado, and when she reached Clara, she grabbed hold of her with her gloved hands.

"You will not marry this . . . this . . . man. I won't allow it."

Clara tried to pull away, but her mother held fast and continued, "You can't marry him. I've had it on the best authority that he is a convict and a womanizer."

"Don't hurt my mama," Hunter said as he moved to put himself between the two women. Curtis gently pulled him to his side. Maddy quickly joined them.

"You have raised hoydens who are most disrespectful to their elders. I knew you were unfit to keep them here."

For a moment Clara thought her mother's eyes actually glowed red. She blinked hard to clear her vision and found they had returned to their normal color. Her mind was playing tricks on her. No doubt the result of her anxiety.

Her mother pointed a finger at Madeline and Paul. "You knew this man was no good, yet you allowed him in your home."

"Mrs. Oberlin, if I might interrupt," Pastor Cosgrove said, stepping down from the pulpit. "Curtis makes no attempt to hide his past. He paid the price for his indiscretion of youth—served time and bore the ridicule and despair that comes with a life of sin."

"So you don't deny it." Her raised voice made Clara cringe. "I would think you might at least have the good sense to hide it from decent folks."

Clara knew there was nothing anyone could say that would stop her mother's rantings, but she felt she had to try.

"Mother, decent folks don't try to hide the truth, nor should they want it hidden from them. We all have things in our past that we'd rather folks not know or at least not dwell on—including you, Mother."

"Well, I never!" Her mother dropped her hold.

"I have to say," Pastor Cosgrove interjected, "I believe it is time to put an end to this."

Clara's mother turned to look at him with such disdain that Clara felt sorry for the older man. "What are you saying?" her mother demanded to know.

"Only that this couple has come to me without pretense and asked to be married. Both are of legal age and have met all the requirements of the state and church. I am going to have to ask that you either take your seat so that we may continue, or leave."

Her mother's face turned scarlet as she sputtered out her protest. "I won't . . . will not be . . . ordered about by you . . . or anyone else."

"If need be, madam, I will ask that my elders help escort you from the sanctuary. This is a house of God, and as such I require reverence and civility." The pastor took a step toward Clara's mother, and she backed away.

"If you strike me, I will have you thrown into jail."

The pastor didn't flinch. Instead, he stood still and simply laughed. Clara bit her lip, knowing it was the worst thing he could have done to her angry mother. She looked to Curtis for help, but it was too late. Her mother muttered something incoherent and turned on her heel to storm from the church.

For several moments no one said a word. The shock of the scene was so much that Clara wondered if the pastor would even continue with the ceremony. She didn't have long to wonder.

Pastor Cosgrove went back to his pulpit. "Before we continue, I want to say that I am quite troubled at the knowledge that gossip has been allowed to run rampant in our little town. For a complete stranger to come to our community and be told all the details of one forgiven man's past . . . well, I'm deeply ashamed for whoever is responsible. If that person is a part of this congregation, I hope you realize the gravity of what you've done."

Clara had a feeling she knew who might be responsible. Naomi Bittner never had any trouble sharing what she knew, but there was no sense in throwing out accusations. They'd had enough trouble for one day.

"Can we still get married?" Maddy asked, breaking the tension.

Several of the people near the front heard her question and laughed softly. Pastor Cosgrove's expression softened and he beamed Maddy a smile. "I think that would be the best thing to do. Don't you?" Maddy gave a solemn nod.

Pastor Cosgrove asked the congregation to bow in prayer. "Lord, we ask your blessing on this family. Marriage is a serious commitment that will require a great deal of patience and understanding. We ask that you would bless Curtis and Clara with both, as well as happiness and love. We ask that you would bless them along with Hunter and Maddy and make them a family strong in Christian faith and love for one another. Amen."

"Amen," Clara murmured, hearing others do likewise.

The pastor smiled. "Dearly beloved, we come here together in the sight of God and man to join this couple in holy matrimony."

Clara's heart had just settled to a fairly even beat when she heard the church door open once again. She couldn't help but turn to see if her mother had returned. She felt the blood drain from her face as her brother-in-law came forward with her mother not far behind.

"I demand you stop this wedding!" Otto called out.

Clara began to tremble. It was like a nightmare that wouldn't end. It was all her fears rolled into one menacing threat. Curtis put his arm around her waist to steady her, but already Clara felt herself growing dizzy.

"On what grounds?" the pastor countered.

Clara began to sway. How could her mother and Otto do this to her?

"On the grounds that the woman is already engaged to marry me."

That was all Clara heard. Her knees buckled and she felt Curtis's strong arms wrap around her. Then there was nothing at all.

23

"Did Uncle Otto kill my mama?" Clara heard her frantic son ask as she began to regain consciousness.

"No, your mama just fainted. She'll be just fine in a minute. See, she's already starting to wake up," Aunt Madeline explained. "Why don't you and Maddy come with me and Uncle Paul? We'll go for a walk so that your mama and Curtis can have a talk with your grandmother and uncle."

Clara opened her eyes as the cloudiness cleared from her mind. She found herself lying on the front pew with her head in Curtis's lap. Seeing her mother and Otto scowling at her even as Pastor Cosgrove tried to speak to them, Clara sat up abruptly and fought the dizziness that resulted. In a moment it was gone and she squared her shoulders for battle.

"Are you all right?" Curtis whispered, scooting closer.

"I'm fine. Embarrassed to have fainted," she admitted, "but fine." She glanced around and found the church had been emptied except for her family and Pastor Cosgrove.

"We've temporarily postponed the wedding," Curtis explained.

"It's not postponed, it's canceled!" Her mother broke away from the pastor and came to Clara. "You might not have listened to me, but Otto has a claim on you and you must listen to him."

"Otto has no claim on me. Not now—not ever." Clara got to her feet and fixed her brother-in-law with an expression of displeasure. "How could you? How could either of you act in such an embarrassing manner?"

"We're acting for your good, Clara." Otto stepped closer. "You aren't making sensible decisions, and given that Adolph died only a few short months ago, it's to be expected. However, that's why more rational minds must intercede on your behalf."

"I have my aunt and uncle as well as Curtis to help me. I don't need you or Mother to interfere. Neither of you have ever had my best interests at heart."

"How can you say that?" Otto looked quite hurt, but Clara was beginning to realize he was a consummate actor.

"I say it because it's true."

"Clara, we need to talk. Alone." Otto looked at her with pleading in his expression.

"But I don't wish to speak to you alone, Otto. There's nothing you can say to me in private that you can't say here in the company of all."

"I think there is. I know it will be easier for you to hear me without the distraction of the others. Just give me a chance, and if you still wish to stay, I will leave without another word."

"Nonsense!"

Clara heaved a sigh at her mother's declaration. She supposed the sooner she let Otto say his piece, the sooner she could rid herself of both.

"Please, Clara," Otto said in a hushed tone.

"Very well." She looked at Curtis. "Give us a few moments alone."

"Are you sure?" Curtis's brow was raised in skepticism.

"I am. Now that they've ruined the wedding, I might as well deal with them so they can return to New York."

"I'm not leaving here without you!" her mother declared. "If you don't cooperate, I'll—"

"Mrs. Oberlin, please refrain from making threats. I'll talk sense into Clara, and then we can all arrange to go home," Otto interrupted, offering Clara his arm.

Clara walked past him, refusing to even touch him. She didn't stop walking until she was out of the church and some distance away, where a small grove of aspen were rustling in the wind.

She turned to face him, knowing he'd be on her heels. She crossed her arms against her body and narrowed her eyes. "So speak your mind."

"You don't need to be angry, Clara. I only want to save you from a life of heartache." Otto had the audacity to smile. "You know how I feel about you. You know I have loved you from afar—the children too. Haven't I always been good to you?"

"I'm sorry that you love me, for I do not love you. Furthermore, I will never love you. I have only ever loved one man, and he is Curtis Billingham. Even your brother knew that I was in love with someone else. I never lied to him about it. In fact, I used it to try to convince him to release me from our engagement, but he wouldn't."

"He most likely knew that this man's life wasn't decent. Adolph no doubt loved you enough to keep you from this . . . degradation."

"Adolph loved himself—his business—and if he loved anything else, I was not privileged to know it." She sighed in complete exasperation. "Otto, go home. Take my mother and leave as soon as possible. I'm not going to marry you, and I'm not going to return to New York . . . ever."

His expression grew dark, and for a moment Clara wanted

to back away. She suddenly felt afraid, remembering that her own husband feared Otto would end his life. Nevertheless, she stood her ground—even when he moved closer.

"I had hoped to keep our discussion civil, but given your misguided intentions, I have to allow that you are temporarily unable to make a rational decision in this matter. Therefore, I will make it for you."

"You aren't in a position to make that choice, Otto. You are neither my father nor my husband. You are my brother-in-law. Nothing more."

He smiled in such a way that made Clara most uneasy. His eyes betrayed his anger as they narrowed. "I know that your mother threatened to take the children away from you if you refused to return to New York. I am prepared to stand beside her in that. Together we have enough friends and money to make any judge see that you are completely insane."

Clara shook her head in disbelief. "Why? Why would you do that? Why do you hate me so?"

"I don't hate you. I love you. Just as I said. I cannot let you make such a monumental mistake." He fingered his mustache. "What parent would lead their children into something that wasn't in their best interest, or something even dangerous? I don't want to take these actions, believe me. But to keep you and your children from harm, I feel I must."

"I'm no child, Otto, and you are certainly not my parent."

"No, I'm not, but for the sake of my niece and nephew, I will do what I must."

Clara tried to think of some way she could reason with him. The contents of her husband's journals came to mind. She might be making a mistake in bringing it up now—it might very well result in Otto fleeing the authorities—but Clara felt it was her only ammunition.

"I don't think you will." She relaxed her arms and drew in a long, deep breath. "You see, I know all about you and the treasonous actions you and Adolph participated in. Not only that, but I know that you were responsible for killing him."

She had never seen such a look of shock on anyone's face as Otto had on his. If she had pulled a gun on him he surely wouldn't have looked more surprised. Clara took the opportunity to continue. "I know that you and Adolph belonged to a consortium of spies who were responsible for a great many tragedies, including the sinking of the *Lusitania*."

"And just how do you know this?" His tone suggested that she was simply making it all up.

"It's enough for you to know that I have proof and that I'll use it."

"Even at the risk of your children's lives?"

Clara shook her head. "My children will face no risk."

"They will if you go to the authorities." The shocked expression was replaced by one of renewed confidence. "If you say anything against me, I'll tell them that you were just as much a confederate in our organization as anyone." He smiled again. "I'll offer to give up all kinds of evidence that will incriminate you and bring in half a dozen witnesses. You'll be jailed and probably sentenced to die . . . because, although extremely rare, they do execute women in New York."

Clara felt her breath catch. She knew that the journals made clear that she knew nothing about the espionage. She knew her husband had commented in them more than once that he hated the risk he'd put her and the children in. But would that be enough if Otto gave sworn testimony to suggest otherwise?

"I can see you realize the severity of such a declaration. Perhaps now that we both understand what's at risk, you will give up this nonsense and return to New York to marry me."

It was hard not to strike the man. The smug look on his face left Clara no doubt that he was enjoying the situation. She forced herself to say nothing for the moment. She had to have time to think. She definitely needed a plan.

"I can't give you an answer right now. I need to pray about it."

Otto looked as if he might refuse her, then nodded. "You have until morning. I will come to your aunt and uncle's ranch for your answer, but we both know what it will be. What it must be."

Clara gave the slightest nod and headed back to the church without another word. She saw her aunt and uncle at the wagon with her children and Curtis. Everyone seemed to be waiting with great interest to know what had transpired between her and Otto Vesper.

She forced a smile and let Paul help her into the wagon, where she joined her aunt and the children. Curtis sat on the driver's seat with Paul, but that didn't stop him from questioning her.

"What happened? What did he say to you?"

Clara glanced at the children, whose expressions were ones of fear mingled with curiosity. She couldn't talk about any of this in front of them. Still, she needed to say something that would put them at ease.

"Uncle Otto was just worried about Hunter and Maddy and whether they were really happy in Montana. I assured him they were, but he plans to come see the ranch in the morning and get his final answer." She looked at her aunt. Madeline seemed to realize the impact of Clara's statement. She nodded and reached out to pat Clara's hand.

"We will all be praying, I'm sure."

"We don't have to pray," Hunter declared as if the matter were unimportant. "Mama already knows that we're happy. She doesn't have to ask God." Maddy nodded, but her expression had grown quite serious as if she too knew there was far more to this.

Curtis had turned to look at Clara. The frown on his face left her little doubt that he understood the gravity of the matter. Once the children went for their Sunday afternoon nap, Clara would explain the entire situation to him as well as Madeline and Paul. Until then, it was best she keep things as calm as possible.

⚬⚬⚬

"I never heard of anything so underhanded." Madeline paced her front room, shaking her head.

"I ought to go into town and horsewhip him," Paul added.

"He won't get away with this," Curtis assured. It was hard for him to keep from riding back into town to deal with Otto personally, and had it not been for his physical limitations he might have done exactly that.

"I appreciate your support, but I don't think anything will keep Otto from making good on his threat. Perhaps if I promise him that I won't go to the authorities regarding his espionage, then he'll be satisfied. Maybe I could give him the books as proof."

"No, because once he has those, you'll have nothing with which to restrain him," Paul said.

"Paul's right. You can't give him those journals, and I don't see how you can withhold the information from the authorities. His actions have cost the lives of many," Madeline replied.

Clara shook her head. "I don't know what I can do, then. He seems to have no qualms about joining Mother on her threat to have me declared insane so that they can take the children. They know the children are the only thing I would fight for—

give my life for." She sighed. "I can't help but feel the situation is impossible."

"With God, all things are possible," Madeline murmured.

"She's right," Curtis said, coming to Clara. He hated seeing her so troubled. He took hold of her hands. "We know the truth and so does God. I think we have to trust Him to give us the wisdom to deal with this. Perhaps we should spend the afternoon in prayer—here—together."

Paul nodded. "I think you're right, Curtis. The sheriff plans to visit us soon and then we can explain the matter to him, but if we spend the time between now and then praying, we're sure to find a greater peace."

❧

"Now do you understand what I expect for my money?" Otto looked at the two sleazy characters who stood before him. He'd located them only the night before. Neither one looked like they'd had a bath or decent meal in some time.

The taller of the two nodded. "We're gonna watch the Sersland Ranch and take the two children."

"Yes, but no one must see you or know that you're there. The first opportunity that presents itself, you need to take them and leave as quickly as possible. Now, you're certain you have a place where you can hide them?"

"Yeah, we got a place," the other man replied. "Don't you worry about that."

"You'll have to bind them and gag them. I'm sure they won't go without a fuss. However, I don't want them hurt in any way. Be kind to them; tell them you don't plan to hurt them and that they'll be returned to their mother very soon. Better still, I'll give you some extra money and you can buy them some candy.

I can't imagine any children would care much about their surroundings if they are given all the candy they want."

The tall once scratched his chest through his threadbare shirt. "Speaking of money—where is it?"

Otto took his wallet from his coat pocket and produced several bills. The man's eyes widened at the sight. Otto knew he risked having the men simply knock him in the head and take his money, but he also knew that he was far smarter than either man.

"You'll get this half now and the other half when the job is done to my satisfaction. I won't carry the money on me, so you needn't worry that someone might . . . hold me up." He smiled and handed the money to the man. "Now we shouldn't be seen together. Are you certain you have mounts to get you out to the ranch?"

"We got 'em. Don't you worry none," the short man answered. "We'll head out to the north in case anyone sees us and wonders where we're bound. Then we'll circle back around to the west and come up on the ranch through the trees. Like we told you, we used to work for Sersland, so we know the lay of the land real good."

"Perfect. I hope you have some provisions with you as well. I want you positioned in such a way that you can observe me after I leave the ranch and head back to town. If Mrs. Vesper isn't in the rig with me, I want you to take the children. I don't care if you have to camp out there all night. Do you understand?"

The two men exchanged a look, then nodded. The short one spoke. "We understand, mister, and we know what we're doing. You just make sure you have the rest of our money."

Otto could only hope the men were as competent as they assured him they were. He took the rig he'd rented and followed the road west to where his cohorts assured him he would eventually reach the ranch. The road was nothing more than a dirt path as far as Otto could see. It was certainly not an easy drive. The rig bounced around in such a fashion that Otto actually wondered if he'd even make it. Why couldn't these barbarians have an automobile he could rent for the day?

The trip, however, gave him time to formulate his plan. Clara said she had proof of his involvement. She'd even accused him of being involved in Adolph's death. That could only mean that she had the journals. He had been afraid they'd turn up, although he'd never expected Clara would have them. Ever since she'd confronted him the day before, Otto couldn't shake the feeling that his days were numbered. He silently cursed his brother.

"You no doubt detailed everything, including my involvement. How else would she know?" He cursed aloud. "I'll just have to get them back. There's no other choice."

He saw the ranch from a ways off and thought it a rather pastoral scene. The house and surrounding buildings appeared, at least from a distance, to be well kempt. The rolling hills were more brown than green from a lack of water, but the evergreens and aspen dotted here and there made up for that. There was a sort of pretty stream that flowed to one side of the ranch. He supposed it a fine home . . . for some, but certainly not for him.

He brought the horse and rig to a stop near the front of the house. The log structure and wide porch reminded him of a hunting lodge he'd once been to when he was a boy. It was a pleasant enough memory, but certainly nothing he wanted to repeat.

He secured the lines, then made his way to the porch. Otto gave a quick glance back toward the east, where the grove of trees that his hirelings had described stood. It would afford them adequate coverage in case any of the adults should be nearby.

"I heard you drive up," Clara said from the other side of the screened door. She looked surprisingly at peace. "Won't you come in?" She opened the door for him.

"Thank you. I hope we can conclude our business quickly."

"You didn't bring Mother? I thought surely you would want her here cheering you on," she said sarcastically.

Otto entered the house and glanced around for the others. "I'm sure your defenders are no doubt close at hand."

"Absolutely." She jerked her chin up in a defiant pose. "I believe there is strength in numbers." She motioned to the room at her right. "We'll sit in here."

"Do we really need to sit?" Otto lowered his voice to a whisper. "I thought my comments were quite clear on what would happen if you didn't agree to marry me."

"We are civilized people," Clara replied. "Even here in the wilds of Montana we believe in offering our guests refreshment after a long, dusty drive." She moved into the room and waited for him to follow.

Otto was surprised that her supporters weren't already seated in the room. "Where are your aunt and uncle?"

"They're in the kitchen. Aunt Madeline is preparing those refreshments I mentioned. Uncle Paul is keeping company with Curtis. Now, please have a seat and try to act in a fashion that befits your training." Her voice was laced with anger, something Otto hadn't expected.

He thought that after having given her time to reflect she would see the impossibility of defiance and agree to marry him. Of course, he hadn't had complete confidence of this. Otherwise, he wouldn't have found it necessary to hire men to steal away her children.

Clara took a seat in a straight-backed chair. She settled her hands in her lap and waited for him to sit. Otto took the chair nearest her and doffed his hat.

"I suppose we might as well get right to the point," he said, but he didn't get a chance to finish his statement before Clara's aunt appeared with a tray.

She looked at Otto with a most disapproving expression, then placed the tray on the small table beside Clara. Then to Otto's surprise Clara's uncle joined them. He led his wife to the sofa and then looked at Otto with a frown.

"I'm sure you would prefer we speak in private," Otto said, looking at Clara.

She shook her head. "I'd prefer we not speak at all, but you have insisted. They know everything. I told them of your threats."

This made Otto nervous, but he wasn't about to let anyone know that. He gave a curt nod, then looked at Clara's relatives. "It really is to her advantage to return to New York as my wife."

"Well, given you've threatened to separate her from her children and have her thrown into an asylum or a jail, I would almost have to agree with you," Paul Sersland replied. "Almost."

Otto raised a brow in question, but Paul said nothing more. Otto turned to Clara. "I have always known you to be a level-headed person. I'm sure you understand that I've only made such threats because I know what's best for you."

"That hardly seems possible," Curtis Billingham said from the arched entryway. "I can't imagine it's ever in any mother's best interest to be threatened in that kind of manner." He leaned against the frame and fixed Otto with a hard look. "But I guess I can't expect much more from a man who has done the things you've done."

Otto felt his anger growing. He found it almost impossible to keep from countering the man's comment with insults of his own. He looked back to Clara instead and found her smiling at the man she claimed to love. For a moment Otto could see the depth of that love in her expression, and it made him most uncomfortable.

She seemed to feel his gaze upon her and turned to Otto. "Would you care for coffee?"

"No!" He hadn't meant to raise his voice, but he was running out of patience. "I would like for us to settle this matter. I want you to return to town with me this minute."

"I'm not going anywhere with you, Otto."

"You haven't forgotten my plans."

She shook her head. "No, but I no longer fear them. You see, we spent a good deal of time in prayer yesterday, and I feel confident of my place with God. I do not believe He will allow for you to have your way."

"And you're willing to risk that? All on this nonsense of faith in a God you cannot see?" He laughed. "I will make it clear to the authorities that you were actively involved in Adolph's treasonous tasks."

"And I will show them my husband's journals."

"That I will declare were falsified for your purpose of seeing yourself acquitted of wrongdoing." He smiled. "I am not without my own faith, but it is in myself rather than some unknown deity."

Clara's expression radiated peace. "He isn't unknown to me, Otto. I have spent a long time knowing God better, and while I have a great deal yet to learn, I know this much. God has already provided for me—long before I was even born. He will see me through this as well. I won't lie for you and I won't lie to God by committing myself in marriage to you."

"You can't hope to win. I have a good many friends who will let the authorities know you are a traitor."

"Will you also let the authorities know that I'm the one who has designed the Vesper Yogo collection?" She tilted her head ever so slightly. "I wonder what people will say when they realize you aren't the artist."

Otto couldn't hide his surprise. He had thought such knowledge wouldn't have reached her. "How . . . how did you—"

"I read the newspaper, Otto." She glanced over to see Curtis's look of surprise. "Despite how my family intends to keep unpleasant news from me, I manage to know what I need to know. How dare you display my jewelry designs and claim them for your own? It was one thing to allow Adolph that privilege, but you promised to reveal the truth."

"And I will. Once we are married I will bring in all the newspaper people and make a formal announcement."

"No, Otto. I don't believe you to be capable of truth. I will create my own jewelry if I am so inclined, but it won't be with you. Now, I think I've made it quite clear that my decision is to remain here. I suggest you leave now."

Otto jumped to his feet, knocking his hat to the floor. He started toward her, then felt a hand take hold of his arm. He turned to find Curtis Billingham.

"The lady asked you to leave."

"This isn't over," Otto declared as Clara's uncle got to his feet. He shook off Curtis's hold. "You'll all be sorry for interfering."

Otto stalked from the house, surprised that no one tried to stop him or threaten him with violence. He climbed into the rig and found Curtis had followed him from the house. Perhaps there would be violence after all.

"Well?" Otto asked, picking up the reins.

To his surprise Curtis threw something at him. Otto ducked but then found that the object was nothing more than his hat.

He took up the hat and pressed it onto his head. He gave Curtis one last hard look.

"You'd do well to change her mind and do it quickly." He slapped the reins against the horse's rump and headed back to town. Once he had his brother's brats in hand, they would all whistle a different tune.

24

Clara awoke on Tuesday morning with a great sense of peace. She was blessed by the support she'd found in her family, but even more by the way God had bolstered her faith. Stretching in bed, she couldn't help but smile. After speaking with Curtis late into the night, they had decided to have a small private ceremony at the house. Uncle Paul had agreed to ride to town and bring the pastor back with him later that afternoon. Soon she and Curtis would be married and all of this would be behind them.

She rose and dressed quickly in a simple navy blue skirt that reached to just above her ankles. Topping this with a blue calico print blouse, Clara smiled at the contrast of fashion. Her wardrobe in New York held satins and silks, laces and tulle. She'd worn embroidered silk stockings and exquisite shoes. *"A wardrobe fit for a queen,"* her husband had once said when encouraging her to go out and buy herself whatever she wanted. Now her clothes consisted of what she'd brought with her from New York, as well as a few simple skirts and blouses, some of which she and Madeline had made.

How simple, yet how much better her life was here in Montana. Clara picked up her brush and began making long strokes through her dark auburn hair. She arranged it in a braid and then coiled this atop her head and pinned it into place as she'd often seen her maid do back in the city.

"There, now I'm more orderly," she said, smiling at her reflection.

After she completed her outfit with cotton stockings and her sturdy boots, Clara made her way to wake the children. Instead, she found their beds neatly made and their nightclothes folded and sitting in place of the clothes she'd laid out for them. They were becoming more and more self-sufficient, and this pleased her greatly.

Clara made her way to the kitchen. The aroma of coffee and ham filled the air. "It smells wonderful in here." Clara pulled an apron from a peg by the door. Her aunt was already busy frying up huge ham steaks.

"Good morning, Aunt Madeline." Clara went to her aunt and kissed her cheek. "Isn't it a beautiful day?"

"You haven't even been outside yet," her aunt teased, "but when you're in love, every day is a beautiful day."

Clara looked around as she tied on her apron. "Where are the children?"

"Out doing their chores. Hunter brought in plenty of wood for the stove and then went off to help Maddy collect the eggs."

Clara laughed. "I was just thinking to myself how efficient they've become. When we first came here, they didn't even know how to dress themselves."

"They're smart, well-behaved children. You've done a good job of helping them adjust to life here."

"I don't think the adjustment was all that hard. In fact, I don't remember ever seeing them as happy as they are now.

In New York they were forced to be silent and remain hidden away in the nursery. Children were rarely allowed at social functions, unless of course it was a birthday party being held on their behalf."

"I'm sure it was different for folks with less money." Aunt Madeline took the ham steaks from the cast-iron skillet and plopped them on a platter. She then turned back to the stove and put more meat into the pan. "Of course, here in Montana it hasn't been that many years since children of all ages were working in the mines. Now you have to be sixteen, although I have my doubts that is always the case."

Clara couldn't imagine children in the mines, but then it hadn't been that long ago that children filled the factories back east. It was something she'd always found appalling. "Having children help around the ranch or farm seems reasonable, but I firmly believe they should be in school otherwise. It's awful to imagine children having to work to help provide for their family." Clara looked around the room. It seemed her aunt already had everything under control. "How can I help?"

"Why don't you go hurry the children along? The boys will be storming the place any minute, starved as usual." She stepped back and opened the oven door. "Oh, good. The biscuits are ready."

Clara nodded. "The children were probably sidetracked by Blessing. They are quite crazy about that pup." She made her way to the back door.

The sun was just up over the horizon, giving the sky and clouds a splash of red, orange, and pink. What was that old saying about a red sky in the morning? Clara mused on it as she made her way to the chicken coop. She wasn't about to let old sayings become a foreboding omen.

"Maddy! Hunter!" She entered the building and blinked at

the darkened room. Her children were nowhere to be found, but the egg basket sat full in the middle of the floor.

Clara picked up the basket. She would have to reprimand them later for leaving the basket out there where someone could have tripped and hurt themselves or the eggs. She headed back for the house. She heard Blessing howling and yipping. It made her smile. No doubt they were all having a grand time playing.

She made her way into the house. "Here are the eggs. The children were nowhere to be found, but I hear Blessing putting up a fuss, so I'm guessing they were distracted."

"Well, don't be too hard on them," her aunt said, taking the basket.

"Oh, I won't be. Still, they need to know it wasn't right to leave the eggs out in the coop. They knew we'd be waiting on them."

Clara exited the house once again and made her way to the barn. Blessing was protesting most adamantly about something. She'd never heard the pup be quite so noisy.

She stepped into the barn. "What's going on out here?"

Blessing's whines were the only response. Clara looked around, gazing up at the hayloft. "Maddy? Hunter?" There was no reply.

A sense of dread began to settle over Clara. She hurried from the barn and went in search of her uncle and Curtis. They were going to be repairing some of the pens out behind the lambing shed this morning. At least that's what they'd decided the night before.

"Curtis? Uncle Paul?" she called out before she could see either man.

"We're back here," Curtis replied. He beamed her a smile as she hurried to join them. "Good morning. You're mighty pretty today."

Clara frowned and shook her head. "Are the children with you?"

Paul straightened. "Last I saw them they were headed out to gather eggs. Curtis and I crossed their path on our way out here."

"I can't find them anywhere." Clara turned a complete circle looking all around for any sign of them.

"I'm sure they just got sidetracked. Maybe they took Blessing out to play," Curtis suggested.

Clara felt her breath catch. "I've already checked on that. Blessing's still in his pen, and he's howling and whining like I've never heard before."

"We did hear some of his complaints," Paul said. "Never thought too much about it, though."

Curtis put his arm around Clara. "Come on, we'll find them. I'll help you look."

For the next half an hour they covered the entire ranch yard and all of the outbuildings, calling each child's name. By now Madeline and Paul had joined the search with Paul heading down to the river and fishing pond while Madeline looked through the house. By the time they came back together on the porch, Clara was convinced that Otto and her mother had somehow taken them.

"But we would have heard a wagon coming up the road," Madeline said, trying to calm Clara's fears.

"Unless they parked it off at a distance and snuck up on the place," Clara countered. "You know them. They are completely capable of such madness."

"She's right," Curtis said, his expression filled with worry. "There's really no other answer. They wouldn't just wander off—especially without their dog."

Paul and Madeline gave slow nods in unison. Clara thought

she might very well be sick. Her stomach churned and she felt the same dizziness she had at the church on Sunday. She forced herself to breathe deep and push away thoughts of what might be happening to her children.

"I'll hitch up the wagon," Paul said. "Curtis and I can go into town and—"

"Not without me." Clara hadn't meant to interrupt her uncle, but she couldn't remain silent on the matter. She wasn't about to be left at the ranch. "Otto knows I'll come to get them. If he and Mother have them, they'll be expecting me to follow."

"I don't like the idea of you having to deal with him," Curtis countered. "If he came here or had someone else come here to steal the children, who knows what else he might have planned?"

"You and Paul can come too, of course. But he won't talk to me if you're there. Once we get to town, I'll go to him and find out the truth." She looked at the trio as if seeking their approval.

"Like I said, I'll get the wagon," Paul declared, then stalked off toward the barn.

"Do you want me to come too?" Madeline asked.

Clara shook her head. "No. Please stay here just in case we're wrong."

Her aunt nodded. "None of you have had breakfast. I'll go put together some ham and biscuits to take along. Those children are going to be hungry." She hurried to the house.

Curtis put his arm around Clara's shoulders. The comfort was too much, and Clara burst into tears. He pulled her against him and held her close.

"If any . . . anything has happened . . . to cause . . . them harm . . ." She couldn't finish. To speak the words aloud might somehow give it power to happen.

"Shhh, we'll get them back and they'll be just fine," Curtis promised. "You'll see."

Clara clung to him, knowing that if she let go, she would collapse in a heap on the ground. Her entire world was spinning out of control and all because of one man's greed and deception.

The drive into town seemed to take forever. Paul and Curtis ate some of the ham and biscuits, but Clara refused. She knew if she ate she'd be sick. Instead, she had forced aside her tears and tried to calm her spirit in prayer, but always she saw Otto's sneering face and heard his threats. Uncle Paul and Curtis remained silent throughout the trip into town, and for once Clara was glad for their silence. She knew they were just as worried as she was, but to hear it in their voices would have been too much.

When the town came into sight, Clara straightened and planned what she would do and say. Otto and her mother were forces to be reckoned with, but they had taken her children and had no idea what Clara was capable of doing in order to get them back. The fact was, Clara herself wasn't at all certain. There was a part of her that wished she'd thought to ask for a gun. It seemed Otto only understood force and violence, so perhaps that was the only way to deal with him. Yet even as she thought of these things, Clara knew she would have great difficulty shooting someone.

Paul pulled the wagon to a stop just down the street from the hotel. "Are you sure you don't want us to come with you?"

Clara was already climbing down. "No. I'll let you know if I need help. I can scream pretty loud if I need to." She looked at Curtis. "Just knowing you're here is enough."

"Be careful, Clara. Your brother-in-law is a dangerous man." She nodded. "I know."

With that she headed down the street and made her way into the hotel. Otto was waiting for her in the lobby. He looked up over his newspaper and smiled. She wanted to grab up the nearest object and throw it at him, but she restrained herself.

"Where are they, Otto? Where are my children?"

"They're safe," he said, not even trying to deny that he had taken them. He very slowly folded the newspaper. "And they will stay that way so long as you agree to my terms."

"To marry you and give you Adolph's journals?"

"Exactly." He put the paper aside and rose. "I'm really a very reasonable man."

"Where are they?"

"Close. You really needn't worry."

Clara turned on her heel. "I'm going to the sheriff."

Otto grabbed her arm and yanked her back. He pulled her hard against him. "If you do, they will die."

She froze. Was he really capable of killing his own niece and nephew? Her heart raced along with her thoughts. How could she deal with this? What was she supposed to say or do except agree to his demands?

"I knew you'd see it my way." Otto released her. "We have no need to involve the sheriff. However, it would be to your benefit to call for the preacher. In fact, maybe we should just walk over to the church and seek him out."

Clara turned to face him. She could see the glint of self-satisfaction in his eyes. Her hands balled into fists, but she forced them to remain at her side. Just then she spied her mother coming down the hotel stairs.

"Does she know what you've done? Is she a part of this?"

"No. And the less you say the better off we'll all be, so behave yourself." He narrowed his gaze. "Or you'll be very sorry."

"Clara, what are you doing here?" Her mother looked at Otto. "Did you bring her here from the ranch?"

"No, Clara came on her own and just happened to find me here reading the newspaper."

"Have you come to your senses, then?" Her mother looked at her with great expectation.

Clara knew that the only way to keep her children safe would be to agree to marry Otto. She looked at Otto, who raised his brow and waited for her to speak. Clara tried her best to steady her nerves. She relaxed her hands and drew them together.

"I came here"—Clara licked her lips and forced the words from her mouth—"to tell Otto that I will marry him."

25

lara could see her mother's look of disbelief change to satisfaction. Clara had never before wanted to defy anyone as much as she wanted to at this moment, but her children's lives were at stake.

"I'm glad you're finally seeing reason," her mother declared. "I will go and have my maid pack immediately." She touched Otto's arm. "I presume you can arrange for our tickets home?"

"Of course." He smiled, his eyes never leaving Clara.

Once her mother was gone, Clara fixed Otto with a sober expression. "I hope you're happy. Now bring me my children."

"In time, Clara dear. In time. First we will marry. Let's head over to the church right now and see if that minister is available to do the job immediately."

Clara knew she had to stall for time. She was forming an idea of how this could all play out without having to actually marry Otto, but she would need the help of her aunt and uncle, as well as Curtis.

"You really know nothing about churches and ceremonies,

do you? Pastor Cosgrove wouldn't even consider marrying us in the church or anywhere else for that matter."

"What are you saying?" Otto's eyes narrowed. "You aren't changing your mind, are you?"

"Not at all. I'm simply telling you that a church ceremony is out of the question. Pastor Cosgrove would consider it sacrilegious, given that I was just to marry Curtis on Sunday. He would also insist that you be a man of God, and since we both know that isn't the case, we will have to rely on a judge to marry us."

"Is there one in this tiny town?" he asked, sounding doubtful.

"My uncle is good friends with Judge Walker. I'll have him arrange for the judge to come to the ranch. Be there at noon." She tried to hide the anger in her voice but knew she was unsuccessful.

"Clara, you needn't disdain our union. You really are quite dear to me."

"So dear that you would put my children's lives in jeopardy? Yes, I can see just how dear I am to you."

He reached out, but she jerked away. Instead of getting angry, however, Otto smiled. "In time you will understand that this is the best for everyone. The children will live the life of privilege they were always meant to live. The trust left them by their father will see to that, and of course you will be well cared for by me."

"Trust? What trust?" Clara could see a look flash over Otto that suggested he regretted his words. "Are you telling me there is a trust fund for my children?"

"Yes. There is. I didn't know about it until recently. Apparently Adolph wasn't completely void of sensibility. There is a large trust for the children awaiting them in New York. It will see them quite comfortable for life—if it's handled properly. I will see to that, however, so there need be no concern."

Clara shook her head. "I understand now why you are so

desperate to marry me. I should have known it would be something like this."

"I'm quite hurt by your declaration," Otto said, putting a hand to his chest. "I've already told you of my love."

"So will the children be allowed to attend the wedding?" She knew it was a risk to ask. Otto could become suspicious.

"As I said, I will produce the children once we are officially man and wife. I have to make certain you will not change your mind." He fingered his mustache and gave a shrug. "I'm sorry."

Clara knew he wasn't at all sorry. She turned and walked toward the door. If she stayed in the room one more minute, she would no doubt say things she would regret. "Be at the ranch at noon, Otto."

"I will, and . . . Clara,"—he waited to continue until she looked back at him—"wear something pretty. I don't want my wife looking like a ranch hand."

She hurried outside and down the street. Ranch hand, indeed. Paul and Curtis paced beside the wagon, and both men stopped in their tracks when Clara drew near.

"What did he say? Does he have the children?" Curtis asked, hurrying to her side.

She nodded. "He has them hidden away and will only bring them to me once we are married."

"Why, of all the low-down, conniving . . ." her uncle muttered. "I'm going to get the sheriff right now and put an end to this."

Clara took hold of her uncle's arm. "No. We can't. He said he'd . . . he'd kill them if we dared to involve the law."

"So what are we supposed to do?" Curtis asked.

"I'm going to marry him." Her matter-of-fact statement caused both men to look at her as if she'd lost her mind. "Come on. Help me into the wagon and I'll explain."

"You'd better be joking," Curtis said, handing her up to the wagon seat. "I'm not losing you to another Vesper."

As they drove, Clara explained. "He has the children hidden somewhere, which suggests to me that he also has an accomplice. Someone must be with Hunter and Maddy to make certain they stay put."

"Unless he tied them up," Curtis said, frowning.

Clara didn't like to dwell on all of the possibilities of what Otto may or may not have done to her children. "Even so, Otto must have help with them. He wouldn't risk us following him and finding them, so I doubt he's the one responsible for seeing that they are fed and can use the facilities. Otto said that until we are married, he won't retrieve them. So my thought is that we convince him we are married . . . without really being married."

"And how are you going to do that?" her uncle asked.

"Well, that's where you come in, Uncle Paul. I wondered if your friend Judge Walker might be willing to participate in a little playacting. I told Otto to be at the ranch at noon. That gives us about four hours to arrange my plan."

"And what is your plan?" Curtis asked, looking even more worried.

"Well, since Judge Walker is retired and no longer has any authority to marry people, I thought he could pretend to marry us. That way, we would go through the ceremony, but there would be nothing legal about it. We would simply convince Otto that the marriage had taken place so that he would bring me the children."

"And what if he doesn't?" Curtis asked.

She met his gaze and saw the deep concern in his expression. "He must. If he doesn't produce them immediately after the wedding, I'll tell him that I won't leave the ranch."

Paul had been driving the team in relative silence, but finally he spoke up. "I think it might work, Curtis. I'm sure Judge Walker will help us out. His place is on the way home, and we can just swing in there and fill him in on the details."

"What about the sheriff?" Curtis asked. "He ought to know about this too, since he wasn't able to meet with us earlier and has no idea of what's happening. If we can have him at the ranch as well, we can turn Otto over to him with the journals, and hopefully that will be the last you'll need to see of him."

"That is a good idea. Then if your brother-in-law tries to make trouble," Paul added, "we'll have the extra help of the law."

"How do we get word to the sheriff? I had threatened to go to him, but Otto warned me against it. I'm afraid of what he'll do to the children if he finds out the sheriff is involved."

"Well, it is difficult but not impossible. Judge Walker has a couple of hired hands, and we could get one of them to ride back into town and see the sheriff. Otto won't know who they are, and if he sees them strolling into the sheriff's office, he wouldn't have reason to think it strange."

"I suppose it's worth a try."

When they reached the turnoff for the judge's property, Clara's nerves were stretched taut. She had prayed for direction—for a way to dupe Otto and not risk her children's lives—and in a few moments they would know whether or not they could put her idea into play. After that it would take waiting until after the ceremony to see if Otto would uphold his end of the bargain.

He must. Lord, I cannot bear the thought of losing Hunter and Maddy. Please give us your justice and mercy in this matter. Justice for Otto and mercy for my children.

Paul brought the wagon to a stop and set the brake. Without

a word Curtis climbed down from the wagon, then reached up to help Clara. Once she was on the ground, she could see that Curtis was in pain.

"You've overdone," she said softly.

"I've only done what was necessary." He rubbed his thigh. "It's not all that bad. My back is stiff and sore and my leg aches, but nothing hurts as much as my heart for our kids."

Our kids. It touched her deeply to know he already felt the children belonged to him as well. She reached up and touched his cheek. "I know. It's only one of the many reasons I love you. You love my children as your own. I couldn't ask for anything more."

He pressed her hand to his cheek. "We're going to see this through. I promise you, I'll get Hunter and Maddy back to you if it's the last thing I do." She nodded, knowing that he spoke from the heart.

Paul led the way and knocked loudly on the front door. In less than a minute, an elderly woman opened the door.

"Well, Sarah Walker, aren't you looking pretty today?" Paul declared.

"Oh, go on with you, Paul. You always have been a charmer. What can I do for you?" She looked around him to where Clara stood with Curtis. "I see you brought us company."

"Is the judge in? We need to speak to him. It's rather urgent."

"He is," Mrs. Walker said, stepping back. "Won't you all join us? We were just sitting down to breakfast. We take our time with such things these days. Have you eaten?"

"We had a bite on our way into town. We had to leave the ranch rather abruptly this morning. I'll explain it all when we see the judge."

She led them through the small foyer past the front room and on into the dining room, where Judge Walker sat reading a newspaper. He lowered the paper and put it aside at the sight of his visitors.

"Well, I must say this is a surprise. To what do we owe this visit?" he asked, then motioned to his wife. "Bring some more coffee and cups, Sarah. And some plates."

"I already planned to do just that." She smiled and gave Clara a wink. "He doesn't realize I've been hostess to this house for forty years."

Clara forced herself to smile and give a nod. She was far too worried about the children to waste time with coffee or a meal. Curtis squeezed her hand as if understanding. She felt strengthened by his nearness.

"Sit down and tell me why you all look so grave." The judge waited for them to take a place at the table.

Paul spoke up first. "We have a bad situation on our hands." He gave a brief account of Clara's past and of her brother-in-law's participation in espionage and aiding the enemy. Sarah served coffee and put plates of food in front of them. When she'd finally taken her seat, Paul continued to explain about the children and Otto's demand that Clara marry him.

"Of course, he told Clara she couldn't go to the sheriff—not if she wanted to see the children again."

"Despicable." Judge Walker was clearly perturbed. "I've always hated to see the weak being attacked or taken advantage of by the strong, but this goes beyond that. I am completely appalled. So what is it you want from me?"

Clara lost no time. "We need you to marry us—Otto and myself."

"Well, I can't say I expected that request." As he buttered his toast the judge looked at Paul as if he hadn't heard right. "Not only that, but I no longer have any authority to do the job."

"She doesn't want you to really marry them. We just need

the pretense of a wedding at the ranch. We're hoping that once Vesper believes himself to be married to Clara, he will produce the children and then we can reveal the truth and have him hauled off to jail."

The judge smiled. "That, I can do. Tell me when you want to hold this . . . wedding."

"At noon." Clara drew a deep breath and continued. "My brother-in-law has the children hidden somewhere, presumably with someone. He wouldn't say anything more than that. We need to reach the sheriff and have him out at the ranch to take Otto into custody. However, I don't know if he'll bring the children or arrange to have them delivered, so I hardly know how this will play out."

"He could even have them hidden away in town. If that's the case, you might have to return to town in order to get them back."

"I had thought of that but figured it unlikely. I know my brother-in-law. He's a man of secrecy and is conniving. He wouldn't risk someone seeing or hearing the children, so I'm guessing he has them locked up elsewhere . . . away from town."

The judge nodded. "That makes sense. He's obviously thought this through. I'll get one of my boys to go for the sheriff and have him come here as soon as he is available. Then we can ride out to your place, and that'll give me time to explain everything. Hopefully we can be there well ahead of time."

"I have no way of knowing if Otto knows who the sheriff is, so you might want to have him stay out of sight." Clara looked at the people around the table. They meant the world to her, and it touched her deeply that the Walkers would care enough to go to such extremes.

"I'll make sure he does just that," Judge Walker replied.

"Now, you don't fret about anything. We'll see to it that the children are safe and sound before anything else happens."

"Thank you." Clara looked down at the plate of food and picked up a piece of bacon. She didn't want to be rude after all the trouble Mrs. Walker had gone to. "Thank you for this as well."

⁂

Otto hummed a tune as he walked back to the hotel. As they'd previously arranged, he'd met with one of his cohorts and learned that the children, although frightened, were well and unharmed. They didn't like being tied up and gagged, but Otto couldn't care less. He'd given the men money in order to feed the twins, then instructed the men to have them out at the ranch by one o'clock. He figured that would give the judge plenty of time to perform the ceremony. The men were to keep the children hidden until he was able to step out onto the porch. He would stand there bareheaded if everything had gone as planned, and they would know they could let the children go. However, if he came out with his hat on, things hadn't gone as planned, and they would need to take the children back to their shack. Either way, Otto would meet up with them later that night to give them the rest of their pay, and if necessary deal with the children.

He smiled. He wouldn't have to hurt them. Clara would cooperate as long as their lives were at risk. In the future he would no doubt be able to control her through the twins. If she failed to do as he wanted, Otto would threaten to send them away to boarding school or simply arrange it so that she was unable to see them.

It was all going to work out just perfectly. Finally he would have his brother's ledgers, Clara's designs, and the trust fund. He breathed a sigh of relief. Once he was back in New York, he would abandon further work for the enemy and bide his time. The war wouldn't last forever.

As he entered the hotel he found a very impatient Harriet Oberlin waiting for him. "Where have you been?" she demanded to know.

"Taking care of a few loose ends. I had to rent a carriage for us. The drive out to the ranch is none too pleasing, but given the fact that it will be the last time I ever have to endure that trip, I'm more than happy to make it."

"It is abominable. I've never understood why anyone would live out in the middle of nowhere." Harriet gave a shudder and shook her head. "I've always hated that ranch."

"Well, soon you'll never have to worry about it again. I won't allow Clara to be making any more trips west." He drew out his watch and checked the time. "We should probably leave in an hour and a half. That will give us plenty of time to reach the ranch by noon. It would also be wise to have all of your bags readied for the trip home. I've checked the timetable, and if we return immediately to town, we can make the afternoon train."

"That would be grand," Harriet replied. "My maid is already arranging for my things. Will you need assistance as well?"

"No. I brought very little with me and can tend to it myself."

"I suppose there will be a great deal of luggage to bring back from the ranch. Perhaps a small carriage won't accommodate it, and I wouldn't count on Clara's aunt and uncle to be of any help."

"Clara can just leave it all behind. I'll buy her whatever she and the children need once we've returned to New York. Besides, I'm sure she left plenty of her wardrobe behind at the house." He smiled, feeling quite satisfied with the turn of events.

"I don't like any of this." Curtis paced the front room, his limp quite noticeable. "I wish there were another way."

Clara felt sorry for him. There was a time when his body would have allowed for him to take matters into his own hands and fight Otto physically, but his injuries made even the ride to and from town quite painful.

"It's the only way I could think of." She pulled back the lace curtain and looked out for some sign of Otto and her mother's carriage. Would they bring the children with them? How she longed to hold Hunter and Maddy. She knew they must be terribly afraid, and that grieved her as nothing else could.

Curtis came behind her and pulled her back against him. "I'm sorry. I'm not helping matters."

"It's all right. I'm not sure there is any help for this—except prayer. I feel at such a loss. I've never been separated from them like this." Tears filled her eyes. "I keep thinking they might be hurt. I know they must be terrified and . . ." She couldn't go on.

"Shhh, don't get yourself all worked up." Curtis turned her to face him. "It's going to be all right."

She looked deep into his eyes. "I want to believe that."

"Then do. Otto has done a lot of terrible things, but I don't think he'll hurt Hunter and Maddy."

"He most likely killed his own brother. Why would he refrain from harming his brother's children?"

Madeline appeared just then. "They're approaching. Curtis, you'd better get out of sight. I don't think it would be wise for you to be here when they arrive."

Curtis nodded. He bent and gave Clara a gentle kiss. "I won't be far."

She didn't want him to go but knew he must. He couldn't very well stand at her side while she pretended to marry another man.

"I'll be fine." She wiped her tears and sighed. "I'm sure it will all go as planned."

Madeline led Curtis from the room. She spoke to him in hushed tones too low for Clara to hear. No doubt they shared some last-minute plan or suggestion. Clara pulled back the curtain once more and saw the dust cloud that rose up from the road.

Clara let the curtain fall back in place and checked her dress. She hadn't wanted to change, but Otto had requested it of her, and she didn't want to do anything to rile him. The mauve-colored gown fell to the floor in a more or less straight line. It was comprised of two pieces. One was a simple sleeveless shift of silk with tiny black beading at the squared neckline. Over this was a pleated silk and lace coat of the same color that hooked at the waist with black frog closures. It was by far the nicest gown she'd brought with her, but after today she intended to burn it.

Her aunt and uncle entered the room with Judge Walker. She wanted to ask her aunt if the children were with Otto and her mother. Instead, Clara glanced at the window once again and bit her lip to keep from crying. Otto and her mother were alone.

"Hunter and Maddy aren't with them," she said, turning to face the others.

Madeline nodded. "Your uncle already told us. Try not to worry. They must be close by."

At the knock on the front door, Paul left momentarily, then returned with Otto and Clara's mother. Otto smiled approvingly at Clara's appearance, while her mother immediately began to fuss.

"Your hair is done up quite plain." She turned to Madeline. "You could have helped her to style it more fashionably."

"My hair is fine, Mother. Please don't go on so."

Her mother fussed with the collar of the gown. "Where are the children?"

Clara stiffened and looked at Otto. "Well, they are . . . that is to say—"

"I asked that they not be present for the ceremony," Otto explained. "I prefer we not tell them until we're back at home in New York City. No sense startling them with yet another change in their life. Better to return them to the comfort of their home and familiar surroundings."

"This has been their home all summer," Madeline protested. "And they're quite comfortable and familiar with everything here."

Otto gave her a rather curt nod. "I'm sure they are, my good woman, but I prefer it this way. They will join us shortly."

Clara took hope in that. "Well then, we should probably get on with this. Judge Walker no doubt has a great many things to attend to back in town."

"I still think you should wait a few months." Harriet's comment took everyone off guard. It seemed all eyes turned her way, and Clara wondered what her mother was up to.

"You're the one who told me I needed to remarry, Mother."

"Yes," Otto added, stepping closer to Clara. "I thought we both agreed it was for the best."

"Well, it hasn't even been six months. People will talk"— Harriet shook her head—"and not in a beneficial manner."

"You should have considered such things before nagging Clara to wed," Madeline said in a huff. "You really should be ashamed of yourself, Harriet."

Clara's mother looked at her former sister-in-law with

disdain. "I have nothing of which to be ashamed. I have only helped to arrange a stable life for my daughter and her children. There is nothing dishonorable about that. And, although they are marrying much sooner than anticipated, it is a good match, and therefore I will approve."

"Well, thank goodness for that," Madeline replied sarcastically. Paul put his arm around her and she fell silent.

For several long moments no one said a word. Finally Judge Walker went to stand in front of the fireplace. "If you're both ready, we will proceed with the wedding."

"I am more than ready," Otto said, taking hold of Clara most possessively. He all but dragged her to where the judge stood waiting. "I'm sure she is as well."

"Yes." It was the only word she could force from her lips.

Judge Walker recited the words Clara had heard at every wedding she'd ever attended. He spoke of the importance of marriage and asked if anyone objected to this union. Clara kept her mouth clamped tight for fear she herself would offer just such a protest. Everything in her mind and soul revolted against this ceremony, even if it was a pretense.

"Clara, will you take this man?"

Clara almost smiled at the judge's omission of words. He didn't ask her to take this man as her lawfully wedded husband.

"Yes," she whispered.

"Will you take this woman?"

"Most assuredly, yes," Otto declared with a broad smile.

"Place the ring on her finger."

Otto frowned. "I didn't think to bring one."

"It's not important," Judge Walker declared. "You can always get one later. As for the ceremony, that's that."

Otto looked momentarily confused. He glanced at Clara and then to the judge. "That's all?"

"Yes. Your ceremony is concluded. That will be ten dollars for my services."

"Well . . . I suppose . . ." He turned to Clara and surprised her by pulling her into his arms. "I'm at least going to kiss the bride."

Clara was too stunned to react. Otto held her in a crushing embrace and pressed his lips to hers before she could say a word.

26

Clara remained stiff in his arms until finally he pulled away and smiled. She wanted to wipe the taste of his lips from her mouth but didn't want to cause a scene.

Otto fished out several bills and handed them over to the judge. "Money well spent," he told the man.

"Well, I for one am glad to have this over with," Harriet said. "The sooner we get back to New York, the happier I'll be."

"I believe we will all be happier," Otto agreed. "Clara, why don't you go gather what little you and the children will need for the trip home. Don't worry about packing up everything. I'll buy you and the children whatever you desire once we return home."

"I see no reason for us to leave just now. The children are hardly in a position to . . . say goodbye to all they've come to love."

"Well, dear wife," he said, emphasizing the words, "they will soon be very glad to join us on this journey. Now, why don't you get your aunt to help you with your things while I finish with the judge regarding our marriage certificate?"

Clara momentarily froze. They hadn't considered that Otto might want legal proof of the union. She looked at the judge, trying her best to mask her horror at the thought that they were about to be found out.

"Oh, we don't do things exactly like other states," the judge said.

"Somehow that doesn't surprise me," Clara's mother said, rolling her eyes. "They are so primitive and backward here in the wilderness."

Otto frowned. "Then how will it be handled?"

Judge Walker smiled. "I will complete the paper work and register it with the state. Then you'll have to wait until a copy comes to you, at which time you can sign it and register it with your state."

Clara knew that wasn't the way things were done, but she admired the neat and orderly fashion in which the judge resolved the matter.

"Very well," Otto said. "I will give you the proper address. I wouldn't want the certificate to go astray. After that, I believe I'll step out on the porch for a bit of air. It's rather warm in here today."

Madeline came alongside Clara. "Shall we go get your things?"

Clara wanted to scream that the only thing she wanted was the safe return of her children. Nevertheless, she nodded and followed her aunt from the room. Once they were well away, Madeline put her arm around Clara.

"Try not to worry. So far everything is going along just fine."

"I thought we'd be found out for sure when Otto asked about the certificate."

Madeline nodded. "I did too."

They entered Clara's bedroom and looked at each other.

It was obvious Clara wasn't going to pack anything, but they would need to at least wait long enough to give that pretense. On the other hand, Clara considered that it might serve just as well to tell Otto there was nothing she wished to take back with them.

"I hate that man," she murmured.

Madeline shook her head. "No. Don't hate him. That just gives him a kind of power over your spirit. It's best to just forget about him altogether."

"I can't. At least not until Hunter and Maddy are safely home. I don't know what I'll do if Otto has hurt them . . . or killed . . ." She couldn't finish that thought. Tears came to her eyes. "Oh, Aunt Madeline, I don't know what I'm going to do if this doesn't work."

"Shhh, it's going to work. You'll see. If all else fails, the sheriff will take Otto into custody and he'll have to tell him where the children are."

"Yes, but what if he doesn't?"

"Well, that kind of thinking is only going to cause further grief. I suggest instead that we pray."

Clara closed her eyes and drew in a deep breath as her aunt began to petition God on her behalf.

"Lord, we know you promised to never leave us—to never forsake us. Right now we're trying our best not to worry about Hunter and Maddy, but, Lord, it's hard. Please bring the children home safely. Help us to foil the dastardly deeds of Mr. Vesper, and give Clara a peace of mind and heart to know that you have heard our prayers and will protect the innocent."

Her aunt continued to pray, but Clara found her mind wandering. God didn't always answer prayers the way people thought He should. What if He didn't give Hunter and Maddy back to her?

Father, they are innocent and they need you so. Please help them.

"Amen."

"What?" Clara opened her eyes and looked up.

Her aunt smiled. "I said amen. Would you like to continue the prayer?"

"I don't think I could concentrate." She fell silent. She'd heard something. Cocking her head, she looked to her aunt, and then the sound came again. It was her children crying out for her.

Pushing past her aunt, Clara ran through the house and out the door. Hunter and Maddy were running across the yard from the direction of the trees.

"Mama! Mama!" Maddy called out between sobs.

Hunter waved his arms. "Mama!"

When they'd closed the distance, Clara fell to her knees, mindless of the silk dress. She opened her arms to her children and embraced them for a long time while all three cried.

"What in the world is all this nonsense?" Clara heard her mother ask.

There were other voices, but Clara didn't care. She pulled back only far enough to see each child's face. "Are you all right? Did they hurt you?"

"We were so scared," Hunter told her, tears streaming down his chubby cheeks.

Maddy nodded. "But we prayed like you told us to."

"Yeah, but we couldn't pray out loud because they put a handkerchief over our mouth," Hunter added.

"I am so sorry. I never wanted you to have to face anything so terrible."

Clara heard the voices growing louder and knew that other people were approaching. She couldn't help wondering if Otto was among them. She hoped that someone had already taken him in hand so that she would never have to speak to him again.

Wiping her eyes, Clara rose and drew the children close as she turned to face her family. Otto and her mother stood only a few feet away while Madeline and Paul remained with the judge at the bottom of the porch steps. To her relief she saw Curtis and the sheriff coming from around the house.

"You act as though you hadn't seen them in years," Clara's mother remarked and rolled her eyes heavenward. "Honestly, Clara, I do worry about the state of your mind."

"Some bad men took us," Hunter said. "They tied us up and put us in a dark room."

"They hurt my hands," Maddy said, lifting her arms to reveal her chafed wrists.

Clara's mother shook her head. "What imaginations those two have. I blame this cowboy country. The sooner we get them back to civilization, the better."

"I quite agree," Otto said, smiling. "Come along, we should probably start back for town."

Shaking her head, Clara pushed her children behind her. "I'm not going anywhere with you."

"But you must. You're my . . ." He glanced at the children. "You know full well why you must."

"Hardly."

Otto turned to face Curtis. The sheriff and judge were right behind him, while Clara noted that a couple of other men she didn't know made their way behind her. Otto looked at Clara and then laughed. "You're too late, Billingham. I've made her my wife and you have no further claim to her."

"I'm afraid you're wrong on that account," the judge said. "You are the one who has no claim to Clara or her children."

"This is preposterous," Clara's mother said before Otto could speak. "I witnessed the marriage myself. That gives Otto all of the claim he needs."

"There was no marriage," the judge replied. "I have long since retired from my judgeship and have no authority to marry anyone."

Otto turned and narrowed his eyes. "Do you mean to tell me this was all a farce?"

Clara lifted her chin in a defiant pose. "It was nothing more." She looked at the sheriff. "Sheriff, this is the man who took my children or arranged for them to be taken. He threatened I'd never see them again if I didn't marry him."

"She's quite insane," Otto declared. "Her mother and I have long been concerned about her mind."

"She's perfectly sound of mind," Curtis said, coming to stand beside her. "Which is a wonder to be sure, given all that you two have put her through."

Clara's mother began to sputter and turn red. "This . . . this . . . cowboy . . . is lying. Clara has never had a strong sense of reality. She's quite weak-minded and needs to be cared for."

"Which I intend to do," Curtis said. He smiled at Clara and then turned back to the others.

"I may not have the power to marry anyone," the judge interjected, "but I've known this young woman for many months now and I can attest to the fact that she is quite sound of mind. I would also be willing to make that statement for any legal purpose."

Otto shook his head as the sheriff took hold of him. "This is madness. Ask the children. They know I had nothing to do with them being taken."

"Maybe you didn't do the deed yourself," Curtis replied, "but you were behind it."

Otto sneered. "You have no proof of that."

The sheriff piped up at this. "There's no need to ask the children. We caught the two men who had them, and they readily gave up your name as the mastermind." Otto's face fell and Clara's mother looked at him in shock.

"Sheriff, if you'll wait a moment, I have some other evidence you'll need in order to see that this man answers to the proper authorities for his acts of treason." Clara turned to the children. "Come with me."

They started for the house with Otto calling out after them. "You know this isn't going to work. You know that I will see you answer for your part."

"She has no part in your treason and murderous actions," Curtis replied.

Clara heard nothing more as she went into the house with the children and Uncle Paul following close behind. "Maddy, Hunter, I want you to go to your room and stay there. You'll be safer there, and Uncle Paul will sit with you until the sheriff takes Otto away."

"Did he really have those bad men take us?" Maddy asked.

Looking down at her daughter's tearstained face, Clara could only nod. She was afraid to say much more for fear her emotions would take over. Instead, she left the children with her uncle and hurried to Curtis's room, where she'd hidden her case. She retrieved the four journals and took them to the sheriff.

"You'll find here a detailed accounting of my brother-in-law and deceased husband's acts against this country."

The sheriff nodded. "I'm sure that will help the proper authorities to put him away for a very long time."

Clara looked at Otto for a moment. "He'll try to tell you that I was also a part of this, but as the journals will bear out, I knew nothing. Furthermore, I am happy to be questioned or even to testify regarding what I did or didn't know."

Otto was kicking up a fuss, but the sheriff's men had him in hand, and when he refused to remain silent, one of the men threatened to gag him. Clara thought that very appropriate, given he'd had her children gagged.

The sheriff took the books and motioned his men to take Otto to the carriage. His hands were now bound by irons, which gave Clara a sense of relief knowing he couldn't hurt anyone anymore.

"I don't understand." Clara's mother came to her. "What is the meaning of this?"

"Otto is a traitor, Mother. He and Adolph were working with the Germans. They were responsible for giving over information that led to the deaths and injury of many people." Her mother's mouth dropped open, and for once she was struck silent.

Clara felt Curtis's reassuring touch as he put his arm around her shoulder. She moved closer, relishing his presence. "Now, Mother, unless you wish to walk back to town, I would suggest you join Otto in the carriage."

Her mother looked to the carriage and then back to the house before letting her gaze settle on Clara. "So you aren't going to return to New York?"

"No, Mother. I'm staying here and marrying Curtis, and together we'll raise Hunter and Maddy and any other child who comes along."

"And if you know what's good for you," Madeline said, "you'll do nothing to cause Clara further trouble by threatening to have her declared unfit and put in an asylum." She put herself between Clara and her mother. "Or I'll see to it that you are the one who gets put away, and I think I can rally plenty of witnesses who can vouch for your unstable mind."

"Why, I never in my life! I am appalled."

Madeline nodded. "As was I when you started threatening

our Clara." She emphasized the word *our* and looked at Harriet Oberlin as if daring her to say something in protest.

Clara's mother gave a huff and stalked off toward the carriage, muttering and sputtering all the way. One of the sheriff's men offered to help her into the carriage and she all but beat him away.

"He won't make that mistake again," Clara said, looking up at Curtis with a grin.

"Not if he's smart." Curtis tightened his hold on her. "Now, what say we go see to the children and then . . . well . . . I think it's about time we had a real wedding—with the right couple."

Clara nodded. "So do I." She elbowed him slightly. "I hope you won't forget the ring."

"No chance of that. I have it right here in my pocket. I have had it there since you demanded I marry you."

Clara shrugged. "Sometimes a girl has to assert herself."

27

Clara sketched various ideas for jewelry while Curtis showed the children the outside of the sapphire mine where he'd been injured earlier in the year. Catching sight of her children caused her to smile. They adored Curtis.

"Daddy, are all the sapphires gone now?" Hunter asked.

"No, but they are getting harder to find," Curtis replied. He bent over and picked up a chunk of dirt from one of the weathering piles. "They're hidden in the dirt and rocks."

Hunter frowned. "Why did God put them there?"

Curtis smiled. "Sometimes the most valuable things are hidden away like that. I think sometimes God just wants us to have to work for them because then we'll really know just how valuable they are. Wouldn't you agree?" He looked over at Clara.

She nodded and thought of how much they had endured to be together. "But good things are worth working for—worth waiting for."

"I couldn't agree more," Curtis replied.

"Are you going to look for sapphires again?" Maddy asked, glancing with great apprehension toward the open trench.

"No. At least not for a very long time. You know the doctor is going to work on my leg again, so it's going to be a while before I can do this kind of work."

"The doctor is going to break your leg again." Maddy's matter-of-fact statement summed it up.

"He is, but then your father's leg will be much, much better, and he might even be able to walk without a limp and so much pain," Clara said.

She put aside her sketchbook and stood. They had taken advantage of the unseasonably warm November day to bring the children out to explore the area. And it was such a beautiful area. Autumn had turned the grass a mixture of gold and brown, and the aspens—the ones that still had their leaves—were a bright yellow. Everything was transformed. Only the evergreens remained looking as they always did.

"Can we climb up to the top of the hill?" Hunter asked, pointing to the left of the dike.

Curtis gave Clara a questioning look. He was still trying to make sure he didn't overstep his bounds when it came to her desires for the children, while at the same time trying to teach her how to let them take small risks.

She nodded, and Curtis gave the children his approval. "You must stay away from the dike, however," he told them. "The area isn't stable enough to play around. The sides can give way without warning. Do you understand?"

"Sure," Hunter replied while Maddy nodded. "You almost died when it fell down, so Mama says we can't ever go in there."

"At least not until your father tells you that it's safe," Clara said, coming to stand beside Curtis. "Who knows if maybe one day you'll want to mine sapphires for a living."

Hunter shook his head. "Nope. I'm gonna raise sheep. Unca Paul said he'd give me some to start out with."

"I'm going to draw like Mama," Maddy interjected. "I like to draw."

"Well, neither of you have to worry about it just yet," Curtis told them. "So why don't you go climb your hill and enjoy the warm weather, because it's sure to change."

The children took off at a run, racing each other up the hill. Their laughter carried on the air, making Clara smile. They were happy.

"Well, now I have you to myself, Mrs. Billingham." Curtis wrapped his arms around her and pulled her close. They'd been married since the first part of September, but to Clara it felt as though they had always been together.

"And are you happy that you have me? Have us?" She sought his face for any sign of displeasure.

He tenderly kissed her lips. "Does that answer your question?"

"Yes." She turned in his arms to watch the twins. "I suppose I just want to make certain you are as happy as I am."

"Well, now that we have your brother-in-law behind bars and your mother returned to Florida, I'm quite content." He tightened his hold on her, pressing her back to his chest. "I never thought a man could be as happy as I am."

"I have some news." Clara hadn't had a chance to tell Curtis about her letter from William Badeau. "That nice government man who helped us with Otto and the journals wrote to tell me that the Vesper offices have been permanently closed and everything sold to pay reparations to those who have suffered because of the espionage done by Otto and his cohorts. He said also that Otto will probably be a long time in jail before they can bring him to trial. It might even have to wait until after the war is finally over. After that, it's anyone's guess as to whether he'll be put to death as a spy or imprisoned."

"Well, I'm just glad to have him away from you and the children."

Clara nodded. "Me too."

"I'm also glad that you plan to keep on creating jewelry. I know you enjoy it."

"I do," she admitted. "And now that we have interest from the jewelers in Chicago to continue making the Vesper collection, I feel that I can help to provide for our little family while you are laid up with your leg."

He sighed and released her. "I wish we didn't have to worry about my leg."

She turned and caught sight of his worried expression. "It won't be so bad. You'll see. The pain you have with it now will diminish greatly after it's set right. Dr. Cosgrove felt certain of that."

"I know, but it's time-consuming, and I feel pretty useless in the meantime. Not only that, but I have to go all the way to Billings to get the work done."

"But it won't be forever. My aunt and uncle are happy for us to stay on with them for the time. Just think, we'll all be together for Thanksgiving and Christmas. Won't that be nice?"

He nodded. "I suppose so. But I would like to have our own place one day."

She reached up and pushed back the hair that had fallen over one eyebrow. "I'd like that too."

He finally smiled. "What else would you like, Mrs. Billingham?"

"Hmm, that's a very interesting question." She glanced to where Hunter and Maddy were starting to make their way down the hill. "Mostly I just want to be a good wife to you. And, of course, a good mother."

He nodded. "And you are certainly that." He grinned and reached out to pull her back into his arms. "No two kids ever had a better mother than you. One day, I hope we have a whole houseful of children."

She smiled up at him. "Do you?"

"Absolutely. Of course, that will mean I'll definitely need to get us a bigger place to live. Madeline and Paul won't be able to house too many more people."

She gave a little shrug. "Well, I would suggest you get to work planning it out and see what we can do about getting it built, then, because in about seven months we're going to need a little more room." She watched him for a moment, waiting for her words to sink in.

For a moment he said nothing but returned her gaze with just a hint of questioning. "What are you saying?"

Laughing, Clara put her hands up to his face and pulled him closer. "I'm saying that we're going to have a baby."

"Truly? So soon?"

She frowned. "Are you upset that it's so soon?"

Curtis looked at her in wonder and shook his head. "No. Not at all. I'm just amazed." Then full understanding hit and he gave out a whoop that caused Hunter and Maddy to come running.

"What's going on?" Maddy asked. "Why is Daddy hollering?"

Curtis gave Clara a quick kiss, then turned to the children. "I'm hollering because you're going to have a baby brother or sister come summer."

Maddy and Hunter exchanged a momentary look of confusion. Finally Hunter posed the question. "Where are we going to get a baby?"

Clara looked with great amusement to Curtis, since he was

the one who made the announcement. He shrugged. "God's gonna give us one. The Bible says children are a gift from God."

"Is He going to give us twins?" Maddy asked.

Clara shook her head. "I doubt it. You see, God gave me twins because your father was a twin, and I suppose God thought that would be nice, and it was. This time, however, I would imagine God will send us just one baby."

"Will it be a boy or a girl?" Maddy pressed.

"It will be a surprise. We won't know until the baby gets here," Clara replied. "But no matter if it's a boy or a girl . . . I know you'll love the baby."

"Well, I think we ought to gather up our stuff and head back to the house," Curtis said, slipping his arm around Clara's waist. "I need to talk to Uncle Paul about building us a house."

"A house?" Hunter asked, eyes wide. "Can I help build the house?"

"I don't know why not," Curtis replied. "I figure we can all work at it together."

"Because we're a family," Maddy said, looking quite serious. "And that's what families do."

"Indeed, Miss Maddy." Curtis gave her a broad smile. "That's exactly what families do."

Maddy and Hunter nodded, making Clara smile. She sighed, feeling her happiness complete. Only a few short months ago, she'd lived with servants and all that money could buy, yet a cloud of gloom had hovered perpetually over her. She'd hoped that the love of her youth would save her, but it too had become tarnished and disappointing. Finally, through patient endurance, she and Curtis had found a love transformed into something deeper, a love centered on forgiveness. An eternal love that Clara intended to cling to forever.

Acknowledgments

Thank you to Betty Smith and Sue Kaul for their help regarding raising sheep in Montana.

Also thanks again to Katie and Randy Gneiting for their help with creating jewelry and information on Yogo sapphires.

Last, but certainly not least, thanks to my husband, Jim, for the history information on World War I and the generous support you give me to do what I love.

Soli Deo Gloria

Tracie Peterson is the award-winning author of over one hundred novels, both historical and contemporary. Her avid research resonates in her stories, as seen in her bestselling HEIRS OF MONTANA and ALASKAN QUEST series. Tracie and her family make their home in Montana. Visit Tracie's website at www.traciepeterson.com.

Sign Up for Tracie's Newsletter!

Keep up-to-date with news on Tracie's upcoming book releases, signings, and other events by signing up for her email list at traciepeterson.com.

More From Tracie Peterson

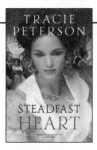

Brought together by the Madison Bridal School in 1888, three young women form a close bond. In time, they learn more about each other—and themselves—as they help one another grow in faith and eventually find love.

BRIDES OF SEATTLE: *Steadfast Heart, Refining Fire, Love Everlasting*

You May Also Like . . .

At Irish Meadows horse farm, two sisters struggle to reconcile their dreams with their father's demanding marriage expectations. Brianna longs to attend college, while Colleen is happy to marry, as long as the man meets *her* standards. Will they find the courage to follow their hearts?

Irish Meadows by Susan Anne Mason
COURAGE TO DREAM #1
susanannemason.com

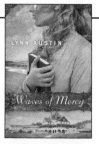

In 1897 Michigan, Dutch immigrant Geesje de Jonge recalls the events of her past while writing a memoir, and twenty-three-year-old Anna Nicholson mourns a broken engagement. Over the course of one summer, the lives of both women will change forever.

Waves of Mercy by Lynn Austin
lynnaustin.org

Ainslee didn't plan on running the McKay's West Virginia tile works alone. While her brother looks for a buyer, she hires talented artisan Levi Judson to keep the business going. But when she develops feelings for Levi, can their relationship survive the secrets they've been keeping?

The Artisan's Wife by Judith Miller
REFINED BY LOVE
judithmccoymiller.com

✒ BETHANYHOUSE